EVERY GUN IS LOADED LONG BEFORE IT'S FIRED.

DOUBLEHELIX IS WHERE THE BULLET GETS CHAMBERED—THE MOMENT A LIFE, A FAMILY, AND A PRESIDENCY ALIGN DOWN A SINGLE BARREL.

DOUBLEHELIX

BOOK ONE IN THE HELIX PROJECT

J.L. CALDER

Copyright © 2025 by J.L. Calder
ISBN 979-8-9930023-1-6 (paperback)
Published by Dwyer Street Press

CHAPTER ONE

He stepped out of the metro station at Federal Triangle and into the icy wind, shoving his hands deep into the pockets of his overcoat so they wouldn't freeze instantly.

"Fuck me," he muttered, running his tongue over his gums to keep them from freezing.

After the initial blast, Mike Green flipped his collar up so it hit the strands of dark brown hair that had overgrown throughout the winter and found themselves creeping down the base of his neck. Then he lit a cigarette and walked parallel to the Mall.

As he traveled along Constitution Avenue, the thick, gray material of his Armani suit rubbed against his overcoat, making a soft, hypnotic sound.

He loved that sound. He loved that coat.

The central character of the hard-boiled detective novels he penned wore one exactly like it. His gumshoe character, Joe, could transform from a womanizing alcoholic burnout into the brilliant mind unpacking the case with a single flip of the coat's collar. He donned it like a superhero's cape, shielding himself so the bad guys couldn't figure out what he was hiding. The coat was practically a supporting character in the cult-followed novels.

Mike had written himself into that character trait. He'd always needed a shield, a mask, a coat—something to hide who he really was.

But no one knew who he was anyway.

He lowered his head as he passed a bookstore that took up most of the city block. It was only March, and already a window dressing teased fans about a summer release. "WHO'S NEXT?" it read, over the curvy silhouette of a 1950s-style femme fatale. "THE THIRD NOVEL IN THE GESTAPO JOE SERIES: COMING THIS SUMMER".

Coming this summer, if I can fucking write it, he thought. Three books in one year was a lot, even for a good writer, never mind one who'd started writing by accident and likely only landed a book deal because some publisher was afraid of the people he was friends with.

Mike Green hadn't even been an English Major when he shat out his first story draft. He signed up for the elective credit because it was at a time he could still make happy hour. That was all that had mattered senior year.

His assignment had been to write a short story. Ten pages. Nothing. Three acts at three pages each—twelve-point font and a pixel and a half of spacing—roughly three thousand words. Mike could spew three thousand words easily when he was high. With the pleasure center of his brain opened wide and serotonin moving freely on a wave of chemicals, Mike's typical introversion took a back seat to the charming and handsome devil who wore the overcoat.

He'd sat down in a beanbag chair on the floor of his Georgetown apartment with a huge cup of black Folgers and tried like hell to come up with an original thought. When none came, he opted to steal one from the newspaper next to him.

Senator Richard Stockton was above the fold next to the headline: **SENATOR DENIES TREASON CLAIMS,** but his roommate, Tom, had already defiled the photo of his father with devil horns and a goatee, scratching the letters of the caption so they read: **SENATOR DIE ON CAM.** There was no love lost between Tom and his father. Mike couldn't relate. Rick Stockton had gotten him out of too many jams to think unkindly about the man. Plus, without a father of his own, Rick had been the only real stand-in for the role.

In any case, Mike moved past the headline, telling himself he'd never write anything that even resembled a Stockton story despite there being many good ones hiding in his Virginia closet.

He picked up a police blotter further back in the paper, scribbled down the details—stole them, technically—and wrapped them in nine pages of pulp just to turn something in. The paper came back with a Post-It that read:

"Mr. Green, this alcoholic, fedora-wearing womanizer is a rip-off we've all seen before. And it's not long enough. No credit. Rewrite, please."

Within a week, his detective had grown some unsavory tactics, a little charm, and the nickname "Gestapo Joe". Mike's Crim-Justice major helped him nail the procedural elements, and twenty-two pages later, he had a story with a whiskey bender and a sex scene that bordered on too inappropriate to hand into a female professor.

She passed him. Then she offered to mentor him.

When twenty-two pages turned into three hundred and twenty-two pages, she floated the manuscript to a publisher, and with what Mike suspected was a follow-up call from Rick Stockton's pit bull of a fixer, he had a book deal, with the first in stores in time for graduation and the summer pool-read rush of 1995.

Suddenly, he was responsible for a detective series, a "franchise" with a release minimum—a summer sizzler and a holiday fireplace read—and he'd still never had an original thought.

And he never did touch that treason case, even though the players had all been white, handsome, and rich Washington Power Elite—politicians who'd mixed their families up in a scandal around stealing secret Naval fleet movements and selling them over cigars. He wouldn't write that story. He wouldn't do that to Tom, and he wasn't a fan of political thrillers. They hit too close to home.

The biting wind came in gusts, so Mike kept his face down until he reached the National Archives building, a stone monstrosity with columns reminiscent of Ancient Greece and a vertical wall of steps looking down over Constitution Avenue. He bypassed the public entrance and used the employee door located on the side of the building.

Mike gave the brass door handle a yank and stepped onto the laminate flooring in the vestibule. No marble on this side of the building. Nothing to impress the masses who shuffled in off buses to look at the Constitution. Here, it was only a dingy security station with a metal detector and a rotating set of faces making twelve dollars an hour to keep people out. Guys were usually pretty pliable when you offered to quadruple that for a single entry.

"Eddie," Mike said, recognizing the night guard. Ever since he'd realized his best idea gathering came at night, he'd made it a point to befriend the graveyard team employed to keep folks from doing exactly that. The archive had business hours, guard rails in place so librarians could protect and maintain order in the annals of history. *Fuck that*, he thought.

"Well, if it ain't Mr. Gestapo Joe himself." Eddie stood and shook Mike's hand. The lumbering guard should have retired a decade before. "Haven't seen you in a while."

"Yeah, been researching over at Suitland."

"Suitland? Over by the Naval Intelligence office? You doing a political thriller?"

"I don't know what I'm doing, that's why I'm here."

As they spoke, Eddie passed him a tray to deposit the contents of his pockets. He may have intended to let him through the building after hours, but he was at least going to make the visitor pass through the metal detector.

Mike removed four things from the oversized coat pockets: his wallet, his keys, the type of top-bound notebook detectives carried to take notes in, and a small velvet ring box that looked very much out of place with the rest of the items.

"A little inspiration?"

"A little plagiarism."

The tray slipped out the other end of the conveyor, which Eddie hadn't even bothered to look at as it went through.

"You're all clear. But hey, no slipping out of here with any originals. They'd have my ass."

"I'd never do that to you, Eddie."

Mike deployed a smile—a toothpaste ad-worthy grin that dominated his face, revealing a perfect set of white teeth and two dimples that had been letting him get his way since he was a teenager. A mask that sent up a smoke screen of warmth and sincerity. It worked to disarm men and women equally. So did a hundred-dollar bill, one of which he passed to the guard for his part in the clandestine activity. Washington had taught him there wasn't anything money couldn't solve.

The older man slipped the bill into his pocket with a happy chuckle—eight times his salary just for letting an insomniac writer work at night wasn't a bad take.

Softening his steps so they wouldn't click so prominently when the floor turned to marble, Mike slid into the darkness. He side-stepped the Rotunda and glided over a stanchion aimed at keeping people in the public vault, before pausing a moment. He knew the location of the security cameras and the exact path of travel to stay in their blind spot. He zigged where it zagged, and their waltz was complete. Washington had also taught him not to leave evidence, even when the crime was innocuous enough.

Nearly a third of the way down the corridor was a research room that welcomed students and scholars during the day, but currently sat empty. Mike slipped through the darkness, across the room of tables, and glided effortlessly over the pull desk. The only thing that came close to the rush he got from opiates was a hit of adrenaline, and sometimes, committing a victimless crime like trespassing was enough to tickle that itch when he didn't feel like scoring.

Once in the backroom, he helped himself to the cave of treasures—filing cabinets that stretched out on all sides like functional green wallpaper. The History of Everything. If he dug back far enough, no one would even recognize the stories as rip-offs. If he picked something from the '50s, he didn't even need to think very hard about adapting the period details. Pick an old file, jot down the facts, and then wander home with his collar flipped up, existing in the mind of a detective. That, plus a great deal of prodding and criticism from his editor, and he'd have a story. Easy.

Mike pulled out his key ring and pressed the button on the tiniest blacklight, searching for the near-invisible UV mark he'd left on the last filing cabinet he'd looked through. Once he'd located the UV dot, he got to work.

The first file he reviewed was a 1935 aggravated homicide over cattle. The second, a moonshine case. A third file, a fourth, but nothing appealed. It was all crap. The stories were crap, he was crap, he had always been crap, and he was kidding himself if he believed that being an author was a sustainable endeavor when he had never had a good idea.

He leaned back against the chilled surface of the cabinet, pinching the corners of his eyes and attempting to quiet the intrusive thoughts and focus on the silence until there was nothing.

Nothing in the room. Nothing in his head. Nothing.

Though that wasn't entirely true. He'd had a song stuck in there since he woke up that morning. Not even a song, more like a low, haunting vibration trying to become one.

Or I'm in withdrawal, he thought. Usually, when the detox started, it started in his teeth. Clenched, grinding, chattering. Always the teeth. Never had it been a melody loop.

The low, repetitive beat cycling itself on repeat filled the emptiness of that room, syncing with his heartbeat. He couldn't identify it, couldn't even hum along with it, but his eyes shot open, and Mike stood abruptly, moving in its time. He crossed the room, abandoning his systematic approach to file sorting, and wandered deeper into the archives' central nervous system. His right hand skimmed the file cabinets' surface, never touching it with his skin, but reading it like invisible braille until the beat in his mind got louder and his fingers coiled involuntarily around one of the handles. One case file dominated the drawer.

"I've never even seen a black file folder," he mused, removing the intriguing collection of notes. Then he flipped open the folder and gagged. He'd seen dead bodies before, but this one didn't seem clinical; she was still suffering even in death.

He touched the color glossy and shuddered as the pain ran through his body, entering at the abdomen and traveling upward, sucking the wind out of his lungs and ending with a thud to his head. He sank to the ground to hold the full weight of the folder in his lap.

The victim lay on a metal morgue slab, a sheet shielding her from the chest down, but the coroner hadn't closed her eyes. They stared out cold, hard, and blue. When Mike had seen dead eyes before, they had looked like foggy, lifeless remnants —a film skimming a vessel that never housed a soul. Not these. Hers were still radiant, still hypnotizing—almost still alive even though her makeup had been worked into a raccoon's smudge around them. No, it wasn't makeup; she'd taken a horrific beating.

Yet her lips rested in something of a smile, as though the death that came for her was a relief from whatever had come before. As he stared at the brutal carnage, he couldn't imagine what horrors this had been preferable to.

"What is your story?"

And if I can't figure it out, maybe I'll write it.

Minutes went by, how many he couldn't tell, enough to trace the outline of her face, to imagine her voice, to form a bond— enough minutes that the orphan child he'd hidden away inside had time to grow attached and become afraid of losing her even if she was already gone.

Strands of hair clumped against her bloody skull, but he could tell they were wavy and dark, and that the sun that had warmed her milky shoulders had been trapped in her hair in fire streaks, the same way his looked in childhood when he'd been innocent enough to play outside. He finally flipped to a new photo.

One neat gunshot wound to her temple.

The exit wound had taken off the back of her skull but left her beautiful face intact. Close-range stippling and GSR told the story: This was an execution.

The old stone building suddenly went very cold. Mike reached for his overcoat and slid it on, but he couldn't look away. It was like cable news covering a disaster, running the same ten seconds of footage, but he still watched it, waiting to notice something with his pseudo-detective's brain that no one else had seen. Fingers broken in a struggle, but a giant diamond on her left hand. A gouged line in her wrist from some kind of cord.

She'd been attacked but not robbed. Restrained but still beaten.

She'd been tortured.

He flipped past the photos of her head and her hands, moving downward, but when he saw a flash of the next image—the one of her body—he slammed the folder closed. He couldn't see her cut open like that.

Scanning the autopsy for the cause of death, he caught other hints of her suffering.

Laceration…

Anterior puncture…

Self-inflicted…

The pages vibrated. The shaking in his hands was usually the first sign of what would follow—the feeling he would never admit was a panic attack. He shoved the whole folder away in favor of the written report that followed.

"CIA letterhead? Where the fuck did I end up?" He checked to make sure no one was watching, though he couldn't shake the feeling that someone was. He fanned the pages, all of them redacted, keeping him from knowing her.

An FBI file logged by the New Orleans field office looked the same. Page after page, a black marker skewed the case notes. Whoever she was, whoever she'd been, the U.S. government was now hiding her—or trying to erase her.

A global mosaic of agencies had seemingly weighed in on whatever transpired, each providing some context that had been immediately erased from the record—except the one logged by MI6.

Mike dragged his fingers along the rows of censored lines until he found the page where the British Intelligence Service had either gotten sloppy or not cared enough to keep their Sharpie out.

[SIS-MI6 // FILE: 002-1-9-68 // STATUS: CLOSED]

OPERATION CODE: ["ORANGEBLOSSOM" // D-10-F]

CLASSIFICATION: // EYES ONLY //

AFFILIATION: MI6 (EXTERNAL ASSET)

LIAISON AGENCIES: CIA / SVR / FBI

HANDLER: [REDACTED]

ASSET NAME: [REDACTED]

ALIAS(ES): [REDACTED]

PEN NAME: DELILAH GRENNAN

"Delilah Grennan," he whispered, jotting the name in his steno pad. It wasn't a legal name, but if she published something, he wanted to read it. An author always left part of themselves in their work, and if that were all he could get, he'd take it.

BIOGRAPHICAL DATA:

DATE OF BIRTH: [REDACTED]

PLACE OF BIRTH: [REDACTED] / USA

CITIZENSHIP: DUAL (UKRAINIAN-AMERICAN, NATURALIZED)

KNOWN ASSOCIATES:

BROTHER (1): [REDACTED]

BROTHER (2): SERGEI [REDACTED] – KIA

PARTNER(S): JACK GRENNAN – KIA / DMITRI [REDACTED] – KIA

CHILD: [REDACTED] – PRESUMED KIA

SUMMARY NOTES:

LINK TO SEN. RICHARD STOCKTON III: **DISMISSED**

CONNECTION TO [REDACTED]: **INCONCLUSIVE**

STATUS:

ALL KNOWN ASSOCIATES: DECEASED OR PRESUMED DECEASED

CASE FILE STATUS: CLOSED

OPERATION TERMINATION: CONFIRMED – 22 NOV 1995

"Link to Senator Richard Stockton dismissed? Jesus, Rick, what?"

He thought about driving straight to Falls Church and asking his surrogate father what the actual fuck he was doing being linked to a girl's torture, but doing so would be admitting he was committing a light treason and open up a separate discussion. Still, there was an exactly zero chance Mike walked out of the archive and forgot about anything he'd seen. Maybe he'd work the name into conversation and see what happened.

PEN NAME: DELILAH GRENNAN

Pen name.

It gave him an idea.

As he slid the folder back into a drawer, a surveillance photo dropped to the floor. The girl—still alive—stood with a young man, photographed through a telephoto lens in the kind of wide-open town squares found across Eastern Europe. Someone—one of the agencies—had deemed her important enough to track as an asset, yet disposable enough to let die. There hadn't been justice. There hadn't even been a resolution.

He tucked the photo into his overcoat pocket, made sure everything else was in its original location, untouched, and returned to the employee door.

"Taking off for the night?" Eddie asked, standing again.

"Yeah. I think I got what I came for."

"I don't need to search your pockets, do I?"

Mike deployed his smile. "Come on, now…"

"I'm just playing with you, Mikey. Have a good night."

A good night. He was carrying a stolen intelligence photo, talking down a panic attack, and ruminating over a murdered Russian girl. His night was going to be something, but good probably wasn't it.

Not without at least a shot of whiskey.

CHAPTER TWO

As he moved up Constitution Avenue, Mike hummed what had finally morphed into the song in his head. The bookstore he'd passed—the one taunting him with a poster of his own procrastination—sat between him and the nearest bar, which moved it up Mike's list of priorities one notch. He ducked inside and went for the first salesperson he found near a computer.

The girl was busying herself with closing tasks, showing no interest in helping another customer. She ignored him until Mike's incessant tapping on the counter grew irritating, and she finally looked up.

"Busy?" he asked with sarcasm.

"We're closing."

"I get it, but you aren't closed yet. Mind looking something up for me?"

"There's a computer at the—"

"Please?" He let *the* smile take over his lips, creeping across his face until she couldn't help but smile back.

"Sure. What are you looking for?"

"Anything by an author named Delilah Grennan. G-R-E-N-N-A-N."

"Grennan… I have a Jack Grennan, contributor to a medical journal. Oh, wait. Delilah Grennan."

"That's it."

"A short story and one novel. Both were pulled by the publisher a few months ago and are no longer in print."

Figures.

Just his luck that something would offer a glimmer of interest only long enough to find out he would never have it. That was the story of his life—the whisper of possibility lost in the scream of reality. "Bummer."

"Wait, it should have been pulled, but the novella shows in stock. If it's on the shelf, I'll give it to you."

"Are we in the habit of banning books again?"

"On occasion," she said, leading him over toward the fiction stacks. "If someone tries to assassinate the president, and the book is basically a how-to manual, they'll yank it."

"Ahh, makes sense."

"Let's see now… GR…"

The girl bent forward, getting a clearer read on the books that filled the 'Gr' shelf, and for a second, Mike found himself distracted by the curve of her jeans. His amygdala was screaming, begging for a hit of something to open it up, and it was willing to settle for anything between an opioid and a handjob.

She ran her finger across his spine, or rather, the spine of his novel, *"Widows Make the Best Lovers,"* locating the short story wedged in next to it. As she removed the novella, he worried that she'd catch the small photo on the rear jacket next to it and recognize him. Fine if it made her want to offer up that handjob, not fine if it made her want to talk about what the next book was going to be. He nudged the stack so the space collapsed and hid his printed face from her before she noticed.

брат

"Here you go. How do you pronounce that?"

"I have no idea," he said, adding his smile as he flipped the book open to check that the text was in English, unlike the title.

The girl waited to see if he wanted it or if she'd have to pull it as the publisher intended. "Can I interest you in a cheesy detective novel to go with it?" she said, waving her arm at the end cap holding his latest endeavor.

"No. No, I'm set there."

"Well, here…" she slid a slip of note paper his direction, and he half expected it to be her phone number. "You could check that new Amazon website for her other one. I wrote the title down for you. If you really want it, you can try calling the publisher."

"Who's the publisher?"

"Fifth and Lex."

Shit.

The same house published him, and while that certainly made it easier to get a hold of someone there, the conversation would very quickly turn into 'where the fuck are my pages, Mike?' and that wasn't a conversation he was ready for. His hands started to shake again.

"Thanks. I'll pay for this up front."

"We can't sell it, actually, since it's been pulled. Just slip it in your pocket."

She'd set him up for the perfect come-on line, but he had too many things to juggle already: a deadline, a new book to read, a girlfriend whose engagement ring he carried in his pocket even though he wasn't convinced he wanted to give it to her. He needed to check at least one box off before he added anything else to his plate.

Mike left the chain bookstore and pointed north toward Logan Circle, debating whether to stop for a whiskey or power through and drink the top-shelf bottle at home. The grinding in his molars answered the question for him, and he slid into the next doorway he came across.

Another few blocks, and he could have graced the lobby bar at the Jefferson Hotel and added whatever drink he chose to a tab that ran permanently for members of Stockton's inner circle, but the trip felt out of the way, and the risk of running into someone who knew him was too high.

The last thing he wanted was to speak to someone. His mind was too occupied, vacillating between invented conversations with a dead Russian girl and the forced dialogue that might become his impending novel. Despite the popped coat collar and the brisk air, the dead girl continued to insert herself into his mind as Mike filled in the blanks of her life with tales of his own concoction. In reality, he was crafting an imaginary friend out of a dead person.

An imaginary friend for an imaginary guy.

He tapped his fingers on the bar to get the bartender's attention, the same way he'd had to flag down the bookstore girl.

"Yo," Mike finally called out.

"ID?" the bartender asked.

"What? Still?"

"What are you? Twenty-two?"

"Twenty-three."

"Babyface. Skip it, I guess. What'll you have?"

"Can you make me a drink called The Placebo Effect?"

"Come again?"

"Double Johnnie, straight. Black if you have it."

The bartender reached into the well and brought up the heavy glass bottle with the black and gold label. He turned it over a double-wide shot glass and filed it past the grip grooves, then slid it over.

Mike knocked back the liquid heat, slid the glass back across the bar, and felt the sense of impending failure start to pass.

"Another?" the bartender asked, already holding the bottle up.

"Yeah, what the hell."

The second shot brought the quiet home. He let his eyes flutter for a second, thankful to find the brief nirvana in a substance he hadn't needed to stroll the H Street Corridor to find, then lit a cigarette and left a ten on the lacquered bar top.

He cared less intensely now. He could read Delilah's story now. He could write a book that was already being advertised now.

He could go home now.

His mind was empty for those few blocks, a welcome reprieve from the running chatter and the low-grade melody looping through there previously. Once he'd penetrated his doorway, the overcoat went onto a hook as if he were a king hanging up his crown for the night. Moving in a ritualistic pattern, he turned on his coffee maker, shed his suit for a more comfortable pair of sweats, and returned to grab a fresh cup of brewed coffee.

His contacts were out, his glasses were on, and the only thing left to ready the room for a night of serious creative exploration was the removal of his beanbag chair from the closet where he secretly still kept it. It had been the chair he'd sat in to write his first novel, and now, he was superstitious about starting one without it. Only he had no intention of starting his own novel yet.

He pulled брат from his coat pocket, along with the photograph he'd lifted from the National Archives, and stared at them both. He couldn't look at her face without his mind superimposing the horrors that found her at the end of her life. This book, with the Russian title that meant "Brother," wasn't going to tell him what led to her death; it might not tell him anything at all, and he'd be stuck there still wondering why this girl had a grip on him, still itching for a fix, and still without even the hint of an outline. The book vibrated in his hand—or the tremors had returned—as he peeled back the cover.

The 'Agitation', they called it. Sometimes the 'Unrest'. The word 'revolution' was never uttered, but we knew what we were doing that summer and every summer before that. Those of us who sat on granite. Those of us who sat in blood. I held hands in the cold. He held a pistol to a woman's head. We both knew what we were choosing.

August 1991. Mike could see Kiev in his mind. The summer the Revolution took hold. The summer before that: a student protest in the town square nicknamed the Revolution on Granite, and earlier that year, the Ukrainian Wave, a peaceful protest where three million Ukrainians held hands from the Polish border to the capital. He could see it playing out like he had lived it, when the truth was, Mike Green probably couldn't have found Kiev on a map without help.

A piercing digital shriek broke his concentration.

"Jesus Christ," he muttered, the book dropping from his hand. He crossed to the kitchen and lifted the telephone's receiver as he simultaneously searched for the bottle of Johnnie Walker he knew he had tucked away somewhere.

The caller ID read: 703.

703 was the suburbs.

Only one person would be calling from the suburbs at that hour.

"Yes?"

"Where the fuck are you?" A party raged in the background behind Tom Stockton's inebriated inquiry.

"Well, you called my apartment, so…"

"You know what I mean! Why aren't you here?"

By 'here', Tom meant the Stockton Compound, a mansion tucked at the end of the same cul-de-sac where Mike's adopted parents lived. He should have been living on his own in the city, but Tom had lost that privilege a year earlier when he'd overdosed.

As his college roommate, Mike had been counseled on what to do if he ever found Tom unconscious, overdosed, or having accidentally killed someone. The answer was not to call the paramedics. The answer was to call the firm of terrifyingly powerful political consultants that Rick Stockton employed to make those things go away. He was to dial a woman named

Lindsey and say, "Play 13." He ran Play 13 once, and Tom was still alive, so apparently it had worked.

"You're asking why I'm at my own apartment and not your house? I live here for one…"

"Stop being a fucking prick. It's my last night of freedom. By tomorrow, the Senator and Mrs. Stockton will be home from 'the trail', and this place will be filled with ass-kiss campaign contributors smoking his pole because they were invited to dinner. I'll have to go back to smiling on camera and wishing I was fucking dead."

"Shit. I forgot."

"How could you forget?"

Mike swilled a rip from the bottle he'd located before continuing the asinine conversation. "Buddy, if I had to remember every time you were throwing a party, I'd have time for precious else."

"Whatever, it's only midnight. Come now."

"Nah, dude. I'm tired."

"I've got something that will wake you up."

Tom rubbed his nose and sniffled, conveying his suggestion. He'd gone to rehab after the overdose. It hadn't taken. Now, instead of trying to keep him off drugs, Lindsey just tried to make sure the drugs were clean.

"I'm not driving out to Falls Church to watch you ride a rail."

"Why not? You never sleep anyway."

"That's also why I don't do cocaine anymore."

"Hate you."

"If my mom looks out her window and sees my car at your house, I'll never hear the end of it."

Tom paced the porch, straining to see if Jennifer Green's lights were on. "Whatever, she's not your real mom anyway."

"Wow. Dick."

If they hadn't grown up on the same street, the wild-child Tom and brooding introvert Mike would never have been friends, but Jennifer Green had the hutzpah to knock on the senator's door one day and say, "I think our sons are the same age, and I'd like to arrange a play date." It hadn't been on Mike's behalf, but on her own. Befriending a senator was always a smart move, especially one with aspirations for the White House.

Mike and Tom had become inseparable after that. Uniquely damaged only children navigating a shitty world together from Falls Church to Georgetown, and now seemingly back.

"I'm playing! I love you. Come over," Tom whined.

"No, I've got plans with a Russian girl."

"Wait, seriously?"

"No."

"Because if you're serious, I'd let you off the hook. I'd even go tell Kristin for you."

"Kristin?"

"Yes, Kristin. You know, the crazy chick you bought a ring for but have wisely opted not to give it to."

"I'm familiar. What's she doing there?"

"Waiting for you, like I am! Show up, or I'm going to tell her you were off banging a Russian chick."

"Whatever. I don't even think she likes me that much."

"Come on! Be here now!"

Tom punched a button on the cordless phone to end the call as a pair of headlights rolled to a stop in front of the guest house he occupied when he had the grounds to himself.

For a moment, the figure that emerged in a dark blue uniform looked like a cop, though security knew better than to let those onto the property without the presence of Lindsey Decker or one of her fierce associates. Once the headlights faded, no longer creating a blinding silhouette, the young man's Navy uniform revealed his identity.

"AJ? What are you doing here?" Tom asked. "Lieutenant Commander Buzzkill reporting for duty?"

"I'm just making sure you're alright, Tom."

"You mean reporting back to my father?"

AJ—whatever that stood for—was a military-edition Ken Doll, minted from a Washington mold for the express purpose of following orders—all light hair and crisp edges, pretty enough to distract from the fact that he was always on a mission. He was a nice enough guy, and they might have been friends under different circumstances, but if he had ever had fun before, it had been so long ago he'd forgotten how.

"I haven't spoken to your father in months. Lindsey asked me to check in."

"Oh. Lindsey. How stupid do you think I am, AJ? If my father's campaign manager-slash-lawyer asks you to check up on me, it means you're reporting back to my father."

"Everyone just wants to make sure you're ok."

"No. Everyone wants to make sure I'm not ruining his chance at the White House! Well, here I am, AJ, not foaming at the mouth or anything."

"Mind if I come in?"

"Why? So, you can interrogate everyone? Confirm that they're Stockton Loyalists? You still wear the uniform, but you're moonlighting for Lindsey Decker and Associates."

AJ stood quietly with his hands in his pockets, neither confirming nor denying.

"What the hell," Tom said, throwing the door to the guest house open. "See? The other cursed offspring of the ruling class. Everyone I'm 'allowed' to be friends with. All of us represent each other's mutually assured destruction. You're in the club, too, AJ. Stay! Get some strange! I won't tell your dad if you don't tell mine!"

"I'm good." AJ stepped off the porch, returning toward his car, but then stopped. "Hang in there, Tom. It's almost over."

"The campaign is almost over. Then the eight-year prison sentence starts."

Both young men held each other's gaze, trapped in the same prison of obligation—a duty to each of their fathers that neither had signed up for and neither could escape from. One had embraced it fully, wearing the uniform and muttering 'yes, sir,' while the other had wholly rebelled against it, doing everything he could to sabotage the ascent to the throne. Neither had been successful at enjoying life.

Mike was the lucky one, Tom thought, not having a father to deal with at all.

CHAPTER THREE

Mike had fallen into plenty of odd obsessions before: a video game phase around thirteen, a juice cleanse in college—as if drinking nothing but apple juice for a month could reverse the effects of all the drugs he had done. One could even argue his writing career existed because of an obsession with walking around in a coat pretending to be a detective.

Yes, his hard-wired need to fill the hole inside had left him vulnerable to obsession—*addiction*—to anything that offered to complete 'the Void'. A place. A feeling. A person.

Delilah's novella was currently filling it—a puzzle piece in the exact shape of the chunk taken from him when he was dumped at St. Augustine's Catholic Orphanage hours after his birth. And he knew another incomplete soul when he saw one. This writer hadn't stolen her thoughts from a newspaper; she'd lived them.

That's why she's innately better at this than you are, the voice in his head told him. He downed two more whiskey shots, trying to shut that voice up. Negative feedback loops were hallmarks of personality.

At the top of the last paragraph, Mike's eyes gave out, and he slept briefly, crumpled in a pile on his bean bag chair. Visions of candy-colored buildings and scrolled iron railings mixed with images of blood spatter and redacted pages in his subconscious, polluted by the secret file.

He woke next to the empty bottle of whiskey, his neck bent like a crowbar, when the sun moved around to penetrate the only window with a sightline to the living room.

A normal person would have seen daylight and forced themselves up. Instead, Mike pulled himself to the bathroom to find help going back to sleep. Drugs, in this application, were the solution, not the problem. Or at least that's what he told himself.

He popped the medicine cabinet open to review the stash of little orange bottles labeled with other people's names that he'd acquired with his own cunning and the use of a certain smile.

DELORES PEMBERTON: ALPRAZOLAM 0.5 MG PO BID FOR ANXIETY

DAVID PIERCE: VICODIN 5/500 1 TAB PO Q4–6H PRN PAIN, NTE 4/24H

ALVIN BROODY: LORAZEPAM 1 MG PO PRN INSOMNIA

As needed for sleep. That's the one.

He popped two milligrams, to be sure.

In ten minutes, it would slow his mind until there were no images of dead girls, no screams or gunshots. He stared at the ceiling, waiting for the peace to take over, waiting for the chatter to stop. It looped in his mind like a radio caught between stations, cutting in periodically with a whisper bouncing off a satellite.

He tried to visualize anything but dead bodies: California. The beach. A petite brunette with a wicked smile... no, she was going to detour him into something else.

He focused on the ocean; each wave, swelling on an inhale and breaking on an exhale, counting backwards, until his mind let go.

Spokoynoy nochi.

The fuzzy chatter had finally crystallized into five clear syllables, and though he hadn't understood them, they bounced off the walls of the room, not the inside of his head. Something comforting, yet forceful, pressed against his eyelids, holding them closed though he badly wanted to look for the source of the voice. Then he heard it a second time.

Spat, Meisha.

Despite a logical understanding that he was floating away on benzodiazepines, Ativan had never spoken to him in Russian before. In a woman's voice. It had to be the book bleeding into his consciousness. Had to be. And it didn't matter what language he fell asleep in, he was about to find peace.

Or not.

A ringing phone shattered the spell and whatever gentle pressure the pills had exerted on him.

"What?" he snarled into the receiver by his bed, hoping that if he didn't open his eyes, he could end this call quickly and reclaim that warm sense of slipping away.

"Oh, did I wake you?" The accusatory voice on the other end of the line belonged to Kristin, the girlfriend he'd left sitting at Tom's party the night before because he couldn't summon the interest to deal with her. At one time, she'd filled the Void in Mike's soul, but either the Void was growing, or she was shrinking.

"What do you think?"

"I think you need to get up and meet me for lunch like you promised."

28

Mike rolled onto his side, lit a cigarette, and exhaled into the phone. No version of this call would let him go back to sleep.

"Rain check? I didn't go to bed until after four."

"Yeah, neither did I! I sat there waiting for you to show up, and when I found out you weren't coming—thanks for the call by the way—I had to drive back into the city in the snow."

"Why didn't you call me earlier? Better question, why did you even go to the party in the first place? You hate Tom. You hate Republicans."

"You really want to do this now?"

"No, but I don't want to have lunch either."

"You're a ten-minute train ride away, and you owe me, get here."

The line went dead in his ear.

There was, of course, a scenario where he took the phone off the hook and rolled over again. Kristin would wait fifteen minutes, then call again. When he didn't answer, she'd weigh whether she had time to drive to Logan Circle, bang on his door, and scream at him before heading back to The Hill. The strong odds were that she'd wait and give him his ration of shit after work, and by that time, he'd have had a nap and could take it.

But now he was awake.

And hadn't eaten solid food in as long as he could recall.

"Goddamn it," he grumbled to himself.

Waste of fucking Ativan.

Mike plunged his cigarette into a cup of brown liquid next to the bed. Whether it had once been whiskey or just water already tainted by a previous butt, it snuffed the ember with a hiss. He got out of bed slowly, pulled on the same discarded suit he'd tossed to the floor the night before, and started toward the Old Ebbitt.

Five months earlier, he'd been sitting in a booth at the Ebbitt reading the proof copy of his Christmas release, *Murder, I Hardly Know Her*, when Kristin first approached him.

"Sorry, have we met before?" she said, first passing the table, but returning to speak to the tall, dark stranger. "You look familiar."

Mike lowered the book so that the rear jacket, displaying his photo, was concealed before he looked up at the woman.

She was stunning—a red-headed knockout he'd have placed out of his league if he thought she was hitting on him. What he actually thought was that after several days of interacting purely with characters of his own making, one had finally leapt from he page; the murderous femme villain with her hourglass figure arriving to slip poison into his drink.

But what a way to go.

"I think I would have remembered that," he answered.

"I know I recognize you. Did you go to BU?"

"Georgetown."

"Do you work on The Hill?"

"No, but if you do, maybe we've crossed paths at the Stocktons'."

"As in Senator Richard Stockton? I'd never be invited to socialize with the enemy. I work for Senator Rothschild of Massachusetts."

"Then you're the enemy," he said, leveling her with his trademark smile.

The model-worthy redhead sat down across from him and helped herself to his water glass. "I'm the enemy? Because I work for a senator who didn't commit treason and then lie his way out of prosecution?"

"Because you work for a senator who led a failed witch hunt against a patriot."

"Oh my God!" she said, laughing. "Seriously? Are you on his payroll?"

"I grew up in the house next door."

"How completely awful for you."

They sparred a while longer, and before she left, he got her number. The next night, they went on a proper date that ended in proper fucking. Things moved quickly, but Mike had a habit of latching onto people.

Now, he carried a two-carat ring in his pocket, because it seemed like the thing to do when your life settled into something resembling adult stability. But each time he'd planned to give it to her, something would happen—some inconsistency that would gnaw at him—activating the tingling hairs on the back of his neck, whispering *don't*.

The brass revolving door twisted him into the dining room of the hundred and fifty-year-old restaurant, where he could already see Kristin seated in a green-velvet booth behind her menu.

"Hey."

Kristin squinted at his two-day-old suit, squishing his nose into judgment just before he took the seat opposite her.

"Still wearing last night's suit? Do you want to talk about it?"

"My suit?"

"No. What you were doing last night *in* your suit, while I was at Tom's."

"Oh. I went to the archives to work on notes, picked up a book on my way home, and got caught up reading."

"So, while I was watching three separate congressmen's daughters get roofied, you were reading a book? In a suit?"

"Basically, yeah."

"Are you seeing someone?"

"Like dating or therapy?"

"Ugh. Maybe you should think about doing both," she groaned, returning to the menu.

"Come on, Kris. Tom throws a thousand parties, I forgot until he called, and by then I was in the zone."

"The book zone."

"Yeah, I found this file in the archives…" Mike lowered his voice before he continued. "Completely redacted dossiers from the CIA, FBI, KGB…"

"The KGB doesn't exist anymore."

"The FSB, SVR, whatever—I don't read Russian, and the text was completely blacked out anyway."

"You stumbled upon a redacted intelligence file in the research stacks? How old was it?"

"Last year. And I don't think it was meant to be an intelligence file. I think it was a murder case. She was killed in New Orleans."

Kristin finally showed interest in him. "So, who was this woman who had every agency tracking her?"

"I don't know. All I found was the pen name Delilah Grennan, so I stopped by the bookstore to see if I could find her publications. That's what I was reading."

Kristin stared, blinking, perhaps analyzing whether or not she thought the whole thing sounded like horseshit, or maybe waiting for him to keep talking about this murder.

"So who killed her?"

"No idea."

Kris buried her face in the menu again. "So you have no idea who she is or why she was killed, but she's more important than me? Only you would slide down an obsessive rabbit hole like that."

"Well, MI6 had a note dismissing a link between her and Rick…"

"Rick Stockton with ties to a murdered girl. *Quelle surprise.*"

Mike lowered the menu he'd only been partially scanning to begin with. This was one of those moments that kept the ring shoved firmly in his pocket; a fork in an otherwise normal conversation where he had to decide if he wanted to stand up for himself and risk a fight, or shut up so he could order a ham steak in silence.

A double dose of sleeping pills should have nudged him in the direction of a quiet breakfast, but the simple fact that he probably wouldn't even remember being there gave him the courage to double down.

"I know you think a Stockton presidency is going to unravel the fabric of America, but you know every time you sling an arrow at him, you're insulting my family."

Kristin met him where he was. "The Stocktons aren't your family. You're just the sad orphan kid who grew up next door and managed to keep their asshole son from OD'ing in college. The minute he's in the White House, you'll be a name on a Secret Service visitor list, assuming you even get that far with your background check."

"Rick Stockton is the closest thing to a father I've ever had."

"I'm sorry, I just don't care for the man."

"And yet he opens his home anyway, knowing that you're reporting everything you hear back to your boss."

"I wouldn't do that to you."

"Right."

Kristin tossed her menu to the side and reached for her tiny crescent-shaped purse. "Look, if after five months you still don't trust me, I don't know what we're doing here."

She stormed off in her dramatic way, only slowing to pull on her coat before the blast of winter air hit her from 15th Street.

Mike had another decision to make: order that breakfast, which would hopefully soak up the bottle of whiskey and two sleeping pills wreaking havoc on his stomach lining, or follow her out into the cold and try to salvage the conversation. Was she worth it? Probably not. Did that matter to a man who'd been passed around foster homes?

Almost never.

He remembered the tenuous optimism each time he had been placed. The hope that his life would finally find consistency, and then thinking it was his fault every time it didn't work. Kristin was a pain, but she was at least consistent. Mike jogged out onto the street, flipping up his collar as he called after her.

"Kris, wait. Don't be mad." He punctuated the ask with his famous smile, but the dimpled grin that won over security guards and bookstore girls was lost on the woman he was dating.

"Mike, you vacillate wildly between indignantly selfish and morbidly codependent, and some days I can't deal with it."

Kris reeled, her coat flying out behind her as she left him there fumbling in his pocket for a cigarette. All he could find was the ring box, taking up all the space.

"Buddy, can I bum a cigarette?" Mike asked, turning toward a shaved-head observer, who'd been watching their exchange as he leaned against the wall smoking.

"Yeah. You need light, too?" the observer asked, with a thick Slavic accent. He fished through the pockets of his leather jacket until he located the cigarette and the lighter, and tossed them both in Mike's direction.

Mike sparked the end of the smoke and drew in a sharp inhale. "Thanks, friend."

CHAPTER FOUR

"I need those pages! You've missed deadlines before, but this is borderline breach of contract."

The coffee maker couldn't brew fast enough. His overcoat already hung by the door, his suit traded in for a Georgetown sweatshirt and pajama pants, and he had hit the blinking button on his answering machine. That was when his agent's voice started screaming at him through the speaker.

"First three chapters! End of day tomorrow, or we risk not going to print on time. Your screen adaptation will be off the table. Get me those damn pages!"

Mike groaned, slumping into the stupid bean bag chair to try and conjure something—anything—he could put to page. Forget plot. Forget a three-act structure. The words weren't even coming. It was all initial pronouns and filler words, crap that would scream 'amateur,' and 'imposter,' and make his agent wonder why she'd ever bothered.

He shoved his laptop aside mid-thought.

Delilah's book was still lying on the floor next to the empty bottle, wedged open to the final page where it fell when he'd dozed off. He poured himself a coffee once the machine had caught up to his desire for it and picked her book up, scanning the final passage.

The dissolution of the Soviet Republic had launched Kiev into a free-market spiral, but something about Christmas Day—a holiday I'd never been allowed to observe under the Soviet embargo—made me walk to the mansion, the one where my brother now lived and worked, in the unsavory current beneath corruption.

Maybe I wanted peace. Maybe closure.

Snow had driven people inside, back to their stoves or the few pieces of coal they'd scrounged. That night would fall well below zero, and those who survived it would face eight more weeks of ice. My clothes were threadbare. Where would I get money for new things? Everything we had, my father gave to the avoritety. I tried to feel sorry for myself, but I knew most people had even less.

The mansion floated behind a mist; the frozen air mixed with the smoke that poured from their chimneys in clouds. What they burned that night could have seen my family through the winter. Instead, it twisted skyward in grey columns. Whatever they needed more of, they would just take.

Like my family.

There were none of us left to take—not once my brother chose to live beyond those walls, beyond that iron gate that separated good and evil—once he'd chosen a corrupt politician as a father figure, because he no longer saw one in the man who had raised us.

I wrapped my bare fingers around that iron gate, knowing my skin might freeze. I wanted to scream. I wanted to curse God on His own birthday for turning his back on us—or never existing at all.

Instead, I sang.

A window on the upper floor cracked open, and my brother's voice rang out in harmony. My soprano ached for forgiveness—forgiveness *for not being able to save him, for letting him walk toward evil and away from the light. His baritone resonated with achievement. The dark side paid better.*

My brother finished the verse with a smile and shut out the cold.

I walked slowly home to die.

Morgue photos flashed in his mind. He set the book down on its face so he could stare at her author photo—the blue eyes, still alive, and the dark hair falling to her shoulders, framing her cheeks. He wondered what she would look like if she'd had reason to smile.

He couldn't imagine what it would be like to have a brother—let alone lose one. Losing people who didn't matter was terrifying enough. Losing someone who did? That would kill him. The night he'd found Tom unconscious, a cloud of sputum gathering at the corners of his mouth as he seized—that was the closest he'd come.

He'd dialed Lindsey, as instructed. Within minutes, a wave of people arrived—a clean-up team. Her lanky associate, Sarah—a girl who'd always seemed a touch too sweet for the work she did —had sequestered him in the Jefferson Hotel before anyone knew if Tom had survived the overdose. Thirty days later, Tom was out of rehab. They hit H Street that night.

H Street.

He didn't need H Street when he had a stocked medicine cabinet.

"Thank you, David Pierce, and your post-surgical pain," he muttered, grabbing the Vicodin bottle from the medicine cabinet and pouring out three of the elongated white tablets. Mike bit down to crack the time-release coating. The powder inside burned his tongue with its bitter poison, but that was part of the self-inflicted punishment.

Any desire to start his first chapter had drained away with Delilah's epilogue. Whether the story was fictionalized or not, someone had gone through that. Someone had seen their government fall. Someone had seen their family oppressed by the oligarchy.

Someone had been murdered for telling the truth.

What had he been doing in 1991? He tried to remember. He'd turned eighteen, moved out of Falls Church, and into off-campus student housing at Georgetown. Rick Stockton had started covering his tuition in exchange for keeping Tom out of the headlines—or a jail cell. He sure as hell hadn't been watching his world crumble.

He stared at the ceiling and let his thoughts take over— thoughts about Kristin, deadlines, Delilah, and her brother. Thoughts about what it must be like to be related to someone by blood, about the voice that had whispered to him as he was trying to fall asleep, and the whiskey that had probably led to the voice that had whispered to him as he was trying to fall asleep. Three Vicodin, two Ativan, a bottle of whiskey, and two pots of coffee in less than twelve hours was a lot, even for him. And not one page to show for it.

He was acting like Tom.

"By tomorrow, the Senator and Mrs. Stockton will be home from the Trail, and this place will be filled with ass-kiss campaign contributors..."

If Rick and Annabelle Stockton were having a dinner party in their own honor, the Greens would be expected to be there, and he couldn't bail on Tom two nights in a row.

"Goddamn it," he grumbled, fishing his suit out for the third time.

The Lexus rarely saw the road, spending most of its time tucked beneath the building in a parking spot against a wall. Mike only kept it for nights like this—when he was dragged to Virginia and the Metro was too much of a hassle.

He navigated toward the George Mason Bridge for the slog to the suburbs. The suburbs: ultimate symbol of surrender. You know you've given up when you move outside the city, he always thought. And he had so much time to think in the grinding winter traffic, reduced to one lane by a snowplow.

He thought about which route to take, where to stop for gas, and which radio station to listen to. He thought, and thought, and it was happening again—that thing he'd never admit was a panic attack.

His fingers tightened around the steering wheel so they wouldn't shake.

Mike fished around in his overcoat pocket, past his wallet, past the ring, past the still-empty notepad, and finally found the pill bottle. When the car came to a stop, he dry-swallowed the blue tablet and waited for it to take effect.

Fifteen minutes. Until then, he was stuck. Stuck in traffic, stuck in that car, stuck in the empty shell of his writer's block.

Usually, the highway was the best place to work out plot points. Work through dialogue. Unlock structure. The speed of driving echoed the flow of ideas. Inching along in gridlock, horns blaring, was not inspirational. He rolled forward and then locked his brakes quickly as two children stepped into the lane.

"Sorry!" their father called out, with the polite wave motorists offered when one did something stupid to the other.

"All good, brother."

The man wasn't much older than Mike, maybe thirty, and was already responsible for corralling an eight-year-old boy and a six-year-old girl out of traffic and toward the snow-covered park. The tiny girl turned and waved, too, before shoving her brother into a snow bank.

So that's what having a sister is like.

Had Delilah done that to Sergei? Had their father taken them to the park, or had life been too hard in Soviet Russia to enjoy? And hadn't the un-redacted MI6 document said…

KNOWN ASSOCIATES:

BROTHER (1): [REDACTED]

BROTHER (2): SERGEI [REDACTED]– KIA

SUMMARY NOTES:

LINK TO SEN. RICHARD STOCKTON III: **DISMISSED**

STATUS:

ALL KNOWN ASSOCIATES: DECEASED OR PRESUMED DECEASED

A horn blast tore through his thoughts.

"Excuse me, asshole, I'm unraveling here."

He cranked the wheel and pulled into a loading zone out of the way. He was like the girl in the story, ill-equipped for the weather and having no business being out in it, but he couldn't shake the feeling that the impending panic was coming from inside the car and he needed to get out.

He left the Lexus idling and strode away, testing whether he could dodge the suffocating anxiety by moving away from it. Best case, he could leave the panic behind, freeze it from his body with a few deep breaths of cold winter air. Worst case, his car would get towed from the snow route zone, and he'd be spared from this whole fucking dinner thing anyway.

Fine by me.

Beyond the spire of the Washington Monument, the White House loomed.

The White House.

The point of that night's dinner was almost certainly to rally Rick Stockton's most prominent supporters for one big push before Tuesday.

Super Tuesday.

D.C. politics didn't interest him in the slightest, but Rick Stockton treated him like a son and had supported him financially—and legally—more than once. He was being compensated for being Tom's responsible friend, but he would have done that anyway. Plus, he wasn't sure he should be the benchmark for responsible. Rick had to know that.

All he had to do was keep Tom alive until November. Alive and out of jail. Alive and off the front page for doing some stupid thing like dating the wrong girl, or making a joke in poor taste.

Just pretend he's your brother...

ALL KNOWN ASSOCIATES: DECEASED

The Xanax finally hit in a soothing wave. The panic left his body. Sure, it might return the second he got back inside the car, but it was too fucking cold to keep standing there. Time to face reality, or at least a chemically balanced version of it.

Not even his Gestapo Joe overcoat could protect him from the snow and the campaign at the same time.

CHAPTER FIVE

The drive took longer than Mike hoped, winding him through mind-numbing stretches of country highway. He exited, passed a lone lit intersection, and turned onto a street flanked by Colonial-style homes, including the one he grew up in. The Stocktons' sprawling estate sat at the end of the cul-de-sac, nestled along the forest line.

The guards recognized his car, or the digital surveillance system had already scanned him as he approached, and drew the electrified gate back automatically.

"They feeding you guys tonight?" he asked the poor freezing bastard posted in the guard shack.

"Nah, but we have coffee, and a space heater from the Regan era," the guard joked, holding up a pathetic-looking thermos.

"I'll slip you a doggie bag."

"You know, Mikey, I don't care what they say about you, you turned out alright."

"Don't let that get out."

Mike tossed out his smile as he rolled up the window. With his luck, Annabelle Stockton would be serving some kind of cold soup for dinner, and he'd have to renege on his offer to feed the guards. Even though the Greens had never had a staff, he'd spent enough time at the end of the street to know that to be successful in life, you had to make friends with the armed dude who worked the door.

The long driveway sloped gently toward the main house, a Greek-Revival with two-story columns trying like hell to imply it was the Truman Balcony. Typically, Mike would pull down the service driveway and park along the kitchen door, but this didn't feel like a slip-in-the-side kind of event, not with the number of cars parked out front already.

Two chauffeured town cars.

An SUV with a distinct military vibe and a government-issued license plate to match.

Jennifer Green's Acura, because God help her if she had to walk sixty feet.

And a BMW.

Kristin's BMW.

"Aww, fuck me. Here we go."

Mike stepped from the car, straightened his suit, and rapped on the door with the enormous brass knocker.

Tom answered, ahead of the Stocktons' housekeeper by a pace. A ring of sweat clung to his hairline as he fought through his parents' cocktail hour in stage two withdrawal. Anyone with half a clue what a junkie looked like would have clocked Tom Stockton immediately: the sallow skin, the bags under his eyes—Mike was surprised that no one had shoved him into a room and locked the door to keep him out of sight.

"It's not that hot in here, buddy. You ok?"

"No, I'm not ok. I'm dying here. They swept the place when they got home and dumped my stash. Are you holding?"

"Just so happens…"

Mike passed his ailing friend Delores Pemberton's bottle of Xanax, the one he'd already dipped into along the way, as he slid his overcoat down his arms.

"Xanax? That's it?"

"What were you hoping for?"

"Something that would take the pain of this dinner away."

"Take two."

"I'm going to take more than two. You want one?"

"I pre-gamed on the way over. Kristin is here?"

"Yeah, she's held up with your mom."

"Oh, great." The 'oh great' was sarcastic. Nothing good ever came from his girlfriend and his mother conspiring against him in a corner. "Who else is here?"

"The Holstons, the Mayor of D.C., and the CNO."

"CNO?"

"Chief of Naval Operations."

"As in the Joint Chiefs?"

"That's the one."

"Heavy guest list."

"Yeah, no kidding." Tom poured out two of the small blue pills and chewed them like children's vitamins. "Top off?"

"Yeah."

Mike reached for the bottle, but retracted his hand quickly when he saw his mother rounding the corner from the salon to the grand foyer.

Jennifer Green was the very portrait of a D.C. Society matron, as though she subscribed to a newsletter that told her exactly where to place the gold brooch and how to style her hair into a bird's nest on her head. Her voice pierced the air with a tone and volume that managed to sound both accusatory and judgmental, even when she wasn't making an accusation or passing judgment.

Tonight, she was doing both.

"There's my son, late as always." Jennifer leaned in for an embrace, then recoiled. "How many days have you been wearing this suit? Marta..." She called for the Stocktons' housekeeper as if the woman worked for her directly.

"Ma'am?"

"Can you steam his coat during dinner? It smells like the inside of a pack of Camels."

"Marta, don't bother. I intend to keep smoking. Also, you don't work for her."

"It's ok, Mr. Green. I'll take care of it. Your coat isn't the worst thing I've cleaned." The woman had been with the Stocktons since she arrived from Cuba in the eighties. His coat was definitely not the worst thing she'd cleaned. Not even that day.

Marta draped the coat over her arm and offered Mike a reassuring smile—the kind, he realized, he got from her more often than from his own mother. He mouthed 'thank you' before she winked and disappeared into the back-of-house corridors where the laundry and serving dishes could pass free of witness.

"Tom, give us a minute," Jennifer instructed.

"Yep." It was a relief to be excused from that interaction, and he disappeared up the stairs to hide the bottle now floating around in his pocket.

Jennifer caught Mike's face in both hands and studied him closely. A passerby would have mistaken it for a tender moment, a mother gazing at the child she raised, as she welcomed him to an evening of conviviality. It wasn't. She was looking for dilated pupils.

"You're high."

"No. Just really, really tired."

"Were you here last night?"

"You know I wasn't. You would have seen my car."

"What were you doing then?"

"You've been talking to Kristin."

"She said you were in a mood."

"A mood to not talk about Kristin."

"Well, that's fair. She is a Democrat." Jennifer looped her arm through his to guide him into the salon, where the tray-passed hors d'oeuvres and sparkling wine lubricated the guests before dinner.

The attendees were gathered in a cluster, anchored to the jolly voice holding court on the far side of the room. Laughter erupted at a punchline that had probably been off-color, given the eye-roll and head shake Annabelle Stockton gave as she separated herself to attend to the kitchen staff.

As the reactions subsided and the men parted to refresh their drinks, Rick Stockton rode out the tail end of his chuckle. Inside, he was a fierce political animal, but his surface gleamed like a man you'd want carving the holiday ham or delivering the State of the Union.

"Mikey! How ya been, kid?" Stockton crossed the room with his arms spread wide and slapped a powerful handshake on his son's best friend.

"Good, sir. Thank you." In this room, around these people, it was always 'sir'. When they were both sneaking a highball in the middle of the night and telling dirty jokes, then he was Rick.

"How have things been here?"

"Usual, or I'm sure you would have heard otherwise."

Rick waggled a finger at Mike like he was in on a private joke they were telling. The gesture was a trademark move that found its way into both Rick's public and private life. "I understand the last car was peeling out of the driveway this morning when our plane touched down."

"I couldn't speak to that, sir. I was working last night."

"When do I get the proof copy for my collection?"

"As soon as I manage to write the damn thing."

"Ehh, relax about it, kid," the senator said, clasping him on the back. "It'll pop in there when you least expect it."

A Navy uniform hovered in Mike's periphery, knowing better than to interrupt Rick Stockton when he was schmoozing, yet hovering close enough to insert himself at the first pause in conversation. Stockton pivoted like the professional he was when he saw the man lurking.

"Admiral, do you know my son's friend, Mike?"

"I don't. Pleasure, Mike," he said, extending his hand. The regalia was intimidating enough, but the grizzled man's face personified calculated power—the type that wouldn't hesitate to launch a nuke from a submarine.

"All mine," Mike said politely, despite noting that there hadn't been anything pleasurable about the walking incarnation of the Military Industrial Complex.

"You're friends with Tom?"

"Mike's the smart one. Keeps Tom walking the line. He's a lot like your boy."

"Let's hope that isn't true," the admiral scoffed.

"How is AJ? Mike, you'll excuse us?"

"Yep. Of course."

The admiral and senator stepped out into the hallway to speak in hushed tones, leaving Mike momentarily alone and debating where to loiter so that he'd be the least impactful to the gathering. Across the room, Jennifer Green held court, cornering the mayor's wife and the future First Lady hostage with her posturing, planting the idea for the Secretary of Education seat in her friend's mind for a year later, when cabinet appointments were being made.

Tom had disappeared.

He had nothing to talk to the mayor about.

The gathering was as awkward and uncomfortable as he'd predicted.

"You look as bored as I feel."

Mike knew the voice without turning around.

James Langham—a nice enough step-dad and the political equivalent of a beard—had married Jennifer Green around the same time Mike and Tom discovered pot. A woman couldn't be taken seriously in D.C. without a husband any more than a professional educator could be taken seriously without a child. Being her decor was all they had in common, but it was enough.

"I lost Tom, and I'm hiding from Kristin."

"Wise. Want one?" James held up his bourbon neat. The mid-fifties financial planner kept an easy hand in one pocket of his trousers and the other swirling the ice in the glass that hadn't had time to start sweating.

"I shouldn't."

"Well, that's a first."

"I'm trying something new."

James shrugged and moved off toward the brass bar in the corner, where that evening a bartender had been hired to pour the drinks. He could hold his own with the men when the discussion turned to horses—betting or riding on—but in the meantime, he would simply shuffle along on the sidelines where his wife kept him.

Mike veered back toward the front foyer, angling to find Tom in the less populated parts of the house. As he moved down the hall, Kristin popped out of the senator's private office. Both were equally startled to see one another.

"When did you get here?" she asked, tugging the door closed behind her.

"Five minutes ago. What were you doing in Rick's office?"

"I needed to take a call from my boss. I didn't think anyone here wanted to be reminded that I work for Rothschild."

"Probably right. I'm surprised you came."

"It would have been inappropriate to cancel at the last minute. Can we not make it weird all night?"

51

"Fine by me. I need to take a leak."

"Charming."

Mike continued to the powder room beyond Rick's office. The saturated scent of whiskey and coffee, undiluted by even a single glass of water, poured from his body. It was no wonder his head hurt. He was dehydrated, toxic, and his blood sugar would have been low enough to kill him had he not slid a flaky little spanikopita-something in his face as he left the salon. He needed an aspirin. Or four.

As he rifled through the medicine cabinet, Rick's office door slammed on the other side of the wall. The voice speaking was too low and quiet to carry through the drywall, but the vibration hummed for about a paragraph.

Rick Stockton was clear when he screamed his reply. "What do you want me to do? I don't even have the nomination yet!"

"Goddamn it, Rick! You roped my family into your attack on the president, and now you're just going to let Jacoby burn it all down on his way out of office?" It took a huge pair to raise your voice to Rick Stockton, and now that it was raised, it sounded like it belonged to the admiral.

"I didn't rope you into shit, Jay! You handed me those documents willingly because you fancy yourself SecDef someday. As for your kid getting involved, that one's on you!"

Footfalls charged in the direction of the dining room, but Mike loitered beyond the powder room door, giving them a head start. He knew that anyone who realized he was a writer would treat him like he was a reporter, assuming he'd take anything he heard to print. He wouldn't, but the admiral was terrifying. All of

Rick's associates were. Mike may not have held any actual political power, but he was raised to mingle in the rooms where it was traded, and that meant also knowing when to give it a wide berth and disappear.

CHAPTER SIX

"Friends, before they plate dinner, I want to take a moment to thank you all for your support on this run-up to Super Tuesday."

Rick Stockton was at home at the head of the table, sleeves rolled to the forearms to project casual command, and a glass raised to incite a toast. To his right, Annabelle gazed at him with practiced admiration. She was every bit as calculated and shrewd, and if they won, she'd be just as responsible. But her perceived place was at his side, and she played it to perfection.

To Rick's left sat the Holstons, Ron and Susan. The junior senator from Arizona and his wife had been glomming onto the Stocktons—or rather, "bringing youthful energy to their sage wisdom"—since 1991.

The rest of the table filled out in descending hierarchy of importance: the admiral, the mayor and Mrs. Mayor, the Greens, Tom, and finally Kristin.

"The next nine months are sure to be a wild ride, but thanks to my ... allies in this room tonight..." Rick paused to land the line. "I know we will all have a seat at 1600!"

"Here, here!" Holston said, rising with his glass to stand at Rick's side

"Of course Ron's in agreement—he's hoping to get the nod."

"I'll bring you a swing state!"

Holston wasn't waiting around for "the nod." That decision had been made in a back room or a brandy-soaked study years ago over cigars and the threat of blackmail. His act was a rehearsal for the future cameras.

"To a Stockton-Holston ticket!" Annabelle cheered.

Everyone erupted in a chant of "Stockton-Holston '96!" And a chorus of clinking glasses. Everyone but Tom and Kristin.

Her eyes radiated hatred. It went past not being a registered Republican. Her disgust for these men was at a cellular level, indoctrinated in her youth. She stared into their foreheads, her disgust tucked behind the polite gaze of dinner party decorum. It wasn't enough to draw comment, but Mike recognized it. He'd seen her disgusted enough times to know exactly what it looked like.

He had also seen Tom about to throw up enough times to recognize that, too. The sweats had passed, leaving a sallow, clammy chill in their place. The bloody prime rib being plated in front of them couldn't have been helpful either.

Tom needed air, and if not air, he needed to go outside so when he hurled, it wasn't on the mayor of D.C. Mike nudged him under the table and tilted his head in the direction of the patio.

"Excuse me, everyone. I'm going to step out for a cigarette," Tom said.

"My son, the proud supporter of our best Virginia crop. I've tried to get him onto cigars, but no dice."

The table laughed at Tom's expense before Mike could jump in to back him up.

"I like a good Republican crop, too," Mike said. "You'll excuse me with him?"

They stepped through the kitchen onto the side patio, where they were allowed to smoke without polluting Mrs. Stockton's potpourri dish fragrances, and sparked two cigarettes.

"Do you think there's a smoking patio at the White House, or is this another thing I'm going to have to give up when they drag me there like I'm on house arrest?"

"You actually are on house arrest."

"No, Lindsey made that go away. You should tell my dad that you need a roommate. I bet he'd let me live with you again. I bet he'd even pay the rent like college."

"I don't need your dad to pay my rent anymore."

"Come on. It would be fun. Like old times! Us, living in the city, hitting the clubs. You and me..."

"And your Secret Service detail. You'd still be the First Son."

"Fuck, you're right." Tom kicked a bench that sat up against the house and then paced, agitated and unraveling. "He can't win. I can't live like that. I need to do something to make sure he loses. Or at least convince him that I should live out here. Maybe if I got sick, or hurt myself..."

"Tom, don't talk like that. I don't have time for a 5150 right now."

"I could just tell my boss about that black folder he's got sitting on his desk." Kristin strolled out onto the patio and plucked the cigarette from Tom's hand.

It really would be that easy. Or Tom could reveal something—anything—to her. The drugs. The parties. The list of D.C.'s

56

daughters he'd been with. None of it was about the senator directly, but the raging black sheep could siphon votes away anyway. Or, there were any number of questionable dealings he'd overheard that would have been enough for whoever Rothschild's Lindsey was to use against him.

"Stop it. Both of you," Mike said, stamping out his cigarette. His head was throbbing, and he wasn't ready to have a whole conversation with Kristin.

"Right. Fight with me at lunch, shut your mom down when you get here, and now bail on your best friend. We're in the 'systematically shut everyone out' phase in the Gestapo Joe universe. Who's next, Mike?"

Who's next?

The clock was running out on his deadline, and he hadn't written a word. Every time he had stared at a blank page that day, it had filled up with rip-off versions of a Ukrainian girl fighting the mafia, and he hadn't figured out how Joe fit in yet.

He gazed out over the grounds, past the guest house now repurposed as a Secret Service bunkhouse. Beyond that were the stables. A faint smell of horses floated in the air. Shit and smoke, all he was missing was coffee. And his overcoat.

Mike's brain had taken a break from creative contemplation while he was forced to be social, but the chill in the air and the mist over the fields had forced it to return to thoughts of dead girls and detectives.

"I need to go home."

"Here he goes," Kristin said, stamping out her cigarette.

"I need to make my deadline."

"You and your responsibilities. You're as bad as AJ. At least he'd feel obligated to stay and make sure I don't slit my wrists."

"Who's AJ?"

"Lindsey's new ONI Barbie. And perhaps my new best friend if you're going to ditch me every night."

"It isn't you, Tom. He's avoiding me because the only thing he's more loyal to than your father is his commitment to hiding in his apartment and dissociating."

"It's literally my job."

"Jesus, do you need me here for this?" Whether from the detox or the cold, Tom had started to shake. Even if he wasn't in enough agony already, watching them bicker would've driven him back inside.

"I don't even need *me* here for this." Mike tossed his butt into the standing ashtray and aimed for the kitchen door.

"That's it? You're walking away again?" Kristin asked.

He halted, with one hand on the door. "Again? You walked away this afternoon."

"And I came out here to apologize."

"Hell of a way to tee up an apology."

"Yeah, I'm out," Tom said, sliding toward the kitchen door.

Mike opened the door for Tom and waved him through before facing her again. "You were saying?"

"I was saying, I know I shouldn't insult your relationship with Rick. If he can separate his business and personal life, so should I. And I shouldn't chastise you for the time you spend researching or writing. That's fundamental to who you are."

"Then why do you keep doing it?"

"Because we've been together almost six months, and I don't know where this is going. I guess I'm just feeling insecure. Can you relate?"

"I mean, obviously."

"I know I'm equally guilty of putting my work first, so let's spend a little time tonight making each other the priority. "

She pressed herself against him, sliding her hands around his chest. For a moment, he forgot he was angry, forgot the toxic way she controlled him by threatening to return him to the orphanage in his head. She pulled him into a kiss, and he gave in.

"Now, that's better," she said once she'd dragged her lips away from his. "I'll follow you back to D.C., you can give me your parking spot, and then you can tell me why this file you saw got into your head."

"The file?"

"On the Ukrainian girl…?"

"Did I say she was Ukrainian?"

"You obviously did. How else would I know that?"

Anything was possible; he hadn't been sober in days.

"Kris, I appreciate the interest, but if I stay up tonight at all, it needs to be to finish those pages. I need to write three chapters in twelve hours. Just give me a day. I'll make it up to you."

"I'm going to hold you to that."

She took him by the hand and led him back into the kitchen, where Marta was already waiting with his coat in one hand and his uneaten dinner wrapped up for him in the other.

"You're so good to me, Marta," he said, kissing the loyal housekeeper on the cheek.

"I know, *mijo*. It's because I can see no one else is." She shot a protective glance at Kristin—the woman she felt had infiltrated her household and was using her boy.

But Kristin had already moved on.

"Go out the side, baby. They won't even notice you've left."

CHAPTER SEVEN

Once he'd passed his to-go bag to the guard at the gate as promised, he turned the heater up, the radio on, and settled into the rhythm of the road, hoping it would yield something he could put on the page. The drive home carried him down a two-lane highway lit only by headlights—the kind of uninterrupted stretch that made his mind wander to places where it found words.

If he could only think past the glare ricocheting off the rearview mirror.

"Everyone on the road is an asshole today," he muttered. Talking to himself—he chalked it up to brainstorming, not lunacy. "I need a plot line... an alcoholic detective with questionable morals plot line..."

"I resemble that remark."

Gestapo Joe materialized in the passenger seat—Mike's self-portrait with his popped collar and his cigarette in hand. The only difference was that the detective version liked to sport a fedora.

And wasn't real.

A normal, sober person would have called him a hallucination. Mike called him a "character he was working on."

"You got anything constructive to say over there, or are you just here for the ride-along?" Mike asked.

"I'm keeping you awake because you kept popping Xanax, you shitbag."

"You're one to talk. That a bottle of Jack in your hand?"

"Booze is a good detective's talisman. Whiskey never made anyone crash a car."

"That is patently false."

"Focus. What kind of trouble am I going to get up to in this book?"

"You tell me."

"Ok, go with me on this: Guy gets killed. Wife is guilty. She gets away with it because she blows our hero."

"We did that already."

"Right. Ok. Guy gets killed. Wife is not guilty. I bend her over a desk."

"Neither of us is any good at this. It's a miracle I have a career." Mike adjusted the mirror again to bounce the irritatingly close tailgater's lights out of his eyes.

"I got it…" Joe said. "Guy gets killed. Wife is guilty, but really, she was framed, see, and she's not guilty. I get her off, so she gets me off."

"Just…shut up. None of this is working."

"Ok, ok, ok. I've got one more…"

"How about girl gets killed?" Delilah suddenly occupied the passenger seat where Mike's alter ego had been a moment earlier. Blood oozed from the side of her head where the skull had been blown apart, but she still smiled—just like her morgue photos. "Because this story, I can help with."

"Jesus fucking Christ!"

Mike swerved, locking his brakes in a reflexive jolt, which sent his tailgater friend jerking wildly onto the shoulder.

"Maybe if you hadn't been up my whole ass since the Arlington County line, you'd still have your front fender!" Mike screamed into the mirror at the direction of the displaced follower.

"Meisha, ignore it," Delilah said. "I'm your story."

"Can you be my story with the rest of your head intact, maybe?"

"I'm sorry, that's part of the story. Part of our story."

He rolled the Lexus to a stop at the next exit and turned to the passenger seat, but she was gone. Joe was gone. Mike was alone, like he had always been. Only the song was still in his head.

It was after midnight when he finally turned into the underground parking garage, after looping 395 more times than he cared to count. He'd traced his thought paths: Georgetown, where Gestapo Joe was born. Maryland, for no good reason. The Washington Monument. Something about its weird two-toned stones looked like a mistake someone hadn't cared enough to undo, and he had always found that relatable.

After he'd stood in the cold staring at the spire long enough that a Capitol policeman clocked him twice, he got back in the car and pulled quickly onto Thirteenth Street, cutting off a dark sedan with a dented fender. It honked, but still let him enter the lane.

"Sorry," he muttered, offering the motorist an apology wave. "Guess I'm the asshole now."

Both cars edged north.

Plenty of people drive north.

But not all of them stay on your bumper.

The headlight's beam stayed fixed in the rearview, occasionally catching the flicker of Joe's fedora in the rearview as Mike strained to see the driver. The blinding glare obscured the figure, riding his tail to Massachusetts.

Plenty of people take Thirteenth to Logan Circle.

"At least you're back in my head," Joe said. "Good sign, maybe I'll see some action tonight."

"Don't count on it," Mike muttered, pulling into the underground garage.

The subterranean level smelled perpetually of fresh paint and cold metal, except in the summer when the humidity hung inside and made it smell like baked trash. The elevator came quickly, lifting him to his fourth-floor apartment before the cold could creep in from the trash chute and claim him.

He peeled off his coat and gave it a sniff. Marta had managed to mask the smoke and whiskey, if not perform a dry cleaning miracle, in the short time she'd had it. She'd even tucked the diamond ring back into the pocket, though if he were propping up a side-by-side list of things she'd done for him compared to Kristin, he should have let Marta keep it. He didn't know how much she was paid, but it wasn't enough, and a stone like that might double her net worth.

He took a moment to pour ground coffee into a filter and hit brew before pressing play on the flashing answering machine light.

"*Mike, so help me, at least call me back and let me know you didn't OD on opiates or something trying to crank out these pages. Call me in the morning and give me your treatment. I can probably get you an extra week if we can show that the delay is because you're writing the screen adaptation at the same time. Wink-wink. Help me help you.*"

The message ended with a beep, and the drag of the tiny tape inside rewound to start again the next time she called him.

"You're on to something with that, Lucy, but if I call you back, it's going to be to ask you to find me a copy of an out-of-print book."

Tom was now in possession of Delores Pemberton's Xanax, but Mike still had David somebody's bottle of Vicodin. He flipped open the medicine cabinet, popped two tablets, and bit down. As the mirror floated closed, a dead girl watched from over his shoulder.

"Fuck! Would you stop doing that?"

"Doing what?" Delilah asked.

"Materializing. Looking like a zombie. Bleeding on my bathroom floor."

"Stop taking the drugs."

"Oh, no. Drugs are going to get me three chapters tonight."

He shoved past her apparition—hallucination? memory?— and flopped to the beanbag chair on the living room floor.

"I'll get you three chapters tonight," she said.

"And you're here because, drugs. I don't tend to interact with my imaginary friends without them."

"I'm not here because of the drugs, Meisha."

"Right. You're actually not here at all, but if you want to tell me that story you teased, I could use a jump start."

He turned to where the vision had stood, but she wasn't there.

"Probably for the best," he muttered, getting to work.

Dead Girls Tell No Tales

Chapter One: Normally, I love a good body. Especially the kind lacking a pulse. But I found this dame in an alley on my way home from Schmitty's. Don't ask what I was doing in the alley in the first place, but it rhymes with "taking a piss." Hold on, I'm getting ahead of myself over here.

Schmitty's.

Yeah, it's two blocks from the station house, ya know. I'd stopped in for a quick tumble. Nope, tumbler. Something to wash the taste of that Betty broad from my mouth so that I could start over tomorrow. I had one whiskey. Glass, not bottle, in case you were wondering.

Schmitty and I talked about the ponies a bit, and then he tells me to beat it, like, so I tossed him a Lincoln for his trouble, and ducked out into the alley. That's when I found her.

She was a foxy broad for one with rigor mortis. Dead sexy, you might say. Neck broken like a little bird. Someone clipped her wings good.

I stumbled back inside to use Schmitty's horn. Called it into the boys anonymous-like because I knew lickety-split the fuzz would be all over that alley, and the last thing I need is to get involved with another dame, especially the cold kind.

I high-tailed it outta there. Let the poor schmuck on nights catch this one. I was headed home. I'd had my share of dames lately and was looking forward to catching a case with a good old-fashioned dead man, preferably one who was unmarried and without daughters.

It was a good plan, a great plan, except the next morning this bird strolls into my office, a dead-ringer for the dead girl, and says, "I need a dick."

"I've been known to be one of those."

I offered to pour her a drink since it was already nine a.m. and drinks don't pour themselves.

"Brandy?"

"No, the name's Margarita, thank you. I need to find my twin sister. She's been missing for two days, and I think someone killed her. They meant to kill me."

CHAPTER EIGHT

The milky light filtered through Mike's bedroom window, though he couldn't remember relocating himself there from his writer's nest. He cleared the haze in his eyes and focused on the clock sitting on his nightstand.

Six.

A.m. or p.m.?

Ultimately, it didn't matter. Either way, he wanted coffee.

Mike stretched long, cracking his neck as he stood. As the coffee pot fired up, he found his laptop to review what he'd written overnight.

Three chapters. Thirty-six pages that launched Joe's next journey, composed in something of a fugue state. The writing wasn't bad. It wasn't publishable yet, but it was enough to keep his agent from sending a sheriff to his apartment on a wellness check.

He unplugged the phone cord, dragging the Ethernet line across the kitchen counter until he could stab it into the port on his computer and start the whirring sounds of dial-up internet.

When the tiny globe in the upper right-hand corner illuminated to tell him he was 'online', he opened an email platform and composed a new message, thankful he could now do that from his own kitchen instead of lugging himself to a coffee shop to send one electronic communication.

To: lucy.dmarco@fifthandlexpub.com

Fr: mgreen101073@aol.com

Sun. March 10, 1996

Lucy—took your advice and got real high so I could crank out these pages. Kidding. Now that I cracked it open, I should be done soon.—MG.

One box ticked. One looming, panic-inducing raincloud lifted.

A peek out the window settled the A.M./P.M. debate— evening—which meant not only had he met his deadline, he'd slept for twelve hours afterward. He'd slept through the narcotic crash, too, and the detox migraine that usually followed.

Rested.

Clean.

Responsibilities met.

He was ready to go—ready to clutch the comet's tail of creativity while it was still within reach.

Ready to revisit Delilah's dossier.

Telling himself he was going to the archives for more research was an inner monologue of lies. Nothing in his manuscript came from sanitized news articles or vintage police blotters. It was passing through his fingertips from his mind.

Or you have help.

If the only way to trigger that help was holding her autopsy in his hand again, he'd risk it—risk the sick feeling in his stomach, or the screams he could hear when he looked at her broken skull. He'd risk a panic attack to feel close to her again.

Mike filled a travel mug with the hot coffee and ventured out into the city streets a new man.

No—as Gestapo Joe.

He stalked the unsuspecting, eyes darting over every detail, cutting through alleys, and noticing the guilty-looking. He watched for something incriminating or odd. It was D.C. at night, plenty of both could be found if you were looking.

Two men huddled on a street corner.

Maybe they're slinging dope.

A woman clutched her purse and walked with her head down.

Trying to make it home without becoming a victim. Or maybe she shoplifted something in that bag.

A guy in a leather jacket walked in the same direction.

And maybe this guy is following me.

The key to thinking like a detective wasn't to look for something suspicious or out of place; it was to assume everything was.

Ooh, that's a good line. I need to remember to use that.

He spun, looking for Leather Jacket again, but he'd vanished.

Because not everything is suspicious in the real world.

At Pennsylvania Avenue, he made a sharp turn, then cut right at 9th Street, passing the bookstore. This time, the poster didn't threaten him as much. He stopped and stared at the silhouette of the curvy dame.

He knew Joe would get mixed up with Margarita. He knew Margarita was supposed to be dead, not her twin, killed by mistake.

"I know who's next, I just need to know who done it."

"The government."

Delilah stood at his side again.

"Thank you for, you know, wearing your whole head this time."

She shrugged.

"I can't do a government conspiracy story. It's too close to home. Although that admiral was an evil villain if I've ever seen one."

"Blame the mafia."

"That could work. Joe sinks into the seedy Havana nightclubs and the dark streets of Miami, chasing Cuban racketeers in '57 Bel Airs."

"It isn't that glamorous."

"But I could make it glamorous. A sexy noir for the screen."

A movie deal had been rumored for a while, though he didn't believe it would happen. Maybe if he wrote a good enough story, he could adapt it and move to L.A. to be one of those film guys.

He wondered what would happen to Tom when he was gone. *Probably nothing.*

Tom would be locked in the Residence with his own Secret Service detail for the next decade. Tom wasn't Mike's problem tonight; Joe was.

"Yeah, who am I kidding? It won't be that good."

"So you *do* like cheesy detective novels?" The cute bookstore girl poked her head out, and Delilah evaporated. "Or do you just like talking to advertisements?"

"Yeah...that probably looked weird."

"Well, I'm glad you came by. I realized you didn't give me your number."

"My number?" *The* smile crept across his face. Female attention hit differently when he wasn't having a panic attack. "What did you want to do with that?"

"Let you know that I found the book you were looking for." She pulled it from her green apron and handed it to him.

A Thousand Words Unspoken by Delilah Grennan

Mike's pulse quickened.

An hour earlier, he had thought his only source of new information would be revisiting Delilah's buried asset file, but he'd just been handed 388 new pages of content.

"Where did you get this?"

"You know that barrel of used book donations? They go to schools, so I have to sort through and pull out the R-rated stuff. This was right on top."

"That seems... planted."

The key to thinking like a detective wasn't to look for what was suspicious or out of place; it was to assume everything was.

"Planted? Throwing out a book in a giant barrel of books, hoping that the exact girl you mentioned it to would find it, pull it out, and happen to see you walk by? Are you one of those conspiracy guys?"

"I mean, there's no way Oswald pulled that trigger, but no."

She laughed genuinely. Not the fake laugh people forced among Washington's elite, and not the compulsory laugh Kristin manufactured out of obligation —simply a genuine, sweet laugh.

Delilah's laugh probably sounded like that.

"It was really thoughtful of you to save it for me. Can I buy you a drink or something?"

"In three years."

Dammit.

"Well, at least you're eighteen, and this whole interaction hasn't been a crime. I owe you a latte then."

"That isn't necessary. I was just being a nice person."

"Ok, well, now I know what that looks like. And I guess I know what I'm doing tonight." He held up the paperback. "Thanks…"

"Kellie."

Mike extended his hand. "Joe."

"Nice to meet you, Joe."

"Actually, it's Mike. I don't know why I lied just then, other than you work at a bookstore and I didn't want you to know I write cheesy detective novels."

He glanced back at the poster.

"Wow, you were talking to your own advertisement?"

"Yep. Getting worse by the second. Thank you for this, Kellie. Goodnight."

She couldn't help but laugh at him. "Goodnight, Mike."

Mike rolled his eyes at his own idiocy and immediately crossed the street to put distance between Bookstore Kellie and his embarrassment.

He buried his head in the first page of the book, disappearing, ready to look up and find himself with Delilah in the Soviet Union, not on the Green Line as it ran through Chinatown. He buried it so deep that he forgot his street eyes and missed the man boarding the train behind him wearing a leather jacket.

CHAPTER NINE

I've never wanted to risk someone knowing me. Not in this house. Not in this town. Finally, I have enough English to write this secretly. Not perfectly, a word or two still slips out in Russian, but I think sometimes if I don't get my thoughts out, they will rattle in my head and shake it apart. My birthday felt like a good time to start something new.

I'm not so naive as to believe I should be celebrated on this day, just... not insulted. I was in the kitchen earlier—the room with the fewest windows, where the chill doesn't bite as quickly. Sergei and this friend of his—Dmitri Zdrastkova—burst through the door already drunk on vodka, their laughter roaring.

They laugh while the rest of us worry.

Sergei unzipped his coat and poured out everything you could imagine: fresh fruits, caviar, cakes. Dmitri was carrying two more bottles of vodka.

"Happy birthday," Sergei said. He tossed a pastry box at me. Cake was a luxury, and yet he dismissed it so casually.

"Where did you get all of this? No one can buy these things unless they're —"

"Don't worry about it," Dmitri cut in. He helped himself to turning down the music I was using to disappear. "Western trash," he muttered.

With his coat off, he caught the same chill I've lived with my whole life, the one that never goes away, even in the summer months. He moved to turn on the stove, but I stopped him. I don't think this boy is used to being stopped.

"Dmitri, we can't afford the gas! Use the gas at your own house. Or sit next to one of your ten fireplaces."

"We only have four fireplaces," he answered, sticking his tongue out. His manor home sits beyond the square, protected by a giant iron gate. When my brother and I were small, we used to sneak over there and try to see inside. This was before we knew who owned this palace.

Ivan Zdrastkova.

Ivan the Terrible.

"What are you writing?" I could barely understand him; he spoke with his mouth full of these rich foods they stole.

"A book about how much I hate you."

I let him pick up my notebook, knowing he can't read English, then I laughed at his ignorance. Even if he picked out a word or two, he'd never be able to tell if what I'm writing is fiction or truth. And I believe no one is ever really telling the truth.

He tossed the notebook back to the table, offended.

"Come on, Serge, let's go."

"Take your stolen food with you."

My brother's eyes lingered on mine, silently pleading with me to stop. He was one of the people afraid to speak up against Dmitri, his so-called friend.

"It's not stolen, and it will help Papa. Please."

We had been close growing up. Best friends. He was the only one who never looked at me like he regretted my arrival, but the light in him is gone, replaced by something darker in Dmitri's shadow. It scares me.

If this darkness can consume someone who has always held such light, there is nothing stopping it from coming for us all.

Mama either pretends she doesn't see it or chooses not to. Her little boy can do no wrong at all—something about mothers and sons...

"I wouldn't know anything about that." Mike rolled to one side, holding the book next to him in the empty space where someone else might lie. If he soft-focused, it was almost like she was there, reading to him in the book's place.

"I don't understand any bond between parent and child. My mother treated me like a burden," Delilah said.

"At least they didn't drop you off at an orphanage and force you to grow up feeling like a prop."

"Maybe because the Soviet orphanages were full." Delilah leaned casually on one elbow, the way girls do at slumber parties. "Orphanages were full. Grocery stores weren't. Criminals controlled the flow of goods, forcing people like my father to give up their salaries in exchange for 'protection'. Under Communism, it was one thing to send the *vory* out to skim from the State, but once there *was* no state, they took from everyone."

"What about the police?"

She laughed.

She did laugh like Bookstore Kellie.

"They were the ones we needed protection from."

"Gangs on police payroll. We have that too."

"That's because young men believe they are invincible, which makes them perfect for carrying guns in their coats and making demands of old men."

The muted argument between Rick Stockton and the admiral flashed through Mike's mind again. "That might have been preferable to the old men making the demands."

"We had those, too."

Delilah rolled onto her back and stared up at the ceiling as if she were remembering...

I couldn't sleep that night. I couldn't sleep any night, but that night my thoughts raced. If I hadn't been awake, I might not have heard my brother come home, but I would have heard him stumble into my room, drunk, and collapse on the floor in a heap.

"You're awake!" His volume control had been lost to the bottom of a bottle. "I got you something."

Sergei crawled across the floor and hoisted himself up, using the side of the bed to steady the spinning room.

"Is it Western Trash?"

"Forget Zdrastkova. Who cares? Open it."

He produced a small green box with a ribbon. Already, I was thinking of things I could use this ribbon for in ways with more purpose than decoration. Inside was a silver necklace—a delicate chain with a feather charm. It was truly beautiful, but inappropriate.

"Feathers. Like they make the old pens with. Because you like writing."

"Sergei, if you could afford a silver necklace, why didn't you fix our heater before winter?"

"You can never just appreciate a nice thing!" he snapped, rising. "Everything to you needs to be some kind of act of servitude!"

"Everything you do needs to be an act of rebellion! What did our father ever do to make you go against everything he stands for and join the Zdrastkovas?"

"What did the system ever do to you to make you want to stand for it?"

Maybe we're both a little wrong in our convictions, but it seems the family is divided down the middle over the Zdrastkovas. My father was friends with Ivan during the war, but that alliance was broken long before I was alive.

Sergei took the necklace from its box and put it around my neck.

"I can't wear this. I'll be robbed in the street."

"No. Soon, everyone will know who I am, and no one will dare touch you."

"What does that mean? Who you are?"

"Keep it. Please. Then I will always know a piece of me is still with you."

It was like... how do you say it... rasstavaniye— a farewell to who we'd been.

I wanted to take the necklace off immediately and hide it, but I'd never worn jewelry. I felt special. Loved. Protected—like the women who came and went from the Zdrastkova mansion. And I hated myself for not hating how it felt.

When I wore the necklace on a date with Pavel Zirkoyu, I looked like one of the fancy European girls who watch his hockey team play abroad. If he is drafted by the NHL, maybe he will take me with him to Canada or the U.S. More empty dreams, I know, but dreams are all I have. I was going to study journalism, but this job is looking more and more dangerous since the Independence. It would be safer to marry a rich *hockey player and emigrate. Plus, his cousin grew up in America and publishes books in New York City! How long should you date someone before you ask them to send in a manuscript?*

Mike closed the book on his thumb to mark his place and folded back the cover to look at the copyright page.

"The hell it is."

No wonder it was yanked. Someone ran a first edition of her journal, thinking they had a *Go Ask Alice* for the nineties, and then she wound up dead. Sergei and Dmitri had both been named as known associates in the British Intelligence Service memo, and their names were still here plain as day. If their names were real, and places were real, the incidents were real too. If she named her enemies, if she went into detail about the criminal consortium her brother belonged to and exposed them, it would have gotten her killed.

ALL KNOWN ASSOCIATES: DECEASED

It had gotten everyone killed.

CHAPTER TEN

Things with Pavel are... how do I want to say... progressing! Tonight, he offered to take me to **ритм**—*a nightclub in City Center. When I told him that I had nothing to wear to this place, he bought me a dress! A bit revealing, but who cares, I'm still young, yes?*

As Pavel waited for me to change into something pretty for him, Dmitri and Sergei returned to the house. Five minutes later, and we could have avoided the confrontation.

"What are you doing here?" my brother asked.

The three men stared and circled each other like stags about to lock horns. Pavel didn't flinch. He stands taller than both of them and planted himself firmly like he would on the ice, about to absorb a hit.

"Taking your sister out."

"You think so, huh? I don't recall giving you my permission," Dmitri said. He tried to stand eye-to-eye, to force Pavel into submission the way he was used to doing, but it didn't work. He flashed his waistband instead.

"I don't need your permission, Zdrastkova."

"No one needs your permission for anything!" I said, interrupting. I had hoped to break up their stare, anchored and fixed on each other, but they stayed firmly locked. "You're not even allowed in this house."

"Guess you'll be leaving," Pavel taunted.

"No, we will." I turned to my brother, refusing to speak to Dmitri again. "Don't wait up for me."

"Which club are you going to?" he asked.

"Why? So you can send a Zdrastkova enforcer to follow us? No, I don't think so." I took Pavel's arm, squeezing myself into the space where his chest pressed toward Dmitri's, forcing them apart. As we passed, Dmitri grabbed my wrist.

"You know he has a reputation?"

"And you don't?" Pavel shot back.

"He collects girls like dolls, and he's a mean drunk."

I looked down at my wrist, clenched in his fingers, choking off the circulation to my hand. "You're worried about him hurting me?"

Dmitri released his grip as if he hadn't even realized that he'd turned violent and turned his stare back on Pavel. "If he does, I will kill him."

I shoved through the door, dragging Pavel away before they could escalate.

We shook this encounter off and still enjoyed the club. Pavel can afford things: bottle service, private tables, clothes to dress me in. I danced to American music as he watched me; my curves accentuated by the fitted dress, the music guiding my hips. I liked being desired. If this is my only commodity, I must learn to cash in on it. Buy my ticket to freedom with the only currency I possess.

My head swirled with vodka and music and desire. I told him to take me back to his house before the rhythm and the drinks wore off, so we could...

A scratching sound pulled Mike from his immersion. A sscccccchhhh. Or maybe a rattle. He slipped the archive photo that he'd been using as a bookmark between the pages and set the book aside, waiting for the sound to repeat.

Maybe it's nothing, pal, because you aren't living in a detective novel.

The second time, the front doorknob twisted—side to side—luckily, the deadbolt stayed planted. Mike held his breath, deciding whether to approach the peephole. One of his neighbors was notorious for coming home hammered and walking into the wrong apartment. The guy was harmless, and usually it ended with an "oh, shit, sorry" and him wandering the fourth floor until he realized he lived on the third floor. The interaction could often be avoided entirely if left to run its course.

The knob jiggled again.

"Wrong apartment, buddy," Mike called through the door.

"Mike?"

He threw the door open to find Kristin standing in the hallway, a little boozy and a lot insistent that she come in. After he leaned into the hallway to confirm no one else was out there, he shut the door behind them.

"Where have you been all weekend?" she asked, peeling off her coat to reveal a body-con dress that belonged in a nightclub more than this living room.

"Here. Working."

"Not answering the phone?"

He had to think for a moment before answering. "I was using the phone line for email. What day is it?"

Kristin looked at her watch dramatically, judging his detachment with a flick of her wrist. "Sunday, but nearly Monday."

"What are you doing here?"

"I felt like some company."

She kicked off her heels and padded barefoot to the kitchen, helping herself to two glasses from the cabinet. As she reached for them, he could see the muscles in her back stretch long one by one, and her tailbone arch up slightly to give her an added inch. She knew he'd notice the invitation.

"Where were you tonight dressed like that?"

"A work thing," she answered, taking a bottle of vodka from the freezer. "You want one?"

He didn't. If it were Sunday night, he'd been clean for two days—almost a record. Part of him wanted to keep it going because if he could go two days, he could go three, and then maybe get off the merry-go-round. Caffeine to rocket him through the day. Opiates to take the edge off—benzos to bring him down enough to sleep. Then, not sleeping anyway and needing caffeine again.

He thought too long about what to say, and she'd already poured the glass, handed it to him, and disappeared toward the bathroom.

Well, fuck it.

He took the first sip. It was unexpectedly sour—not usually his reaction to vodka.

"You would have hated it," she called from the other room. "Everyone wanted to talk about Super Tuesday, and that spiraled into a real-time retelling of the entire Senate Intelligence Hearing of '94. They practically had President Jacoby hanging martyred from a cross and Stockton spearing him in the side to drink his blood."

"You sound almost sympathetic."

"Almost."

She reappeared on the beat, wearing only lingerie —the kind of lacy set that went on sale twice a year in a boutique and was otherwise too expensive.

"Wow. How were you hiding that under that dress?"

"You like?"

He liked her lingerie a hell of a lot more than he liked her personality. Before he could answer, she pressed herself against him and trailed her fingers along his hip bones, sliding them down his thighs.

They moved to the couch. Mike dropped to the cushion and guided her onto his lap, tracing the outline of her body and grazing the lace with his fingertips. The tactile difference between skin and fabric was fascinating—smooth like heated glass as he slid his hands up her arms and down her back, but pebbled like fresh sand when he trailed them across the line of her panties.

I'm fucking high.

It had been a long time since Mike had done E. Tom was a notorious Molly-dropper in college, and for a few months in there, Mike had joined him in rolling through party after party. It always made the lights kaleidoscope until he could taste colors and hear light. He couldn't, but by the time he felt that way, he'd usually forgotten himself enough to let some girl go down on him, and for a few hours, he could pretend he was Tom—carefree and unburdened.

Kristin roofied me?

He knew his head wasn't spinning from a shot of vodka. A professional like him needed the bottle to get anywhere near the level of pliability that he found himself sinking toward. Once the pleasure pills stunted his inhibitions, he'd feel confident and assertive. Every cell in his body would resonate and release, and once the euphoria had passed, he'd start to run at the mouth, a strange side effect of turning off the reservation center of his brain.

Why?

Was he usually so bad at intimacy that she needed him drugged to play along? Was she acting out some fantasy of her own? It didn't matter. He was on the ride now, and whatever this was, it was more enjoyable than her usual disinterest in him as a person, let alone a lover.

She dragged him to the bedroom, spreading herself out across the bed, an unwrapped gift. Every synapse fired, every neuron erupted until Mike collapsed back onto the pillows in a cloud of literal ecstasy.

Kristin uncoupled herself and reached across to the nightstand, grazing her breasts across him as she plucked two cigarettes from the pack. As she lit one for each of them, her eyes locked on something else sitting on the nightstand.

"This is the book, huh?"

"One of them. She wrote two." This was the chatty part of the drug spiral he wasn't a fan of, unless it was creating Joe's dialogue.

"Fiction or nonfiction?"

"Unclear." He paused a moment, not wanting to talk to Kristin about Delilah, but his swimming head was doing its own thing. "The characters feel real."

"You always think characters are real. Your imagination makes them so—it's why you do what you do."

"That's the nicest thing you've ever said to me."

She ignored the jab, fanning the pages and noting the journal formatting and the marginalia he'd already scribbled as he followed along, explicating the text like it was evidence in a case. The archival photo stopped her cold.

"Where did you get this?"

"I stole it from the intelligence file in the archives."

Her tone shifted as she assessed how far down he'd already sunk into this. "Jesus, Mike. This thing is fucking with your head. Maybe you should stop."

"Stop? I'm just getting started."

"Seriously." Her tone was cautionary, as if for a moment she actually cared about him. "Pursuing a rogue investigation is careless. You're going to end up in over your head."

"You know what else I'm just getting started on?"

"What?"

He answered her with a flip, rolling her onto her back and pressing inside of her again. "Not letting good X go to waste."

CHAPTER ELEVEN

The room was still dark, but he couldn't sleep. He'd tried—fighting the draw to stand up, hoping if he tried counting backward the way the nuns had taught him, his mind might retreat to the same place his body still hovered. It wasn't working. He stood.

As he blinked the room into focus, he could see the other beds lining the walls, each holding a tiny inmate. Those children had no trouble sleeping. Maybe because they'd spent all day playing, running, exhausting themselves with each other's company, while he sat alone reading. Their brains were exhausted while his was still turning.

He drifted toward the light seeping in from the rectory. He knew from experience that he could slip out of the ward room and into the playroom, where the extroverted children did their arts and crafts, but he hated that room. The wallpaper was made up of clowns that skewed nightmarish rather than whimsical, and the giant gold cross painted on the wall was worse.

"Michael?"

Busted.

He spun to face the nun and whatever punishment she'd wield for his hundredth infraction. Instead of a ruler, he was met with a smile.

"Can't sleep?"

"No."

"Want to go for a little walk?"

The nun tucked a stray red strand of hair back into her habit and took his hand. She couldn't have been more than mid-thirties, and though he'd only ever seen her eyes and cheeks, they always tried to convey understanding.

The walk would lead him back to his bed along the eastern wall of the ward room, but she would delay it as long as she could, meandering the halls past the staircase that led down to the basement.

"Meisha?"

He froze at the whisper, head snapping toward the sound.

"Michael, come along," the nun urged.

But he couldn't move. At the top of the stairs, an angel beckoned with one finger—toward her bloody skull.

"Meisha, I need to show you something," she whispered.

"Sister Mary Catherine, can we go that way?" he asked, pointing to the empty staircase.

"No, child. It's a basement filled with old files. And no, you can't read them, you precocious little thing. There isn't anything down there for you."

The haunting apparition tried again. "You need what's down there, Meisha!" Her call turned into the scream that accompanied in her death.

Mike's eyes popped open.

"Woof, detox dreams…"

He stretched out his arm, feeling for Kristin, but the space next to him was empty. Warm, like she'd only just left him. The way everyone left him.

Mike pushed upright, teasing his balance before shuffling toward the kitchen in search of water to flush the MDMA.

Instead, he found Kristin quietly fanning the Gestapo Joe notes he'd left in the living room, though she'd never tried to violate his unpublished work before. Her fingertips brushed the scrawled margins as if feeling for something between the lines. He strained to see what part she was reading before startling her.

"What are you doing?"

"Looking for my bra," she said with a smile, dropping the page in her hand. Her eyes flickered for a second before the smile fell away.

"Try the bedroom floor. What time is it?"

"Four-thirty."

"Do you have to go already?"

That part of him that had wandered the night with a nun because he was afraid of both connecting with people and losing them, reached across decades and painted disappointment on his face. He was willing to forget that he'd almost broken up with her two nights earlier if she'd stay and keep the Void from returning.

"I can't very well wear *this* to work."

"Right."

Kristin slipped on the coat she'd tossed aside on her seductive rampage and tucked her hand into her pocket. The motion felt deliberate, but passed before Mike could process it.

"Do you want to come back tonight?" he asked, looking at her hopefully, with the eyes of a five-year-old.

"It's Super Tuesday-Eve. Tomorrow is going to be long."

"So… maybe?"

"Maybe."

She leaned in, but her kiss was limp, the way he was used to it being. Her whirlwind exit left him immobilized in its wake.

Four-thirty.

It was six of one and half-dozen of the other if he'd be able to sleep again without chemical aid, and he already felt stale—from their bodies pressed together, the sweat-laced detox, and from however long it had been since he bothered with a shower before that. Sometimes the ritual of a hot shower was more cleansing than sleep anyway.

Mike stood for a long time with the hot water pouring down the back of his neck. He tried to remember the last few days, how much he'd read, how much he'd written, how much he'd slept. He scrubbed off the feeling of the drugs and the smell of Kristin from his body, hoping for a clean slate—a fresh Monday morning, ready for a week where good things could happen.

He skipped coffee—not yet ready to be caffeinated. The hangover stage had arrived—the headache, the sadness, the awareness that he was alone.

Not if Delilah is with me.

He grabbed her book from the nightstand, bypassing the twisted mess of sheets he had no interest in climbing back into. Instead, he went to the couch. Though it wasn't exactly clean, at least it didn't smell like sex. He could read comfortably until something else demanded his attention...

His bookmark was gone.

The photo he'd lifted from her archive file and used to hold his place wasn't where it had been. Kristin had pulled the photo out to stare at the surveillance snap, but where was it now?

The bedroom? Kitchen counter?

Kristin's purse?

Mike traced the binding with his fingertip. He knew books, and he could decipher a virgin section from one he'd touched. The photo would show up again when the sun rose. Everything always looked better in the fresh light of day.

He returned to the winter of 1991.

Christmas Eve - This evening, we attended church. For the first time in my life, the doors to the cathedral were unlocked, allowing Christians to offer prayers on the Lord's birthday. To be honest, I don't know exactly why I should be one of these Christians.

In the Soviet times, they did not allow this—reason enough to do it —but I've never gone to church or read the Bible. I don't know if I believe—really believe. Mother says her parents were Christians before the occupation. I think father's parents were Jews. No one talks about this. No one talks about anything in this family.

This church holds an odd warmth. A thousand candles glowing brightly, flickering, against a golden altar. Above the altar hung a giant golden cross holding Jesus. I can see why the Soviet State did not want people believing in something larger than what they could control.

How can this religion suggest Jesus has taken my suffering? If he has, he has not done a very good job. But the warmth inside this building reminded me of something. There has never been a church unlocked here in my lifetime, so I am not sure why I have this feeling, but I've seen this golden cross before—just as I have seen people on their knees hoping for something to connect them.

Mostly, I think churches are supposed to make you feel safe, whether you believe or not. I think they will always let you come inside and offer you a place, a community, a belonging. Maybe that's what I'm looking for. I'm looking to find my brother again—or fill the Void left by being separated from him.

Tomorrow, perhaps we all will start over. The Soviets will lower their flag. The Union is over. The States have claimed their freedom, yet I don't feel free. I feel scared of what's next...

The Void.

The gold cross.

Had he read this already, and had the dream because of it? Gold crosses weren't necessarily uncommon. Neither were churches or orphanages or Catholic iconography jammed into his subconscious after growing up with nuns.

But the Void? Capitalized. Named like an entity—or an enemy.

They were bleeding together—her experiences, his memories —but that didn't make sense. Unless he was high. When his consciousness was altered, so was his perception of reality. He had to end the cycle again—break it down so he could rebuild it.

And he had to find that goddamn photo.

He leapt from the couch, flipped on the lights, and set metaphoric fire to everything he wanted to cleanse: the sheets from the bed, the piles of coffee grounds and stamped out cigarettes that made his apartment smell like a bus stop, and the last of the orange pill bottles lingering in the bathroom like little enablers. Everything—everything that served to remind him that he was a mess—went into a garbage bag.

As he slammed the dumpster lid on the discarded pieces of his life, he slowed, noting four shadows at the mouth of the alley. Men. Two wore gold chains that took the morning light and scattered it while they smoked—their eyes fixed on him like they'd already decided what they wanted. The other two barely noticed—staring out into the street, preoccupied. *Or they were lookouts.*

I saw Dmitri today with his cousin and two of his vory, Yuri and Valery, loitering as I left class. The vory extinguished their cigarettes into their palms—Ohh, big tough guys. I don't know if they meant to threaten or impress, but neither worked. Dmitri's cousin, Alexei, seemed preoccupied, staring out at the street.

"Excuse me, guys, I need to get through here," Mike said.

Valery angled himself, forcing Mike to thread past Yuri and his unblinking stare on his way back to the building. *Why did he look familiar? And why didn't I just use the trash chute?*

"My father made Sergei his driver," Dmitri said, catching up to Mike.

"You mean a thug?" Mike asked.

"I mean a bodyguard."

"If he carries a gun and puts it in people's faces when he doesn't get his way, you mean a thug."

"Vladi, neither of us does anything we aren't made to do."

Mike stopped, doing a double-take at the page in his hand.

Vladi?

"My real name is Vladienka," Delilah said, materializing next to Dmitiri. Mike circled the passage as the morgue photos cycled briefly through his mind.

ASSET NAME: [REDACTED]

ALIAS(ES): [REDACTED]

PEN NAME: DELILAH GRENNAN

He was finally getting somewhere.

"You can come visit him, you know. My father doesn't put limitations on my guests the way yours does," Dmitri said.

"I would just need to check my principles at the door?" she asked.

"Sergei would like to see you."

"Sergei shouldn't have chosen to go live in your house then."

"We have an air conditioner unit."

"Oh, well, if you have an air conditioning..." Mike added.

"It isn't my fault that he belongs with us."

"Belongs with you? Is there no limit to your sense of entitlement?"

Delilah met his gaze, the one person who would stand up to him, and the only person he wanted to get through to. She wasn't afraid, even with his cousin and the two impressive thugs tailing them. Mike finally broke the visual chokehold.

"Let's take it inside, guys."

The characters dissolved, awaiting their next chance to continue the narrative.

Yuri still loitered on the street.

Mike turned the bolt on the door and shoved his keys back into his pocket before glancing back over his shoulder. The leather-clad one still took up space on the sidewalk, leaning on a building and smoking.

Like he had at the Ebbitt.

Mike slammed the building's street-level door and rushed upstairs. Once there, he threw his deadbolt and moved to the window, peering from a crack in the blinds to see if the man was still on the street below. He wasn't there. Maybe he never had been.

Get a grip, Meisha.

He released the blinds, noticing how his hands were shaking.

"Not this again." He shook them out like he was flicking away water, and paced the living room twice, talking down the swell of his heart rate. "You do this every time. You start writing a set of characters, and suddenly they're everywhere. This is just you coming down."

Unless it isn't.

"I'm not being stalked by Russians just because I found a book."

Unless you are.

Mike grabbed the phone cord still fixed to his laptop and reattached it to the receiver.

"Stockton residence," Marta answered.

"Hey, *Mama*, is he up?"

"No, *bebe*," she said, laughing.

"Will you have him call me when he is?"

"He finished that bottle you gave him. It's going to be a while."

"Shit. Ok, thank you."

Marta could hear something in his voice she didn't care for. "*Bebe*, is something wrong? Do you need Lindsey?"

Lindsey Decker was a person you only called in case of emergency. Was this an emergency?

You don't even know if this was real. If you call Lindsey with a hallucination the day before Super Tuesday, it won't matter if someone's stalking you; she'll kill you for them.

"No, I'm not going to bug Lindsey today."

"Ok, *mijo*, I'll tell Mr. Tom you called."

Mike replaced the receiver on the wall and strolled back over to the window. No one had reappeared, wearing leather or otherwise.

"I don't have a stalker..." he told himself. Then the idea crystallized.

I do have my antagonist.

CHAPTER TWELVE

Dead Girls Tell No Tales

Chapter Five: I'd spent three days with Margarita, retracing her sister's footsteps through the City of Angels. Brandy hadn't been the going-out type. She took steno at the mayor's office—not even for the mayor, just in the secretary pool. The girls who got put on the desk were always the ones who let themselves get put there if ya know what I mean.

Brandy had an apartment in Mid-Wilshire, one of them art deco places with the gargoyles eyeing the street. Middle floor. Not high enough to get in from the roof and not low enough to crawl in a window unsuspectingly. Whoever killed that girl had done it on purpose, thinking she was the upright version standing next to me.

I didn't see much in that one-bedroom—some hose drying on the line and a nightgown that had never known a man's touch.

"How well did you know your sister?"

"Would you believe I never met her?"

"No. Twins separated at birth is just a bad plot device."

"Yeah, but it still happens. Teen girl finds herself in trouble and can't take care of it —what else is she going to do?"

"I suppose."

I was done looking her over—the gargoyle apartment, that is—and aiming for my Buick when I decided to pop the question.

Not that question.

"So why would someone want to kill you?"

I should've asked days ago, but one thing I always say: nobody's ever telling the truth. Not really.

I was hoping she'd lead me to it—let something slip, drop a dime on some Billy, Mac, or Buddy she did wrong, who'd want to see her neck snapped. Nothing. The dame was sealed up tighter than me.

"Well, we could ask him."

She kept walking, swinging those hourglass hips like the rent was due and everything was for sale, but I stopped dead.

Sure as a preacher shows up on Sunday, there was a Cuban on our tail. Her tail. But my tail was with her tail, so he was, by default, on the collective tail. Smoking a cigar and watching us pass like fish in a tank.

"Keep walking, Joe."

"How am I supposed to keep walking with a jabroni like that clocking our moves? I should go over there and give him a proper shake-down. Or better—call the fellas from Station Two, tell them someone with brown skin rolled into their neighborhood. They'll be over in a second."

"Leave it. I want to see what he does."

"What he does? He kills you tonight when he realizes you're still breathing. I don't think I ought to let you go back to the Century City Hotel."

"Well, not now that you said it out loud. If he didn't know where I was staying before, he does now. You moron."

I was no moron. I burned her location so she'd be forced to stay somewhere else—somewhere of my choosing. Despite both of them girls having names that sounded like something I'd swallow whole, the living one hadn't given me the chance yet.

"I've got a pad over on the Westside. Nothing fancy, hell, it's not even nice, but there's a mostly clean mattress you're welcome to."

"And if he follows us there?"

"That's why I keep this pony in the stable, ready to ride."

I flashed her my pistol, holstered under my arm right where it belonged. She seemed unimpressed, but she didn't have another idea.

Chez Joe could have used a quick wet down before company showed up, but that didn't happen.

"Guess the maid took the day off," I said, tossing a pair of tighty-whiteys out of the way so she'd have a chair, then I hung my coat on its hook. My coat was the only thing that had its own place in that studio apartment, because, without it, how was I supposed to fight bad guys?

She sat right down in that underwear chair to straighten the seam on her hose. Women and their hose—neither ever fit right. Except I was starting to think this one was different. She wasn't all hairpins and lipstick. She was trouble. I liked trouble. Getting in more than getting out.

"I think we've gotten ourselves into enough trouble today, sir. What do you say, we call it a night?"

She lit up a cigarette at the end of one of them shiny black holders carved out of the same stuff they make a piano out of. Then she wrapped her lips around it and sucked.

Wood. That's what they make pianos out of.

Through the crack in the casement window, I could see that jabroni lingering outside. He'd followed us, alright. Planning, plotting, reporting back to his boss—I didn't know, but one thing I always say: Shit's bound to pop eventually.

And it's always easier when the villain finds you.

"Our friend came along after all. You made the right call coming here, so I could keep a private eye on you."

"Then fix me a nightcap," she said, plucking her pillbox hat away from her skull.

"Happy to. What's your poison?

"Belladonna."

With a killer smile, she gave her platinum blonde mane a toss and sent the scent of violets my way.

———————————

Why violets?

Mike had been smelling them—or what he thought were violets—he couldn't have picked a violet out of a lineup, truth told.

Probably the shit I mopped with. That's why I don't recognize it.

He stood and stretched. He'd been drafting pages all night, now that he had the thread: Margarita admitting she might know the mob boss who was behind everything, Joe agreeing to go with her to Miami to confront him, and a leather-clad thug shadowing them to make sure they failed.

Would two strangers travel the world together to find a killer? Would they succumb to the heat of a case and the steam of the Latin underworld?

Yes, they would.

When Mike wasn't drafting his outline, he was reading about demonstrations in Kiev and family secrets—alluded to in hallways, but never uttered out loud. A tight-lipped mother and a despondent father, no wonder a teenage Delilah had attached herself to a mediocre hockey star with a vodka problem.

Two years of her life played out in prose. Players in a Russian soap opera, woven painfully through time and history. Something had happened during the war—something between her father and Dmitri's that loomed like an impending storm, threatening both families but never showing its face. Two men of the older generation forged by battle and splintered by a betrayal buried so deeply that not even their family understood it.

Buried betrayal...

Mike snapped back to the Stocktons' powder room, eavesdropping.

"Goddamn it, Rick! You roped my family into your attack on the president, and now you're just going to let Jacoby burn it all down on his way out of office?"

"I didn't rope you into shit, Jay! You handed me those documents willingly—happily, in fact—because you fancy yourself SecDef someday. As for your kid getting involved, that one's on you!"

LINK TO SEN. RICHARD STOCKTON III: **DISMISSED**

Dismissed or buried?

The 703 area code flashed on his caller ID, as if it were reading his thoughts.

"How many did you take?" he said, answering the line.

"Not enough," Tom answered.

"The whole bottle? What's wrong with you?"

"What's wrong with me? People are coming and going everywhere—congratulating him like he's already won! I can't take it!"

"Want me to sneak you out?"

"Yes! But, no. Press arrives at seven tomorrow. Lindsey would fucking kill me if I went AWOL or was hungover on camera. And I mean, actually send someone to kill me."

The shaved head thug flashed in his mind, stamping his cigarette out with his palm.

"You could come over, though," Tom whined. "Maybe bring another bottle with you?"

"I'm out."

"Fuck you then."

"Dude."

"Sorry, I'm crashing so hard. Score for me, please? I'd do it myself, but..."

Mike considered the ask, then he remembered exactly why he'd been calling Tom in the first place.

"I'll trade you."

"Yes, anything. What do you want?"

"A gun."

"Jesus, why do you need a gun?"

"Oh, have I finally found something you don't have a guy for?"

Tom looked out the window at the long driveway that terminated with the security gate. An SUV with government plates was held there, awaiting clearance.

"I didn't say that. Let me work on it. You work on getting me something to take the edge off."

"Rolling H Street. Another reason I need the gun."

"You don't need a gun for that, you have that boy band smile."

"Bite me."

Tom hung up, satisfied. With relief on the way, he hurried down the stairs toward the din of supporters gathering to shake hands with his father, so they would remain top of mind after he took the oath.

The SUV had been carrying the admiral, who never missed the opportunity to ooze around the edges of power, absorbing it where he could. He'd dragged his son—full dress blues and all—along with him this time.

AJ looked like he didn't want to be there any more than Tom did. He stood perfectly still at the edge of the salon, either trying not to crease his uniform or trying not to get comfortable around people he didn't trust—likely both. Tom hovered in the foyer, his back against the doorway— a bookend behind AJ, close enough to trade words, without anyone seeing them speak.

"Psst, AJ," Tom whispered.

The Navy commander searched for the source of the noise, finally peering around the wall where he found the young Stockton.

Tom shuffled his feet as he spoke. "How'd you get stuck here tonight?"

"Duty, honor, tradition," AJ recited with a hint of disdain.

"Are you allowed to do that in uniform?" Tom asked, nodding to the scotch in AJ's hand.

"Nope." He took a long sip to punctuate the defiance.

"How's the Navy?"

"What are we doing, Tom?"

"Do you know where I can get a gun?"

"What?" AJ stepped into the foyer and pressed Tom further down the hall toward his father's office.

"A gun!"

"Lower your voice."

"Sorry," Tom whispered. "A gun. You know, pew, pew, pew." He mimed firing with his index finger and thumb.

"Pew is more of a laser sound."

"Come on, man…"

"What do you need a gun for?"

"It's not for me. I have a buddy who lives in the city. I guess it's getting rougher in his 'hood, I don't know."

AJ was unflappable, a function of his upbringing and the things he'd already witnessed. He showed no reaction as his mind ran a risk assessment on the ask.

"Never mind, I thought if you knew a guy in an armory or something, it would be safer than meeting some gang banger in a parking lot, but I'll figure it out another way. Thanks for nothing." Tom turned back toward his room.

AJ's mental calculation drew an instant conclusion: The reason he was there, part of the job Lindsey paid him to do, was to protect the Stocktons from themselves. Typically, it meant locating and burying intelligence that would hurt the future administration. In this case, though, it felt like locating an untraceable weapon for Tom Stockton so he wasn't caught—or killed—in the illegal acquisition of one.

"Tom…"

He turned back to face the commander.

"Give me a day before you locate an arms dealer."

"Thanks, AJ. This won't trace back to you, I promise."

"I know it won't."

AJ was too smart to let it. He had been bred to avoid being tied to scandal and was building a clandestine career around the Washington game.

He'd utilize his burgeoning connections to come up with an untraceable weapon and hand-deliver it to Tom tomorrow under the guise of Super Tuesday. Even under the scrutiny of the press and eyes of the Secret Service, he knew he could slip a weapon past the gates without a trace—because AJ McCollister didn't make mistakes. He engineered outcomes.

CHAPTER THIRTEEN

Mike slipped two pill bottles into his overcoat pocket and headed back toward the Lexus parked a few streets away. He'd opted to forsake the seedy underbelly of Washington's junkie boulevard in lieu of a much more sterile means of procurement.

Nurses.

Most nurses were tired, overworked, and under-appreciated —easily charmed by a tall man with a toothpaste smile.

One thing I always say: Give me ten minutes and I'll get a nurse to hand over a prescription.

"Why do you say that?" Delilah asked. She'd been waiting in the passenger seat while he ran into the nursing home for Tom's drugs, even if she disagreed with enabling the habit.

"I don't. I've never said that. I don't know why I said that now."

He'd never seen her so dolled up—hair teased, blush highlighting her cheekbones. She wore her second decade well, but what lived behind her eyes was much older.

He leaned past her, stashing his wallet in the glove box beside the mobile phone he never used. It weighed as much as a brick, with a battery that only lasted ten minutes—when the service lasted that long.

"And why do you make me go to this party?" she asked.

"Because it's your brother's birthday," Pavel answered.

"I might as well not have a brother anymore. He's been gone from my life for a while now."

"Ok, but his rich friends are giving out free vodka, so we go."

I rolled my eyes. It is always this way with Pavel: big crowds, big booze. I think there are even other girls now.

Ivan the Terrible loomed over Mariinsky Park, seated on a dais—a throne—beside his younger brother, Otto. The sight of these brothers turns my stomach. Their eyes feel like spiders crawling across skin, warning you to be afraid.

Their enforcers flanked the perimeter, as people—ordinary people with nothing to give—left alms to the rich. To my brother! A man who needs nothing!

I was furious before I saw the women—hollow, rail-thin girls, probably on drugs. Drugs might be the only way to survive what they're made to do. Ivan deals in human trade as much as weapons. Girls whose fathers couldn't pay, collected as currency for their debts and sold to businessmen and politicians for pleasure. They surrounded Sergei, "gifts" from his benefactor.

I should have left then, but I'd lost Pavel to the crowd. Before I could find him and insist that we leave this world where we didn't belong, Dmitri found me.

"I'm glad you came," Dmitri shouted over the music.

"Why? So I could see how you spend your money on prostitutes?"

"They were presents from my uncle."

"You couldn't say 'Sorry, Otto, we're not interested in getting AIDS?'"

"My choices haven't been my own to make for some time now."

The way his voice resonated with regret, I almost believed him, but it didn't change anything.

"My mother would be appalled."

"Your mother was here earlier."

"What? Why?"

"I don't know. She sat at the head table and visited with my father."

"She would never. Unless she was begging to have my brother released from your prison."

"They looked friendly, Vladi. Not like people locked in some generational feud. I saw them laughing."

"Shut up."

I shoved past him, intent on leaving regardless of where Pavel had gone, but from Sergei's point of view, it must have looked like Dmitri had restrained me. He lunged, grabbing Dmitri by the shirt collar.

"Let go of her!"

"I didn't touch her."

"Not yet."

"You're drunk, Serge. Let's get someone to take you home."

"So you can be alone with my sister?"

"She's not your sister anymore."

The comment enraged him. Sergei swung violently, but Dmitri dodged the hit. His fist landed on my face instead.

I sank to the ground, my world imploding—my mother, friendly with Ivan? Dmitri sounding remorseful? Sergei, lashing out violently? She's not your sister anymore? The scaffolding that held up my understanding slowly crumbled to the ground with me.

Both Sergei and Dmitri knelt to help me, but I didn't want them.

I just wanted to leave Kiev.

I dragged myself up and wiped the blood from my mouth.

"Vladi, I'm sorry!" Sergei said, reaching out to console me, as if I were a crying child.

"Both of you get away from me!"

I pushed them away. Valery and Yuri moved in to remove Dmitri, as was their job, while Alexei pulled Sergei the other way. I was left in the throng of shouting thugs with a bleeding mouth and a broken heart.

"You get away from me, too!"

The steering wheel dipped as Mike absorbed her shove to his shoulder.

"What the hell did I do?"

Delilah wept in the passenger seat, pressing her hands to her eyes to stop the tears until they were smeared into the same black circles he'd seen in her autopsy report.

"You're making me relive this horrible story, and it only gets worse. Watch the road."

Mike snapped his attention to the street in front of him. A military SUV exited the Stocktons' electric gate, requiring more room than the drifting Lexus had offered. He slowed, letting the bigger vehicle pass, then the familiar guards waved him through.

The Lexus eased alongside the kitchen door, and he parked near the staff entrance, giving Delilah one final reassuring look before he tucked the book into his coat pocket and left the warmth of the car.

"This exit is sealed, sir. Go around and check in with the agent at the front," a Secret Service agent instructed.

"Seriously?"

"Let him through—he's family," Tom said, blasting through the kitchen door.

"Mr. Stockton, I can't. It's protocol."

"And so it begins," Mike said.

"Sorry, man, they even kicked me out of the guest house. I'm stuck living upstairs in my old bedroom like a fucking six-year-old."

"Mr. Stockton, the threat level went up in the last few hours," the agent stated.

"Why?" Mike asked.

"I'm not at liberty to say. Do you have some ID on you?

"My wallet is in the glove box. I don't usually need it to walk through my kitchen."

"Your kitchen?"

"Yeah, I told you, he's family," Tom said again.

The agent still hesitated, caught between letting Mike bend the rules and not upsetting a Stockton. "I'll have to pat you down."

"Jesus, I'm sorry," Tom grumbled.

"It's fine," Mike said, spreading his arms and legs apart so the agent could feel along his outline.

"I'll make sure you're on the Green list by morning." Tom giggled at his own unintentional pun. "That's funny. Green list. His name is Green," he explained to the agent.

"So it's not Nancy McPherson?" he asked, pulling the pill bottles from Mike's overcoat pocket and scrutinizing them.

"Oh, for fuck's sake, Agent Doucheworm! You're not the DEA, and he's not a threat to my old man! Do I need to get him

110

out here? Would you rather be on the advance team for Shitfuck-Kerplechistan?"

The agent handed the bottles back to Mike with a scowl and stepped aside.

"You're welcome," Tom said as he weaved through the service corridors to avoid being seen by the gathering number of well-wishing ass-kissers.

"Actually, *you're* welcome," Mike said, tossing him both bottles.

"No, *you're welcome*. I solved your little hardware problem."

"Wait..." Mike confirmed no one else was around. If there was anything he'd learned about that house, it was that someone else was always around. He lowered his voice to a whisper. "The gun?"

"Yeah, the gun."

"How?"

"Navy guy."

"I take it back—you do know a guy for everything."

"And you apparently know a nurse for everything," Tom said, looking at the fresh prescription bottle. "Which do you want? Upper or downer?"

Before leaving the car, Delilah had been on the verge of revealing how things went wrong. Gestapo Joe was nearing the end of Act One, ready to complicate his storyline by sleeping with his client, and Mike was sealed inside a Secret Service perimeter as Washington's elite fawned over their next chosen one. He needed to stay on point.

"Upper. Definitely upper."

CHAPTER FOURTEEN

Tom shut the door behind them. He couldn't lock it— that privilege had been disabled ten years prior—but the entire household was too busy cupping his father's balls to care what was going on upstairs.

He wiped a space clear on the dresser and poured out the pain pills Mike had obtained, then brought the bottom of a weighted water glass down hard, crushing them into chalky dust.

"Hand me your credit card," he said.

"Were you not downstairs for the whole wallet thing?" Mike said. Instead, he pulled Delilah's book from his pocket, bent the stiff cover back, and used its edge to scrape the broken powder into uneven lines. "This is not going to be smooth."

"No, but it'll kick faster." He plugged one nostril and inhaled through the other while Mike opted to lick his finger, collect the powder, and smear the bitter dust against his gums—different delivery, same burn—a bitter bite that seared like a match, quick and mesmerizing. In a few minutes, the rush would come.

Tom flopped back on the floor, his arms falling out wide like he was hanging from a cross, and closed his eyes. The pills he actually needed were Lithium, Prozac, Neurontin—anything that would fix the chemical imbalance in his brain and keep his highs from making him think he was infallible and his lows from trying to kill him. But the president's son couldn't be bipolar. Tom couldn't be treated for depression any more than he could be a drug addict, and so opioids, stolen and ground up, would have to suffice to even him out.

For Mike, the rush began in the back of his neck—a tingle that moved up his scalp and wrapped around his forehead before it infected his mind. A woozy, welcome lightness cleared the usual fog, clamping off the neurons that sent the negative signals— pain, fear, insecurity, inhibition. With those gone, his mind opened. This was his preferred high. He didn't like feeling dull. He didn't like feeling relaxed or complacent. He liked quieting the bad parts and leaving the Void open for something better: ideas, connections, balance, and, if he was really lucky, peace.

The short-lived sobriety he'd held tightly to that weekend had felt promising, but there was no way he could have read the next scene in Delilah's book without a false sense of peace.

Pavel's team lost in a rout, an evisceration that wouldn't have mattered had there not been a scout in the stands that night. What should have been my post-game birthday dinner turned into half the team drowning their sorrows at the bar, while I sat on the sidelines, wondering how long I could pretend that things with Pavel weren't getting worse.

I should have left him there, but I dragged him out before he was too drunk to walk. I just wanted the night to be over. He wanted me to stay with him, but I hate staying now. He sweats vodka through his skin and flops around, snoring. And nothing—no condominium in New York City or beach house in Los Angeles—is worth pretending that he doesn't have other women. He's no different than one of the vory now.

"Stay, Vladi," he said. It was more of a command, punctuated by his fist slamming the door behind me.

"No, I have class tomorrow."

"Stay." He put himself between me and the door.

"Pavel, move. I'm going home."

"I said, stay!" As he growled the demand, he put a hand around my neck.

He threw me down, bouncing my head against the floor. The light faded, the darkness taking over, as he climbed on top of me. I fought. Not to resist him, but to stay awake. I didn't want to wonder what had happened or give him the chance to deny it. I wanted him to know that he was hurting me.

My head rolled to the side as the air left, each blink lasting longer, each moment I lost disappearing in his laughter. Then my hand touched a metal blade. With my last breath of consciousness, I heaved that hockey skate against his head and knocked him away from me.

I only took a second to take in air again before I forced myself up and found the door. Then I walked away from Pavel, a changed person. No one would ever make me feel like a victim again. I'd die before I'd surrender my power.

My dress barely clung to my shoulder, split from the hem to the hip, where he'd tried to lift it from my body. I heard whistles from men who had the wrong idea, calling after me. One followed, moving in and out of the shadows cast by street lights, gaining. I stepped into the middle of the road, trying to stay visible rather than tucked in the shadows.

"You shouldn't be out here!"

Dmitri.

I slowed. I don't know whether I wanted him to catch up, or the shock was wearing off into a concussion.

"Seriously," he continued. "Someone is going to snatch you up and sell you to Bulgarians."

"Someone who works for you?"

When I turned to face him, he saw the handprint on my neck, black against my pink skin.

"Shit. Take my coat," he said, peeling it off and wrapping it around my shoulders. I could feel something weighing it down. Something heavy, like a gun in the pocket.

"What happened to you?"

"Nothing."

"Something happened. Who did this?"

"I'm fine." I continued walking. The longer we stood there in the street, the more likely it was that someone else would show up. Friend, foe—it didn't matter. Adding anyone to the situation would have made it worse.

"That wasn't what I asked!"

"Dmitri, don't. I don't need you to…"

"Say the name, Vladienka!" He shook my shoulders, trying to jar the name loose—trying to make me into an accuser.

"I just want to go home."

"Were you raped?"

"I don't think so."

"You don't think so? I'm going to find out what happened and deal with this."

"If you want to help me, take me home."

He moved closer, like he was going to take me into his arms and use the weight of his influence to create a shield around us. Instead, he reached into the pocket of his coat and drew out his pistol.

"Nothing bad will happen to you tonight. Nothing bad will happen to you ever again."

"Well, that was a lie," Mike said, putting the book aside. He wanted a drink to wash the taste of her blood out of his mouth.

The Stockton house had gone quiet. People had stopped coming to the door, parading through the salon, and shaking each other's hands like they all had a stake in the results of the next day's primary.

He crossed the room, stepping over Tom, who was asleep on the floor, and checked the window to confirm that there were no cars, particularly his mother's, parked outside. With the compound empty of all but its residents, he slipped downstairs.

Mike crept down the staircase and floated around the ground floor like a spirit haunting the common areas. Liquor anchored every room: Wine and beer in the kitchen, brandy in the salon, and a full assortment of Scotch in Stockton's private office. He didn't help himself to the senator's private stash most nights, but he wanted something aged and smoky that could stand in for a cigarette, so he didn't need to go outside. Brandy wasn't his craving tonight.

Unlike Joe.

He stepped inside Richard Stockton's office and focused on the bar in the corner. He didn't want to glance at anything else in the room. The senator shouldn't have had any classified national security documents yet, not until he was the party's nominee and subjected to a security briefing by the Alphabet Agencies as part of his potential transition, but it didn't matter. If Mike accidentally read something sitting on a desk or resting on a chair, it would bleed into a book someday, and then, conscious or not, he'd have committed treason. All he wanted was a whiskey, not a violation of the Espionage Act.

"I ever tell you the one about the penguin with the dead car?"

Rick Stockton's voice startled Mike so hard he nearly dropped the bottle of aged Macallan.

"Jesus, Rick," Mike muttered, collecting himself. "You want one?"

"I want four. Have I told you the joke?"

Mike handed a glass, filled to the rim as instructed, to the senator and sank into a big leather armchair that smelled like the cigars Marta snuck into the country for him.

"No. Penguin with a bad car?"

"Yeah, so this penguin," he said, leaning in to whisper, although no one else in the house was awake. He sipped his whiskey and continued, "...he goes out for an ice cream cone. On the way back, his car breaks down. Damn thing just sputters off the road. Penguin sits there waiting for the tow truck, eating his ice cream."

Mike waited for the punch line, sipping his glass, which was filled about a third compared to Stockton's.

"Tow truck driver shows up, checks under the hood, and says, 'Buddy, it looks like you blew a seal.' Penguin goes, 'No, that's just vanilla ice cream.'"

Mike snorted, stifling a laugh. Rick believed in always having a dirty joke with his scotch; it was anyone's guess where the joke would rate—nestled somewhere between a dad joke and something prosecutable.

"Come on, Green, it's funny. Blew a seal! Get it?"

"I got it," Mike said, finally laughing. "I'll never unsee that image either."

"Good, because I won't be able to tell any of those in the White House. I hear the whole goddamn place is wired for audio." The senator's face turned serious, and he paced over to his desk. "You mind topping me off again, son?"

"Course not…" Mike didn't mind, but he was tallying up the ounces of liquor he'd already poured out and wondering how many more the man could stomach before he wouldn't make his press call. "Something wrong? Other than everything?"

"Wired for audio…."

"Come again?"

"The Secret Service did a sweep today. They found audio devices planted around the compound."

"What?"

"Bugs."

"Yeah, I know what audio devices are. What were they doing here?"

"Hell if I know."

"Where did they come from?"

"Hell if I fucking know that either!" Although he almost always kept it in check in public, the senator was known to have a temper. He regained his composure and started over. "The FBI is going to investigate."

"Guess it means someone thinks you're important," Mike said, attempting to downplay the severity of someone having bugged the office and living quarters of the next President of the United States. The increased threat level that had the Secret Service crawling up his ass made sense now.

"Guess we'll see about that. How's Tom?"

"Asleep. If we're being honest, I dosed him. Just one."

"Will you stay with him tonight? Tomorrow's going to be a fuck, and I'm worried about him."

"Like he said something on the recordings he shouldn't have?"

"God, no. Like he's going to hurt himself during the campaign."

"Are you worried because you think he's sick, or because it would hurt your chances?"

Rick closed the gap between them as if he were going to raise a hand. He stopped short of making contact, but the intimidation was as effective.

"Perhaps it's acceptable to disrespect James Langham, but we don't do that in this house. I believe you know that, Michael."

"Yes, sir."

Being scolded wasn't something Mike had much experience with, and not by anyone with as much paternal gravitas as Stockton had. James Langham's involvement in step-fatherhood had been loaning him a gas card and not telling Jennifer when he found Mike's *Playboy* collection in junior high.

119

"I care about my family and the country equally."

"Yes, sir."

"I need you to keep Tom in line all the way to November."

"Yes, sir."

"Good boy." Stockton patted Mike's stubbled cheek with a gentle hand. "How about a shave, too, huh?"

"Yes, sir."

"Fuck, I have to get some sleep or all they're going to see on camera tomorrow is an old man with bags under his eyes. Rothschild's probably getting fucking Botox or something so he looks fresh as a daisy's cunt tomorrow. Oh, speaking of cunt. There once was a girl named Regina…"

"Please, no. I haven't had enough whiskey for a limerick."

Rick laughed and put a tender hand on Mike's arm. "All right, I'll save it for after the victory speech. Goodnight, kiddo."

"Night, Rick. Say, Rick…" Mike halted the senator's exit.

"Yeah?"

He could see Delilah loitering along the study's bookshelves, examining the galley copies of Mike's series, sprinkled between family portraits of Mike with the future First Family—the back of her head still missing. He badly wanted to ask his surrogate dad what he knew about the dead girl, why he'd been named alongside her death in the first place, even if the connection had been dismissed. But part of him didn't want to know.

"You changed your mind about the 'Girl Named Regina', didn't you?" he said, smiling.

Mike let Delilah fade away. He needed there to be one hero in his world, even if professionals had spun the narrative that way.

"Yeah. Tell me that one again."

CHAPTER FIFTEEN

"Do you believe the duty of the free press is to report the truth even when it poses a threat to their personal safety? What is the turning point between exposing the rot and letting them win? The threat of death?"

A quick two-knock rap on the door pulled Mike from the page that had been his only company all night. Super Tuesday was going to require every ounce of public face he had, and he hadn't bothered to sleep—not when it meant leaving Delilah alone in her crumbling life. Surviving an attempted assault had fueled her quiet rage, igniting it into a full-blown mission to drag the filth eroding Kiev out into the light. In a way, her activism was inspiring, since all Mike could do was pretend.

The knock repeated, and then the door opened anyway.

"Breakfast is at six now," Marta said. She extended a cup of black coffee and a freshly pressed suit in exactly Mike's size. "You have half an hour."

"I thought the press call was seven?" He pinched the corners of his eyes.

"Lindsey wants something called 'B-Roll.'"

"Understood. I'll make sure he gets up."

"If you don't, Lindsey will."

"I'll warn him. Thank you, Marta."

"Thank you, *Mijo*." She passed him the clothes and the coffee and continued on her rounds.

Mike nudged Tom's body with his toe.

"Hey, Lindsey wants you downstairs."

The comment worked better than an alarm clock. Tom was on his feet a second later. "Shit, they're early."

"They want to see you eat your bagel, JFK Jr."

"I didn't ask for this. Selfish bastard, dragging us to the White House because he's obsessed with power and legacy."

"It could always be worse."

"How? How could it be worse?"

"Are you fucking kidding me? You're wondering how your life could be worse than having two parents with an estate worth eight figures who are about to take center on the world stage."

"Exactly! I'm forced to act and dress how they want me to; I'm not even allowed to have my own opinions. It's like living in Soviet Russia!" Tom slammed the door to his en-suite and fired up the shower.

"Prick," Mike muttered.

Tom didn't know what he was talking about. He'd been born rich, raised by nannies, and would never work a day in his life. He hadn't been raised in an orphanage. He hadn't ever wondered if a foster parent was going to put a hand on him, and he sure as shit didn't know what it was like living in Soviet Russia.

Mike dressed in the suit Marta brought and slipped Delilah's book into his pocket, so when the cameras cut away, he'd have something to pass the time other than watching the polls. He started down the stairs toward the dining room, halting on the second-to-last step to steel himself, then forced his trademark smile and stepped into the fray.

A small army of fixers put the last touches on a buffet that rivaled that of a five-star hotel, under the calculated direction of Ms. Lindsey Decker herself. She was still well shy of forty, yet ran the whole of D.C. from behind the scenes, unquestionably in charge of any room she stood in.

The Scotch and Cigar crowd—like Stockton and Holston—trusted her unreservedly, and she'd been manipulating the Stockton narrative since Mike was in high school.

"There! Now, don't let anyone start on that buffet until the video team is in here!" she commanded.

Mike intentionally side-stepped her and plucked a muffin from the middle of the stack, tipping the pastry balance and sending the rolls around it toppling.

"Mr. Green," she said through gritted teeth. "I wasn't told that you'd be joining us today. I guess I should have known." Lindsey didn't like surprises. She was orchestrating every detail down to the type of food they would be eating. A new body at the table hadn't been approved.

"It wasn't planned."

"Is something wrong with Tom?"

"Nope." He tucked a piece of fruit in his mouth and hit her with his smile, though it only worked on her about half the time.

"And how long will you be staying?"

"He's staying as long as he stays," Tom answered, arriving and pulling a second roll from the stack as the catering manager finished resetting the display. Tom cleaned up well when he had to. His blonde hair was longer on top than the sides, and landed just right to play off the sparkle in his eyes. He'd done another hit before coming downstairs. "You don't mind, do you, Linds?"

Lindsey licked her teeth and forced a smile. "Not at all... Sarah!"

Sarah Wallace, a lanky woman with long, red hair, whose habit of perpetual motion lent both to her effectiveness and her lack of body mass, snapped to attention in response. "Yes?"

"Soundbite: 'Mr. Michael Green, family friend and prominent D.C. author.' Mention something about an inked film deal so we soften the Hollywood Dems."

"Got it," she answered.

"The film deal isn't inked," Mike corrected.

"It will be after I say it is. Congratulations." Lindsey booped the tip of his nose and hurried off to tend to her next irritation.

"Come on," Sarah said, wrangling them toward the formal dining table. She was the one who had checked Mike into the Jefferson Hotel the night they cleaned up Tom's overdose. Of everyone on the LDA team, she was the nicest, though it never stopped her from ruling a press conference or deciding who ended up writing recipes in ladies' journals in Akron when they stepped out of line. Rumor had it she was on the short list to be Stockton's White House Press Secretary.

"Want to sit with us?" Tom asked.

"I'm not sitting until after the inauguration."

"Aww, but you're the only reason I showed up."

"And if you truly love me, you'll behave today so I don't have to call in a clean-up team."

"Would my dad *really* have me killed if I ruined today?"

"Your dad, no, but Lindsey, for sure."

"Is that honestly a service LDA provides?" Mike asked. A glimmer of the man in the leather jacket flashed in his periphery.

"Only when the press gets out of line," Sarah said, winking.

"Isn't the role of a free press to expose the questionable morals acting within a free society?" Mike said. The voice came out hardly like his own. It almost came out in a Russian accent.

"The hell it is. The role of the press is to tell the story I want them to tell. And I'm letting them in now, so will the two of you stop... doing anything you normally do?" She flapped about trying to get them into their chairs.

"Yes, ma'am," Tom said, turning agreeable. His crush on Sarah had started the first time she'd prepped him for an interview. When her feminine fingers looped a Windsor knot around his teenage neck, she'd also tied him around her finger. Lindsey may have gotten her way with raw intimidation, but Sarah got hers because Tom just wanted her to like him.

"I need a cigarette. You don't need me for the cold open, do you?" Mike asked.

"I don't need you here at all," Lindsey answered from across the room, capable of doing multiple things at once while still hearing everything that went on in the house.

"Love you, too, Linds," he called out as he pushed his way through the kitchen toward the patio.

Mike sat on the bench outside, lit his cigarette, and spread the leaves of the book open again while he had a few minutes alone.

The Duty of a Free Press in a Free Society.

Two years ago, Ludmilla Butsiah wouldn't have been able to teach this lecture on the free press. A free press hadn't existed. I would argue that it still didn't, but as I was in my final year at university, I wanted to absorb every bit of knowledge I could and try to capitalize on my own future. The one I would have to build for myself, so I didn't need to rely on anyone else to save me.

My peers, those of us who had become adults during the revolution — the first generation of young people with no guarantee of work under socialism — we'd need to make something of ourselves. The only thing I knew how to do was write and question authority. Journalism was a natural path.

I listened to Mrs. Butsiah philosophize on one's duty. Was it the truth? Whose truth? The writer's? The editor's? The publication's? Could whoever paid to circulate the truth buy their version of it? The answer in a truly free society was yes. Yes, to all of it.

"Do you ever compromise your voice to protect your safety?"

"Excellent question, Ms. Stromkovietz. I'd love to speak with you after class."

Stromkovietz. Vladienka Stromkovietz.

Now he had her full name. Mike circled the page number and made another margin note. He had her full name, Dmitri Zdrastkova's full name, and by default, Sergei's full name. He had the years she attended Kiev University, and the streets and cafes she frequented. If he had been a real detective, he'd now know enough about the victim to start retracing her steps, interviewing her friends, and locating her killers.

Mike paused his reading while the idea washed over him.

Go to Ukraine. Walk in her footsteps. Prove that someone in the Zdrastkova organization had motive. Hand them over to Interpol.

Easy.

Not easy. Four global agencies had already done this, classified it, and buried it in an archival ant farm so they never had to think about it again because this one girl wasn't worth the effort.

And if you wanted to start interviewing people, there's someone right inside...

He talked the impulse out of his head as he watched the parade of cars arriving at the compound: press vans, a familiar Acura from next door, a military SUV. The house was getting smaller, and the spotlight was getting brighter. Mike made a fist so no one could see that his hands were shaking and crawled back into the safe space inside the pages.

When class ended, I stayed behind to speak with Mrs. Butsiah.

"Ms. Stromkovietz, I'm glad you stayed. Your question reminded me a lot of your father."

"You know my father?"

"We were comrades when he lectured here."

"He lectured here?"

She seemed surprised that I didn't know this simple truth about my father—more secrets and lies from my parents. "For a long time, in the science department. Please send him my regards. But to answer your question, I think the answer lies only in the individual."

"How so?"

"One should always consider the greater good first and foremost. But, if you have a child, someone you are responsible for, whose life will

suffer if you are imprisoned or killed for your conviction, you must consider your responsibilities."

She reached into the pocket of her cardigan and withdrew a small orange token, which she placed into my hand. Orange was the color used to symbolize subversion during the protests.

"What do you use these for now that your cause is achieved?"

"We have so many more enemies." She beamed. "Are you busy? I'd love to show you something else if you have time."

What else was I doing? Going home to the cold silence that filled our house now that Sergei was gone? Walking past the Zdrastkova mansion, hoping that Dmitri might see me and come running out?

Since that night he walked me home, he creeps into my mind. What if all the years he was cruel it was to try to distance me from the cruelty he himself knows? Because that man who walked me home, holding off everything in the darkness that might have threatened me, was not the same boy who called me Western Trash.

I walked with Mrs. Butsiah to a cafe beyond campus. This isn't a cafe for food, it's a cafe for the internet. Three of her other students were gathered around a word processor, trying to craft a flyer: typeset, columns, copy... it looked like an extracurricular project, but it wasn't.

They gathered not as students, but as a private pact, seeking mentorship. Butsiah was a steward to this collective of minds who wanted to make a difference, and she was gathering them right under the university's gaze. She had probably done the same throughout the entire revolution.

"We could talk about how the police only ensure the safety of the wealthy," one said, trying a headline.

"And how the wealthy buy their way out of trouble," another added.

"You're writing a dissent flyer. You can't just say 'Wealth is Corrupt'. Everyone knows that. Everyone has always known that. To influence impactful change, our words need to challenge, to question, to ignite!" Mrs. Butsiah said.

"You could name Ivan Zdrastkova."

They all turned to look at me, a stranger among them, infiltrating their private and dangerous club.

"Ivan Zdrastkova is a prominent figure in the community, but no one knows why. His generational wealth compounds despite the Soviet collapse after the war, the economic downturn in the eighties, and a revolution?"

"Who are you?" one student asked.

"Ms. Stromkovietz is a promising journalism student," Mrs. Butsiah said. "If you were going to print, your editor would want corroborating sources, proof..."

"I can get proof. My brother lives in the mansion."

She smiled proudly. "Well, luckily, I'm not your editor. Type your voice."

I took my pain, the anger I felt watching Ivan and Otto lord over Sergei's birthday, and my hatred for all the secrets my parents are keeping, and poured them into my writing. The other students helped with font and format. I created this project with them, a collaboration with others who think like me. I didn't even know there were others who think like me.

After it was well into the night, Mrs. Butsiah saved our work to a disk and erased everything from the public computer, like spies, as we donned our coats and went off in different directions into the night.

I've never smoked, but for some reason, this adrenaline made me want a cigarette.

CHAPTER SIXTEEN

Mike stamped out his cigarette and blew the last drag of smoke into the cold.

"Hi, honey."

"Mom."

Jennifer Green never used the staff entrance; she must have come from inside the house and sought him out in the one place she assumed he'd be if not with Tom.

"Exciting day," she said.

"Sure."

"The senator is about to give his first cut-in to the morning shows. Don't you want to be in the breakfast room for that?"

"Boy, do I."

"You've been given something few people get, Mike—a seat at the table."

She meant the metaphoric table in the fabled 'room where it happens'. His proximity to power, Rick Stockton's in particular, was what everyone in Washington was striving for. She could have also meant the literal empty chair beside Tom at the Stocktons' dining set, where the family was playing out a pantomime, threading the needle between average, loving family at breakfast, and a power couple capable of steering the country through adversity.

But in Mike's mind, the table was spread out on a dais in the central park of Kiev. The generation, the control, the power—it was all the same. Only the ideologies were different.

Or they weren't.

"I'm good."

"A little publicity wouldn't hurt your career."

"I said, I'm good, ma."

"Then maybe you ought to leave. If you aren't advancing the story, you're stalling it. As a writer, you should know that."

Joke's on you, Jenny, this kid is no writer. Just a fraud.

Jennifer returned toward the buzz inside. She could have his seat at the table. She wanted to be in the room where it happened and positioned herself conveniently nearby, awaiting such an invitation.

But she wasn't wrong. Why was he there if not to prop Tom up during the most stressful day of his life, even if that stress was self-manufactured? It would be weird for the Stocktons' neighbor-friend to wake up there pre-dawn and then disappear while the cameras rolled. Even with Lindsey's soundbite, speculation would swirl. The opposition might question whether the senator's son was gay, and while they'd find plenty of women to testify to the contrary, that was hardly helpful either.

A mug of fresh, hot coffee appeared in front of his face like an apparition had guided it there.

"*Spacibo,*" he whispered.

"Don't speak Russian around the press," Sarah scolded, waiting for him to take the cup. "This is your five-minute heads up to make yourself presentable."

"Like I just told my mother, I don't need to be in the limelight."

"I'm not putting you in the live feed, I'm putting you in Tom's eye line in case he starts spiraling."

She hovered, tapping her foot incessantly as was her way. After he relieved her of the drink, she used both hands to smooth the folds of his blazer and tame the errant hairs on his head.

"Would it have killed you to get a haircut before today?"

"I didn't know I was going to be here today."

"It's good that you are. Tom's really struggling, isn't he?"

"Tom's fine."

"I'm not asking as a fixer—I'm asking as a friend."

"Then go ask him, Sarah. The guy's had a crush on you since he was seventeen. Would it kill you to go on a date with him?"

"When? When do you think I have time to date?" Her fingers trailed along the final strands of hair she forced into place by wetting her finger and tucking it behind his ear. "Good enough to be seen with the next president."

"You just said I wasn't joining the feed."

"No, but I'm putting you in the family stills."

"Seriously?"

"Your mom will hate it." She grinned, knowing he wouldn't be able to resist.

"I'm in."

Sarah extended a hand to help him up, although it was more symbolic than anything. Every protagonist needed a support character, and in a narrative filled with ulterior motives and clandestine plans, the girl-next-door archetype always radiated warmth enough to fill that role.

Or I need to go spit out more pages so I stop seeing literary tropes everywhere.

Mike took her hand and then quickly let it go before Tom accidentally saw the simple gesture and plummeted into a depression because of her. "Let's do it, Wallace."

"Run the Play, as Rick says."

"Which play is this one?"

"Play 42."

"Am I supposed to know what that means?"

"No one is supposed to know what that means."

She held the door open for him, pointed toward the staircase, and then cleared the Secret Service agent to resume his post by the door.

Dark sunglasses shrouded the agent's eyes even though the morning sky was still gray. He locked into his post, committed to securing the portal as he'd been drilled to do. Stockton had already been assigned protection; it was so certain that he'd win not only the primary but the election. Doing a good job there might ensure the agent was assigned to the president's detail.

"This exit is sealed, sir," he said to the Naval officer approaching the patio in winter dress blues and a pea coat. "I need to ask you to go around to the front, please."

AJ stood tall and straight, calculating exactly what he wanted to say next. He wasn't in the habit of disobeying an official request made by a government agent, but he was holding a padded mailing envelope rolled up inside his jacket that he had every intention of slipping between the exterior wall and the bench where Tom was known to smoke. The agent was between him and his objective, and he wasn't in the habit of failing at his mission either.

"Perhaps you could radio your lead agent and give them my name?"

"Perhaps you could walk around to the front door and give it yourself."

He was no stranger to posturing—the inflated sense of rank some people tried to exert on others—it had never worked on him. AJ stood firm, waiting for the agent to blink first.

"What was your name?" the agent asked eventually.

"Anthony Jay McCollister."

He muttered into his wrist and waited for his earbud to answer. "You said, Jay McCollister?"

"No, Jay McCollister is my father. My name is Lieutenant Commander Anthony Jay McCollister."

The agent tried again while AJ waited, rack-straight as though he were planted on the deck of an aircraft carrier absorbing the movement around him while remaining completely still. Finally, the agent relaxed his stance.

"Sorry, sir. You were listed under Tony."

"The Secret Service was confused by the abbreviation of Anthony?"

The agent ignored the barb. "Could you hold your arms out, please?"

"Is that necessary?"

"Yes, sir."

AJ lifted his arms to shoulder height, every muscle taut. A gun in his coat, he could explain. A gun sealed in an envelope? That was harder.

The agent started high, pressing into the fabric at AJ's collar, then tracing deliberately down his left arm, squeezing from bicep to wrist before repeating the ritual on the right. AJ kept his breath even.

The arms weren't the problem. The problem was pressed hard into his ribs, paper edges cutting faintly against his skin.

The agent switched to the back of his hands, thumping across AJ's sternum in short, practiced taps. He threaded his hands under AJ's arms. The search was about to get interesting—then a voice from the service door saved them both the extra incident report.

"He's on Lindsay Decker's Gold List. He does not get searched," Sarah said.

The agent pressed the earbud deeper into his ear as if the message had been relayed there at the same time Sarah delivered it.

"Apologies, sir."

"It's fine, agent. Thank you, Sarah."

"You're welcome, Commander." She held the door, waiting to bring him into the interior fold.

"One second."

AJ bent and placed a spit-shined leather Oxford on the bench. His laces were tied, though the knot wasn't perfect—it wasn't *regulation*. He adjusted, pulled the lace, retied it with military precision, and then tugged the cuff of his issued trousers taut at the crease. The motion disguised the envelope as it slid from his coat, and he slipped it behind the bench.

"I see all the LDA cubs are here," he said, without missing a beat. "Mama Bear must not be far away."

"She's out there digging a fire line between the senator and your creepy father," she said, pointing into the salon where Lindsey was masterfully moving supporters toward and away from the senator in the order of their importance.

"Think she'd do that for me?"

"She would if you paid her as much as Rick does."

"What's the schedule?" he said, looking at his watch.

"Nice touch, wearing that thing," she pointed at the vintage timepiece she'd added to his collection as part of their last Play 42. "They just finished 'Good Day, USA', did a family photo op, and in ten minutes they leave to open the polls."

"Understood."

"Tony," Lindsey said, catching sight of him and waving him over. She refused to call him AJ. She felt it was diminutive and tied him intrinsically to his father by consonance.

"Ma'am."

"Oh, lighten up. You look like you kick cats for fun. We're about to do the circuit. Ride with us."

"No, thank you, ma'am."

"You need more face time with Future POTUS."

"No, thank you, ma'am."

"Eight years, Tony. Imagine how much power you could accumulate in eight years. Special Intelligence Envoy to the President of the United States at... how old are you?"

"Twenty-five."

"Twenty-five and you could be on the National Security Council."

"You mean, you could have a plant on the National Security Council?"

"You wouldn't answer to your father."

Lindsey dragged her tongue across her teeth. She knew how to appeal to him at his core, and she had opened him up and planted her seed inside. Before he could consider the path she was presenting, Stockton joined them, shaking the young man's hand vigorously.

"AJ, how have you been? Sorry, I was too busy to find you last night."

"No apology necessary, sir."

"You're still at ONI?"

"That's right, sir."

"Good, good. I saw you chatting with Tom. Lindsey tells me you looked in on him a few times while I was on the trail."

"Yes, sir. I like to think we've bonded a bit."

"Founding members of the *my old man's a prick* club?"

"Not at all, sir."

"Right." Stockton wagged his finger. "Gotta run. Always good to see you, Commander."

"Yes, it *is* always good to see you," Lindsey cooed.

She trailed off, one pace behind the candidate, her massive designer bag slung over her shoulder like Mary Poppins, if Mary Poppins had kept imprisoned souls in there.

AJ—Tony—whatever version of himself he was leaning into— retreated to the perimeter of the salon, a shadow against the backdrop, waiting to complete his mission.

CHAPTER SEVENTEEN

The grey skies should have been a warning, but they are so often grey that I didn't notice. I walked toward the university, foolishly thinking only about myself, the things I wanted to achieve, or the places I might see if I were good enough to write for a real publication. Bombs are falling in Bosnia. Europe just formed a unified alliance with a single currency and open borders. The world is unfolding at a pace I've never seen, or at least never been aware enough to recognize.

I was fascinated—preoccupied—by the idea of telling stories of struggle, when my own trauma materialized in front of me. Pavel.

He was waiting for me at the edge of University Park, his coat draped around his shoulders. I didn't register the detail right away, but his arm was in a cast that didn't allow him to dress fully. I did notice the prominent bruising across his broken nose.

My stomach turned. Dmitri must have figured out who had attacked me and sent someone to deal with him. I didn't want to ask. I didn't want it to be confirmed. I didn't want to face this man who'd tried—and nearly succeeded—in violating me.

I turned, but he followed.

"Vladi, I came to apologize."

"I don't want your apology."

"I was upset that we lost in front of the scout. I was afraid I wouldn't make the draft, and then it would take longer to give you America. I had too many drinks."

"You were afraid I was upset, and so you strangle me while you try to have your way? Bullshit."

"I apologized, now can you apologize to me so we can move on?"

"Apologize to you? For what?"

How dare he think I have anything to apologize to him for?

"For telling your brother to send his friends after me!"

"What are you talking about?"

"Look at me!" He screamed, flaring into that violent man I had seen flashes of over the years, and experienced the full power of that night. "They broke into my house! They crushed my stick hand! I've been in the hospital since that night!"

"Who did?"

"Those thugs in the leather jackets that your brother hangs out with! Yuri, Federov, I don't know all of their names."

Dmitri's enforcers.

I tried not to smile. As much as I despise brutality, as much as I prefer words to fists, there is something about redemption that feels fair.

And there is something about knowing that you can use evil for your own good that makes you feel powerful. I shook this terrible notion before it took root.

"I won't apologize to you. You deserved it."

Pavel tried to follow me as I walked faster, toward the classroom building, but he struggled to breathe the cold air with his broken ribs.

"So you don't believe in what they do until it benefits you?" He spat on the ground. "Enjoy being alone!"

When I was younger, that comment would have hurt. I grew up worried about abandonment, and I let people treat me without dignity if it meant they would stay in my life longer. But something changed that *night on Pavel's floor. When I left him sprawling on the ground and wiped the blood from my face, I had a revelation: Nothing is worth filling the Void with something unhealthy...*

The jagged sound of Tom dragging his nose across the dresser's top with a deep snort pulled Mike from Delilah's head.

"Dude, maybe not while the press is still downstairs?"

"What? It's just Vicodin. I'll put on a fucking polo and tell them I fell off one of the horses." Tom leaned down for a second rip of the crushed pill.

"Or, chill out one time. I mean, I get it, buddy, but come on..."

"You couldn't possibly get it! The whole country isn't watching your every move, waiting for you to fuck up so they can hang the loss of their 'hopes and dreams for America' around your neck!"

"No, but I grew up worried that everyone was going to abandon me, and I let people treat me like shit if it meant they'd keep me in their life longer. Take you, for example."

"What the fuck is that supposed to mean?"

"What the fuck do you think it means, Tom? You don't have the market cornered on suffering! You think your life sucks because your parents dragged you along with their drama! Mine kicked me out of their life!"

"I could be so lucky."

Tom slammed the upstairs bedroom door where they'd retreated after the overly staged photos of the Stocktons and their closest family friends had been snapped on the sweeping stairs.

Mike considered leaving. Rick was gone, Tom was irritating, and his mother had no idea whether he was in the house or not. It would be simple—an Irish goodbye out through the kitchen.

Who knows? Maybe I'm Irish.

Except, despite his firm words to the contrary, Mike hadn't had the kind of come-to-Jesus that Delilah had. He could parrot her words, inspired by her suffering, echo them with empathy, but even in pain, he was an imposter. He couldn't claim to have a bigger emptiness than Tom while they were both sitting in the same mansion, pointing toward the White House. And he'd made a promise to Rick over whiskey and penguin jokes.

Just get him to November.

That was his contribution, moral support dressed up as loyalty. But loyalty only guided him so far; Delilah had to carry him the rest of the way through the day's obligation. He cracked the journal open again, choosing someone else's past over his own present.

It was impossible to concentrate in class, wondering if Pavel would still be waiting outside when I left. The room filled with words I didn't hear while I imagined walking to the mansion, rapping on that big iron gate, and demanding to see Dmitri.

But what would I say?

Thank you?

How dare you?

What makes you think you have the right to hurt people…

…even ones who deserve it.

And why?

Why do you care what happens to me?

I left the lecture hall, consumed by my own thoughts, anxious to walk through the fall air, hoping it would clear my head. That kind of winter crisp always let me think the clearest, though I walked toward the Zdrastkova's mansion without realizing. Maybe I was drawn toward my brother, hoping for some touchstone of normality.

I didn't make it there.

Dmitri flew across the sidewalk, appearing from nowhere, and waving a slip of paper that had been crumpled and flattened again until it was creased. "What the hell is this?"

"What the hell is what?"

"It's a circulation calling my father a criminal!"

Everything else I wanted to talk to him about disappeared as my cheeks grew hot, and the blood rushed through my ears. I'd meant to practice my new activism, not print it.

I couldn't let him see the fear cross my face. "He is a criminal. Why are you surprised?"

"Because you wrote it!"

"Accountability is the only way to keep men like Ivan Zdrastkova in check. They can't expect to operate freely under the new Independent State, breaking up families, and claiming people's sons as collateral." Hearing the words out loud made the bile rise in my throat. They were only ever supposed to be text on a screen. "You wrote this, didn't you? No one else's family lost a son to our home."

"It wasn't supposed to be printed... I was just..."

"Just what? Just trying to impress your school friends!? Just trying to make yourself out to be some revolutionary? Do you have any idea what my father does to people who write these things?"

I'd never seen him so enraged, his cheeks flaring with fire. He threw the page in my face. I could imagine him in that moment crushing Pavel's bones himself.

"Let me guess; he breaks their hand."

"That bastard deserved a lot more than what he got!"

"I'm not yours to worry about!"

"Just stay away from Ludmilla Butsiah! Don't be near her when it happens."

He was gone as quickly as he appeared. I knew I had to warn Mrs. Butsiah that she would be blamed for the flyer that I'd written, though she had printed it without my permission. I ran back to the cafe, and when she wasn't there, I ran all the way back to her office on campus.

"How could you?" I asked, breathless from the jog.

She looked at me with genuine confusion.

"How could you print that flyer and post it for the Zdrastkovas to see?"

"Your voice is so strong. It deserves to be heard."

"But you didn't have my permission!"

"You put yourself into those words—on paper—what did you think would happen to them? You sent them out into the world to affect people —to effect change."

"They're going to kill you for it."

The threat stopped Mrs. Butsiah like a needle being ripped from a record. Then she gathered herself and started again.

"Men like Ivan and Otto Zdrastkova don't kill you. They destroy your spirit, killing what you love first. They kept their wealth through the Soviet Oppression because they are oppressors, and that, dear girl, is *what your flyer makes known. That is what your fight is about, and why it had to be published."*

"Whatever they do, they are planning it now. Because of those words you printed. Words that I wrote. You've put targets on both of us."

"Does this answer your question then? The one from class the other night?"

With all that had happened in the last few days, I couldn't even remember what question she was referring to.

"What is the turning point between exposing the rot and letting them win?" she said to remind me. "The answer is, there isn't one. You never let them win."

CHAPTER EIGHTEEN

I sat at the same computer, detailing the threat to Mrs. Butsiah, while she encouraged me to support my hunch with evidence like Pavel's attack.

She had convinced me that nothing was ever achieved without moving through discomfort, and there were enough people like us—the same ones that expelled tyrants and ushered in democracy—who would take up this mantle and stand with us to expose Ivan and the criminal syndicate he runs.

Malkin, Federov, Slavovicj...

Zdrastkova.

She could see the fear in my hands, trembling as my conviction flowed, so she signed her name to the article to protect me. Then she gave it a headline:

WHEN I'M DEAD, IT WILL BE BECAUSE OF ZDRASTKOVA

I knew I was betraying Dmitri. I kept remembering his eyes—the things they must have witnessed—as they admonished me for my words. He is usually a master of shielding his emotions, wearing a public face, and invoking respect, but even he registered fear when he spoke of his father. Men that powerful— men whose children were even afraid to speak around them—deserve to be stopped.

"Son," the admiral said, finally making his way across the Stocktons' salon.

AJ clicked to attention, his elbows rigid, and his thumbs tracing the seam of his trousers. "Sir."

The admiral examined him carefully, attempting to find fault with something—a fold, a crease, a crooked ribbon— but there was nothing to criticize. Anthony Jay McCollister was in perfect form as always.

He snorted. "At ease, Commander."

"Sir." AJ shifted his weight, relaxing his spine, but not his gaze.

"I don't remember requesting your presence today."

"You didn't, sir."

"Then why are you here?"

"I was invited by the Stocktons."

"Really? Which one?"

Admiral McCollister's first hint that his son had regular dealings with the Stocktons had only come the night before, when the guards at the gate had called him "Tony" and waved him through without checking his ID. Until then, he had believed himself to be the only McCollister with a through line to the future First Family.

"All of them."

The comment could have been considered borderline insubordinate, at least to an old-school disciplinarian like Jay. AJ held still and waited for the force that was his father to blow, but nothing came. Not in a room full of potential allies or adversaries. Any admonishment would come later in a darkened study where kingdoms were planned.

"Good. Stay close. He owes you. He owes us both. Seeing you reminds him it's almost time to cash in."

AJ gave the simple, indoctrinated response he'd been reciting since he was eight years old—since his mother had taught him that anything more might invite a reaction. "Sir."

"That's it?"

"What more would you like me to say, sir?"

"Nothing." Jay looked his son over one more time. "As you were, sailor."

The admiral reintegrated into the gathering, leaving his son on the fringe where he believed him to belong. Once he'd folded into the smattering of operatives important enough to get an invitation to the house, but not to have ridden with the senator's entourage, Tom slid into the place vacated when he left.

"Do you have it?" Tom asked in a regular speaking voice that set AJ's internal radar off.

"Keep your voice down."

"Right, sorry. Do you have it, though?" Tom whispered.

"I left it behind the bench where you smoke. No one will think it's strange to see you poking around out there."

"Smart!"

"But watch the agent at the door."

"Right. Where'd you get it?"

"I'm not going to tell you that."

"It's clean, though, yeah?"

"It's clean. Are you?" He could see that Tom's eyes weren't fully responsive, though not as bad as the night he'd driven the boy to rehab at Lindsey's behest.

"Ish."

AJ exhaled long. "This never happened, Tom. You guys get busted knocking over a liquor store or something stupid, and my name comes up…"

"I know."

"Do you?"

"Neither of our dads can have that kind of thing blowing back on them. Trust me. It's all I've heard since I was thirteen years old."

"Only thirteen? They'd have started you at six if you went to Navy Primary."

Tom managed to chuckle at the dry wit. "Well, however you got it, thanks, AJ. I know you don't like helping me out."

"I don't mind helping you, Tom. I just wish you'd get your act together so I didn't have to."

"I get that. Say, you want to meet my buddy? He's upstairs."

"No, I don't want to meet your friend, Tom. I want to be able to swear under oath that I have never seen him before."

"Under oath." Tom scoffed at the idea, as if to suggest that perjuring themselves wasn't all that uncommon in his house. "Do you want to grab a drink or something?"

"I should go before my father sees us *conspiring.* I'll see you around the election, though."

"Sure. Yeah." Tom's expectant eyes fell. "Well, thanks again."

"You have my number if you need something?"

"No."

"I'll tell you what, then. If you need me, call Sarah."

Tom scuffed the tile bashfully with the tip of his shoe, realizing AJ was trying to orchestrate a meet-cute with the fixer he'd spent years convincing himself he wasn't good enough for.

"Fuckin' puppet-master," he laughed, dashing back up the stairs.

"Fucking Butsiah!" Dmitri screamed, waving the headline. He found me as I was leaving campus. He seems to be able to find me anywhere in the city, as if he has spies following me at all times. "You put a nail in her coffin! Maybe in yours!"

"Lower your voice!"

He yelled with no regard for who might hear him. "You aren't hearing me! I was alone with my father when he gave this order! The only way she would know is if you told her! And the only way you would know is if I told you!"

"I had to tell her! She's a mother. Her children would be orphaned."

"You didn't have to write about it! He won't care whose name is on the byline! He's going to know I betrayed him as soon as he sees this — and believe me, someone will show it to him if they haven't already!"

"I don't care what your father thinks of me."

"I care what he thinks of me! Now I'll be given a job…"

"What kind of a job?"

"I don't know, but I hope it isn't you." He started to leave again, as he always does—with me standing there hanging on his last words—but he turned back. "I never wanted this life," he said. "I wasn't given a choice in being my father's son."

"You had a choice in recruiting my brother."

"I wasn't given that choice either. That was your mother's doing."

152

Dmitri joined his cousin Alexei, who I hadn't noticed, and left. Again, I was alone, wondering what events I'd set in motion. If what he said was true—if my mother had bartered with Ivan and the payment had been Sergei, I could never forgive her. She and I weren't close—she had always looked at me like I was just another mouth to feed, like I'd come at the wrong time and never left—but if this is true, she's dead to me.

"Hey," Tom said, opening his bedroom door slowly to find Mike on the sofa in the corner where he'd been most of the previous night and so far that day. "Always reading. You think you'd be smarter."

"You would think." Mike closed the book on his thumb to save his place. Delilah was headed for a confrontation he didn't want to miss.

"Returns have started to come in."

"Is that good or bad?"

"Fuck, I don't know. I hate all this, but I don't want it to change, ya know? That doesn't make sense."

In its own messed-up way, it did. Change was scary, for an addict, for an orphan, for anyone. Change meant the unknown, and the unknown was a Void of its own. Mike understood. He also understood that his best friend was trying to apologize in his squirrelly junkie way for the selfish tantrum he'd unleashed earlier.

"I get it. Like, remember the night we were packing up for Georgetown…"

"We were trippin' balls…"

"We were, but remember, you were acting stoked about getting our own place, but you were freaking out because you had no idea how to make coffee, because Marta always did it for you."

Tom laughed. "Yeah."

"Look, you're going to move into the White House. It's going to be weird. Secret Service is going to be all up in your shit, but maybe you find something cool in that next phase. Maybe the First Lady's platform can include music education in inner city schools, and you can travel around playing for kids who can't afford instruments."

"God, I haven't played in years."

"Or maybe you slink around the press room until Sarah agrees to go out with you."

"Yeah, I could do that too."

"See, you never know, dude. The universe is dragging you in the direction of your fate, whether you know it or not. You weren't given a choice in being your father's son, but you just gotta roll with it."

"You're probably right. Come have a cigarette with me."

"Yeah, let me finish this chapter."

"Dude, your obsession with this Russian girl's story is next level even for you."

"Ukrainian. And I think since I know she's dead, the whole thing reads like that moment in a horror movie where you want to scream at the kids not to open the door because the monster is behind it."

"I hate those movies."

Mike hated those movies too. Suspense was not his genre. He didn't need anything else manufacturing a knot in his stomach.

"Yeah, but it makes you wonder which door your own monster is behind."

CHAPTER NINETEEN

I knocked on the door once I'd summoned the courage to—once my hand had stopped shaking. I was tired of wondering, of lying awake at night with questions and fears. Fear destroys, and, in the end, it only works when you let it burrow through your thoughts. When you look it in the eye, it disappears.

Or it kills you.

The end result is the same.

"Ms. Stromkovietz," Ivan answered. I don't know why I was expecting a servant, some type of housemaid, to come to the door and not the patriarch himself. "Would you like to come in from the cold?"

"No, thank you. I'd like to speak with Dmitri."

"Dmitri isn't here. You're welcome to wait inside."

"Sergei?"

"I'm afraid you've just found me. Only the old folks are in at this hour while the youth enjoy the night."

I could only imagine what they were doing. "No, thank you. I'll come back another time."

"Let me have someone drive you. You've already been attacked once recently."

A chill crawled over my skin. Why would Mr. Zdrastkova know about my private trauma? Was it that important for him to be involved in every chilling detail that took place in Kiev, or did he have to approve the use of his network of thugs to retaliate? I felt further woven into his life than I'd hoped.

"Dmitri will be back shortly, I believe. Give him ten minutes, and if he's delayed, I'll drive you home to your parents."

He extended his hand to invite me in. This man was no monster, at least not the one I'd imagined. And I didn't want to like him, but I found myself unable to look at him without feeling embarrassed—more importantly, poor.

"Can I offer you tea or perhaps chocolates while you wait?" he asked, showing me to the large kitchen and offering me a seat in their banquette.

"No, thank you."

"I'll leave them here in case you change your mind."

He placed the truffles in the center of the table in a perfect pile, some dusted with gold, others dipped in sugar so dazzling it looked like colored glass.

"She's thinking to herself, 'I can't possibly eat these luxuries that I didn't earn for myself through my own suffering.'"

"No, I…"

I stopped. This was not the man to get into an ideological debate with. Not when he had a price on my head and I was in his court.

"Please, go on. I'd rather have discourse with my enemies than find out how they feel from a flyer."

"Sir, it isn't that I require suffering. I just prefer not to inflict it on others."

"I've heard that about you. Convicted. Outspoken. You'd have done well in the Revolution had you been old enough."

I'd popped a chocolate into my mouth without noticing. It burst with a sweet syrup I'd never tasted before. "You have so much influence. Why not use it to improve the quality of life here? To build a country and not a second oppression?"

"Because I'm compelled to improve the quality of life for my own blood first before the masses. It's selfish, I know, but I can affect this directly."

"By eliminating everyone who disagrees with you?"

"Not everyone."

"You're talking about my father?"

"No, though, I still consider Alexander a comrade. We survived the terrors of the front line. I would never wish him harm."

"Then what happened between the two of you?"

"What always happens between two young men: A young woman."

Our talk was interrupted by the creaking of hinges, followed by the slam of the front door — just when I'd found someone who was willing to answer my questions.

"Father, it's done. Can that be the last —" Dmitri froze when he saw me. "What is she doing here?"

"Waiting for you, son. I'll give you your privacy."

Ivan excused himself and left Dmitri standing there in his winter coat, staring blankly. When he snapped into motion, he moved to the sink and began washing his hands.

"You need to leave."

"Your father was about to tell me why he and my father never speak, and yet my mother visits him."

"That's his story to tell."

"Then tell me why you disagree with this life, but recruited Sergei for it."

"You still have no idea? They don't tell you anything, do they?"

"They really don't."

"Ok." He slammed down the leather gloves he'd removed to scrub his hands. "Your father lost all of his money years before the revolution. Your mother came to us with her two babies in tow, begging for his help. He's the reason you're fed."

"She paid off her debt with Sergei's life."

"Better than yours. Do you know what you'd be doing right now?"

I slapped him, but this kind of violence is nothing to him. He laughed and threw his pistol from his pocket to the table.

"I'm the only person in your life telling you the truth, Vladi. If you need to hurt me for that, go ahead, but I didn't cause the feud, and I haven't been the one lying to you. If anything, I'm the one who just..."

"Just what?"

"Nothing. Go home. I'll have someone take you."

"No, I want to hear more about our families..."

"Go home!" he yelled, dragging me by the arm to the front door. He threw it open, but before he shoved me through the threshold, he kissed me.

I'd never known a kiss like this before. Gravity gave way, and the only thing holding me to Earth was him. Then I was standing on the porch alone. He yelled for Alexei to walk me home and slammed the door.

My head was dizzy.

Alexei asked me where I live, and I couldn't remember.

My whole truth unraveled.

159

Ivan wasn't pure evil, my parents weren't being singled out for punishment by him, and Dmitri... Dmitri felt like the puzzle piece that had always been missing from my soul.

The next night, I attended Christmas mass with Mama and saw Ivan again, surrounded by his soldiers under the gleam of that golden cross. My mother kept her gaze fixed on him the whole time. I can't quite describe how. If what Dmitri said was true, she should be furious with him for putting her in the impossible position of giving up her only son. At the same time, I would expect Ivan to show superiority, as he has emerged victorious in this power struggle.

Neither of those was the case. He smiled like he was happy to see her, even for a second, and she nodded the way you would at an old friend across the room. They were like movie characters who would find a way to be together by the end of the film.

My mother struggles with loving a Zdrastkova the same way I do.

I couldn't let on that I saw any of this, though inside I was screaming. How could this man put a price on a child's life, and how could this woman abuse his love to take his money? Ivan may not be the monster I once thought, but he is no Christian. He was probably there to keep half the church's collection for himself. Then again, I am no Christian either. I'm nothing. No one. Lacking even the conviction to speak to my parents or sign my name to an opinion. If I can't forgive them, I cannot be the Christian my mother finds peace in being.

In this way, Dmitri is blessed. The lack of choice means he has no struggle to define his desires. They're handed to him, expected of him, and his wants are repressed for the greater good—a simple life of service.

Imagine that—after everything, I am a Communist.

CHAPTER TWENTY

Mike closed the kitchen door behind him to keep the heat inside and tucked the book into his coat pocket. Tom was already pacing the patio with his cigarette in hand.

"Jeeze, what took you so long?"

So long?

"I read a chapter and flirted with a reporter. Why are you trippin'?"

"There's something out here I don't want the Secret Service to find on their next sweep."

"Domino's delivering coke now?"

"No. I hooked up your piece."

It took Mike a second to remember what his friend was even talking about, then he flashed to Dmitri removing the pistol from his pocket the night they'd stood in his father's kitchen.

That wasn't you.

"Someone dead-dropped you a pistol? Here? Today? Inside the security perimeter? Who the fuck pulled that off?"

"Buddy of mine." Tom honored his agreement not to mention AJ by name and slid his hand down between the exterior wall and the bench's leg. Keeping an eye on the agent posted nearby, he passed it to Mike. "Here."

Mike opened the flap and peeked inside.

"Let me see it."

Neither knew anything about firearms, but they could read the markings: P228 SIG SAUER 9MM.

"Government issue?" Mike asked. "Where did your friend say he got this?"

"He didn't. Do you even know how to shoot a gun?"

"How hard could it be?"

"Fuck, dude. Be careful."

"I'm not going to play cops and robbers. I just feel like if other people are walking around with them, I should."

Mike waited for the agent to sweep the other direction and slipped the pistol from the envelope into his pocket.

I could feel something weighing it down. Something heavy, like a gun in the pocket.

"That might be the worst reason I've ever heard to have a gun."

"What kind of a Republican are you?"

"I'm not. That's the crux of my entire problem: ideology in direct contrast to my emotional construct."

"There were about five words in that sentence I didn't think you knew."

"I read my press packet while I was waiting for you to get down here."

Tom smiled a boy band grin that usually emerged when he was about to swing into a manic phase. He'd spend the next two weeks awake sliding down some obsession, which felt in this case like it might be his father's platform—not because he cared, but because he could potentially impress Sarah—then he would crash, requiring a hospitalization no one would let him have.

Mike didn't have time for it. His commitment to the Stockton family was honored. The Republican Party nomination was a lock. He had hustled himself a G-Man gun. It was time to leave.

He stood and flipped up his collar.

"Mind if I go?"

"You get your little toy and then bail on me?"

"I've been here for twenty-four hours. I brought you drugs. I did the press call. I kissed the ring. My duties are complete."

"And what am I supposed to do? Mingle? Shake hands? *Smile?*"

"Exactly. Life comes for all of us, buddy."

"You do need to leave. You're darker than usual."

"Yeah."

The two threw out a fist bump, and Mike moved off toward his Lexus as Tom returned inside to hover around his father's future Press Secretary.

As Mike rolled his Lexus down the long drive, the senator's convoy breached the gate. He gave it the right of way, lingering until he had the driveway to himself. Before he could inch forward to freedom, Lindsey hopped from the rear of an armored SUV and knocked on his window.

"Mr. Green," she said through the glass.

He inched the glass down only far enough to show his eyes. "Lindsey."

"How married are you to this girlfriend of yours? I heard something about a ring."

Was it that important for her to be involved in every single chilling detail that took place in Washington, or does she have to approve Kris because I'm so close to Rick? I felt further woven into Lindsey's life than I'd hoped.

"I'm still on the fence there."

"Well, come down on the side of it where you aren't dating a senior advisor in the Rothschild camp. Two to one, he's who we face in November."

"You want me to break up with my girlfriend because her boss is also running for president?"

"Yes. Unless you can flip her into being a mole for the campaign."

"Fuck you, Linds."

"We've done that, honey. Wasn't that great."

"Then why'd you do it a second time?"

Mike knew he'd won the round and pulled away from Falls Church, away from that piece of his life that was growing increasingly oppressive.

Highway 66 between Falls Church and D.C. was starting to lose its appeal. When he hadn't been making the drive every other day, it had been the only place his thoughts could flow freely, but this week it was the road where assholes with high beams stayed on his tail and kept him from being somewhere productive.

"Not this again," he muttered, speeding up.

They stayed on his bumper. Mike brake-tapped, hoping to discourage the tailgater—hoping he would back off enough to see if there was a dent in his front fender.

Two assholes don't make a stalker. You're losing it.

Mike distracted himself with the radio. Typically, it would have been tuned to the alternative rock station he'd grown up grunging out to, but the tail end of a classic rock song—the song stuck in his head since the other night—blared instead.

"You're listening to KWDC, and we're taking you back to 1973. Vietnam ended, Watergate was in full swing, and your gas was about to get way more expensive. Where were you, my friend?"

On the doorstep of a fucking orphanage.

He punched the button to make the DJ stop, hoping the Void might fill up with the next chapter he needed to write, or Delilah might join him in the passenger seat.

Neither came to keep him company.

Just the headlights.

He crossed the bridge.

They crossed the bridge.

He exited E Street.

They exited E Street.

So did nineteen other cars. It's a popular route, idiot.

Besides, I've got insurance now, he thought, rubbing the weapon nestled against his hip.

He took the roundabout at Thomas Circle for a three-sixty to see where the other guy got off.

Vermont.

If he were following me, he'd have gone to Massachusetts.

Satisfied, he swung around again, exited, and pulled into his parking garage without any further irritation.

This time, when he stepped inside the apartment, he didn't bother with the deadbolt. He hung up the coat, turned on the coffee pot, and took his pistol to the bedroom. Standing in front of the full-length mirror, he raised and lowered it several times, getting the feel, measuring the weight— programming his muscle memory.

He located the safety.

Should probably keep that on.

But he needed to know where it was in case he needed to remove it. He dropped the mag and re-seated it. It felt exactly how it looked in the movies. He racked the slide to chamber a round, watching his reflection morph into something.

Something that felt right.

"Mike Grennan, LAPD," he said. Then he pushed his trademark smile across his face and tucked the pistol into the waistband of his suit. "But people call me Gestapo Joe."

CHAPTER TWENTY-ONE

Dead Girls Tell No Tales

Chapter Eighteen: Margarita adjusted her trousers—a pair of those high-waisted numbers that had too many buttons to get past easily. They made her look a little like a sailor, if the sailor was an hourglass. I still didn't get why dames would want to wear trousers. If I had legs like a racehorse and a tush that could make a man cry, I'd never hide them behind wool.

"The truth doesn't even matter, sweetheart, only what story you can spin," she said, slamming the car door. It was less of a slam and more the regular amount of force it took to move the steel, done so with the ease and proficiency to make a loud thud. She was stronger than she let on.

"I'm LAPD. I'm not in the habit of spinning stories," I said.

That made her laugh out loud.

"You got something against the integrity of the LAPD?" I asked.

"What integrity of the LAPD?"

We'd been on the road together for enough days that we'd lost the polite filter. Road trips and motel rooms took the glitz off a person real fast. And she didn't have anything left to hide. I'd had my mouth in all of those nooks and crannies already.

I was right when I'd clocked her as different. Yeah, she could set a curl and paint a lip like a proper broad, but unless someone was asking her to, she didn't do it by choice. She'd have rather been swilling straight from the bottle and laughing with too much volume. She was basically a man, with a helluva rack and the ability to walk in four-inch heels.

Wait. None of that sounded right.

You know what I mean.

"No, I want to hear what you've got against the LAPD," I said, catching up to her as she crossed the parking lot of that New Mexico motor inn. "Because, in case you forgot, sister, you came to me for help. Your dead twin fell under my jurisdiction, but this wild goose chase we're doing across the country, looking for some bloke named Fat Ivan with a bald thug in a leather jacket chasing us the whole way. That shit is extracurricular."

She slid cash across the desk to the motel guy. "One room," she said to the moron, before she turned back to me. "Lighten up. For every one of the good cops on the force, you got a goon with a god-complex, and you can't tell me it isn't true."

It was true.

"Now, you're one of the good ones, Joe. Real good, honey. That's why I came to you. You care. You care about the truth. You care about nailing the bad guy, and you're easier on the eyes than I could have hoped for. Now get the bags out of the car."

"Yeah, yeah. Build me up, buttercup, because you need a sherpa."

Since when is being used ok because she's a ten on the Richter scale? And when the fuck did I develop a moral compass?

Mike highlighted everything he'd spent the last hour writing and deleted it, then paced the room, sipping his coffee. When the words didn't come, when the worlds he created started to jumble, blood flow was the key to unlocking it.

Not that kind of blood flow.

Although that might work too.

Margarita had started as a sexy mystery with a dead twin, but she'd started to turn into Lindsey: manipulative, calculating, and ulterior. He was writing her as the last woman he'd seen, because she had left a whiff of her poisonous cloud in his orbit. He didn't want to, but Lindsey was the most influential woman he had ever known.

Until recently.

Delilah had also crept into his character development, in the worst possible way. Joe's essence, his human flaw, the most consistent part of his brand, was his lack of a moral compass. He knew the LAPD had no integrity; it was why he signed up to work there. But corrupt power now felt different. Unattractive. The romantic notions of running unchecked had been stripped away and replaced with the pain of a girl he would never know.

You know me better than anyone.

Delilah was curled up in his beanbag chair, her knees pulled into her chest. "And I think you know what happens next."

"When do you start sleeping with him?"

She fanned her book in her hand until she'd found the passage she was looking for, then she passed it to Mike. "New Year's Eve."

"To 1994," Dmitri said as he handed me a glass of champagne. The fizzy liquid tickled as it went down. I'd had champagne before, I think, but this was the good stuff. The kind that wouldn't leave you with a headache the next morning.

"Drinking in public? Isn't this illegal?" I asked.

We were standing among the thousands in Independence Square. A throng, bundled in fur hats and overcoats to protect against the cold, just to watch fireworks. The square was all rubble and silence—where ideology used to live. The old Soviet monuments had been pulled down, but nothing had gone up in their place—just a half-built gate flanked by scaffolding. A promise. Someday it would be the Archangel Michael, Protector of Kiev—or Kyiv, if we could get it changed back to our own language.

"Don't worry about that. No one is going to arrest us," he reassured me. "Let's celebrate."

"What is there to celebrate? Times are dark."

"I'm celebrating that you agreed to come out with me tonight."

"No, I was going to come here anyway."

That wasn't entirely true. I wanted to purge 1993 from my soul, but it wasn't until he left a note on my bedroom window, asking me to meet him at the Lyadski Vorota, that I decided to go to the square.

"Then I'm glad I'm here to protect you, since there has been an uptick in violence this last week."

Why do you think that is, I wanted to say. People had been found dead in their homes. Journalists. Professors.

Journalism professors.

Mrs. Butsiah and her husband had been shot at close range as they slept. I wanted to ask him about it, and I couldn't do it in the

Zdrastkova mansion. I wasn't sure if I could do it at all. That was the real reason I went.

Since our kiss, I couldn't think of him as a thug, or even as the man who'd stolen my brother. He wasn't a political enemy or a shadow in the background of every event in my life. Dmitri was now a heartache, hidden behind duty, shackled by honor, and suffocated by tradition. He was a blue-eyed boy with lips that knew love but weren't allowed to express it.

"I don't care what the motive is, we're here," he said, clinking our glasses before he refilled them with more of the expensive liquid.

"I asked my father about yours. He wouldn't even speak to me."

"Do you blame him? What man wants to admit failure to his family?"

"What else do you know about it?"

"Is that the only reason you agreed to this? To interview me? Ever the investigative journalist."

There was some truth to the accusation, but it wasn't the whole reason.

"No. I wanted to see you again. After..."

"After I kissed you?"

"After you came home with a pistol in your pocket, the same night Mrs. Butsiah was murdered in her home."

"I always have a pistol in my pocket. You know that." He flashed the edge of the grip for effect.

"Did you...?"

"It wasn't me, Vladi, now stop. No work tonight. Give me one night where I'm not a Zdrastkova. Just one night where I'm allowed to be who I want to be."

"Who do you want to be?"

The countdown began. Thousands in unison: "Ten, Nine, Eight..."

"I want to be the guy kissing you at midnight."

...Seven, Six, Five...

"Unless you tell me not to."

...Four, Three, Two...

"Last chance?"

He cradled my face in his hands and drew me in.

"HAPPY NEW YEAR!"

I let it happen. I wanted it to happen. It lasted so much longer than that first, hurried, confusing collision in his doorway. It lasted until the crowd tore us apart with its undulating celebration.

"Let's go," he said, pulling me away from the frantic chaos.

We ended up at a nightclub, some basement where Western music blared and strobe lights made everything throb in rhythm with the beat. No one made us wait in line. Zdrastkovas don't wait in lines; they walk to the front, parting people with their expansive energy field.

The whole night disappeared. 1993 disappeared. Every question I had disappeared. Vodka helped, but it was Dmitri—the real Dmitri— smiling, dancing, ignoring the people who wanted to offer him free drinks and the girls who tried to get his attention.

He called a taxi to take me home and rode with me to make sure I got there safely, then he walked me to the door to make sure no one was lingering in the dark.

I think he suggested that he come in to make sure no one was waiting to hurt me for the things I'd written, but I may have told him I was afraid of that, so he'd feel compelled to protect me.

All of it was a ruse. The only person capable of ordering that violence was his father, and he was the one carrying it out. I knew that, but I wanted to pretend I didn't. I wanted one night where I could be the person I wanted to be, too.

CHAPTER TWENTY-TWO

I kept my eyes closed as long as I could. Once I opened them, I knew 1994 would look exactly like 1993. Cold. Empty. Violent. And Dmitri would be gone.

He slipped from the bed, and as much as I wanted to let him move away in darkness like a haunting, I couldn't pretend we hadn't just fractured our lives.

"I don't want to leave, but I don't think your parents should find me here," he whispered, sitting next to me when he noticed my eyes open.

I traced my finger under his collarbone, across a fresh tattoo cracking as it healed. The five-pointed star of the vory—issue for killing someone on behalf of the family. I wish I didn't know these things, or why he had a new one.

"Thank you for being with me on my only night of freedom."

"Why does it only have to be one night?"

I didn't want to be that girl—the kind who was always asking when they could see you again, or what the relationship meant. Needy, insecure, fearful—all things I swore I'd never be again, not for a man. But I felt like when he left, a piece of me would go with him, and I was already missing so many pieces.

"You shouldn't be with someone like me."

"Why do you have to be someone like you?"

"To be anything else, my father would have to think I was dead."

I closed my eyes again so I wouldn't have to watch him leave.

Weeks went by before he found me again. I'd seen Alexei outside my house, I'd even seen Yuri following me home from the market, but Dmitri kept himself hidden, as if he had intentionally erased himself from my life. Then he materialized under the platform where they were still building the Archangel. At first, I thought I had been remembering him so powerfully that I conjured him, but I could feel the weight of his gun against my leg.

"Do you want to be with me?"

I was startled, both by his appearance and his question.

"What?"

"I found a way to do it, but I need to know if it's what you want."

"What way? What are you talking about?"

"I'll get us out. All of us. You, me, and Sergei."

"How?"

"I can't tell you that yet. Just trust me."

"Why would I do that? My entire life, people have kept secrets. Lies. Right down to the DNA in my own house! Why would I believe you?"

"Because I'm your best chance at getting out of Kiev."

"I need more than that."

"Because I love you. I always have."

Love? I don't know what that is or if it's what I've been feeling. Maybe you love your best chance at survival.

"Yes."

"Yes, you want to be with me?"

"Yes, I want out of here."

It wasn't the answer he'd wanted, but it was enough. He disappeared again so fast, I wondered if I had imagined it—dreamt of a way to be free. And I didn't want to be that girl, but I could only wonder when I would see him again.

Mike shuffled down the hall to refill his coffee. He'd lost track of how many pots he'd consumed since getting home. It was about thirty written pages and seven of Delilah's chapters ago. That was how he was marking time, not by a clock grounded in reality, but in someone else's events as they created the scaffolding that held him up.

A retch heaved into the toilet bowl as he passed the bathroom. Delilah's raccoon eyes looked up at him, wet, as she cried over the throne. Mike dropped to his knees and held her hair back as she heaved again.

"How far along are you?"

"Eight weeks." She sat back, resting her head against the wall and feeling her abdomen. "It's easy to count from New Year's Eve."

"When were you going to tell me?"

"I planned to tell the baby's father first."

Mama let go of my hair as I sat back, resting my head against the wall and rubbing the place where there was now a child taking form.

"Do you know whose it is?"

How little this woman must think of me. "Of course, I know whose it is!"

"That makes it easier. Who is he? What kind of a man?"

"He's a Zdrastkova," I said, vomiting again.

"I should have known." Mama wet a rag and held it to the back of my neck. "If you can turn your head and not ask where the money comes from, your child would never know want."

"Then why did you choose Father over Ivan?"

"I wanted to know where the money came from, even if there wasn't any."

"And yet he still supported you, and you had to pay this debt back with your son."

"You make different choices for your children than for yourself. You're about to learn that, child."

I've never had a connection with my mother. I wouldn't have guessed an unplanned pregnancy would be the thing to bring us together. When my stomach had settled, we broke the news to Papa.

"Can you accept a Zdrastkova baby into your heart?" I asked.

All he said was, 'I've done it before.'

"I've done it before…" Mike said, looking up from the book and repeating the line. "Sergei wasn't payment for a loan. Sergei was Ivan's son."

"That was the only thing that made sense to me, though it didn't make things better. I was still pregnant and alone." Delilah lay her bleeding head on the pillow next to him and draped her hand across his.

KNOWN ASSOCIATES:
BROTHER (1): *[REDACTED]*
BROTHER (2): *SERGEI [REDACTED] – KIA*

"MI6 listed a second brother? The only one not KIA…"

"Fuck MI6. They didn't know anything, and they didn't care. They left me to die like this."

She took the book again, flipping forward twenty pages. "Here's where it starts to go bad."

"It hasn't been bad yet?"

She motioned to the gunshot wound and assorted brutal injuries mapped across her body. "Obviously it gets worse."

I still need to tell Dmitri he's going to be a father so he can consider the baby in his plans. He won't want a child growing up with the birthright he and Sergei carry.

If he can't get the baby out, I will have to move into the mansion… go to Ivan and present his grandchild as an heir. What other choice is there—an orphanage? What would become of me, a mother who abandons her child? No. Orphans have no chance at a normal life—forever carrying the burden of being unwanted.

"Unwanted?"

In his two-ish decades on Earth, Mike had run scenarios around his own abandonment countless times. He liked to think that he was the sole survivor of a tragic accident, and his parents' dying thoughts were of him, but the truth was likely less literary. He could have been pulled from a drug addict or commandeered by the state. He'd buried those unflattering possibilities at a young age, choosing to keep his birth parents faultless in his desertion, but for all he knew, he could have been a crack baby.

That would explain the drugs.

It hadn't occurred to him that he could have been voluntarily given up, set out like garbage because he didn't fit his mother's lifestyle. Women's Lib was roaring in 1973. Maybe she was simply not interested in motherhood.

"How could that even cross your mind?" he asked Delilah, furious that she'd suggested the option, and that someone had suggested it to his mother.

"Look at everything I was facing…"

"You make a mistake, you live with the consequences!"

"Is that how you've lived your life, or have you had Lindsey Decker and Richard Stockton there to make those consequences go away?"

A slam startled both of them. Mike grabbed the pistol from the nightstand and moved to the window.

Someone closing a car door— nothing worth drawing a weapon over. "It was just a car door," he assured her, returning the gun to the table.

"It's never just a car door, Meisha."

"They can't hurt you, Vladi, you're already dead."

"You're not. You should pay attention."

"To what?"

"Everything."

CHAPTER TWENTY-THREE

I decided to finish school before the baby comes—to feel like there was something I could do for myself. Then maybe wherever Dmitri takes me, I can use my education to do something—be self-reliant, never depend on a man to provide for me. If nothing else, I have accomplished a university degree.

Before she was murdered, Mrs. Butsiah gave me notes on the novella I wrote. It was her revolution story, though Sergei found his way into it, leaking in and adding sorrow. It probably won't ever see print, but it gives me something to work on as the baby grows and my body aches.

Dmitri found out about the baby. I would have told him if he'd found me, but someone—one of his spies—must have seen my growing belly and ruined my chance to tell him myself. I was afraid he'd be angry. This development could have ruined everything he was planning. Instead, he said he'll move faster. "Double Down," I think they call it.

We met under the blaring summer sun—shielded only by the bronze skeleton of our future Archangel—so he could tell me when the plans were moving forward.

"You haven't even told me what the plans are," I reminded him.

"The less you know about my work, the better. You would be worthless to my enemies."

"You think I'm worthless?"

"To my enemies, yes! I am protecting you. I'm protecting our child."

"I can't keep living with secrets, Dmitri."

He exhaled long, resigning himself to open a vault he'd never cracked open before. "I've made contact with the British Intelligence Service."

"British Intelligence Service? How do you even meet someone like that?"

"I was approached. They consider my father a terrorist."

"Approached?" I lowered my voice. If Ivan had people willing to take him a flyer written in anger, he could certainly have someone report this conversation. "How do you know this isn't a trap?"

"They'll relocate us if I can provide them with enough evidence to arrest him and dismantle his syndicate."

"And...?"

I could tell he had more on his mind, something he was leaving out. I'm so tired of people thinking they can 'protect' me by keeping me ignorant. Ignorance is a tool used to control. I refuse to be controlled anymore.

"Dammit, I'm carrying your child, I deserve to know everything!"

He moved us into the center of the square as though he were giving someone a clearer line of sight to watch over us. "My father is planning to meet with the Three Families this fall..."

"Who are the Three Families?"

"The old crime families—Austria, France, and Italy. The men who have owned the trade routes and banks for... I don't even know how long."

"Mafya."

"What else? We're going to drive to these places—take advantage of the open borders so we don't need to show our IDs—and once I have *their identities, their routes, where the arms are going, I'll give them to MI6, and they'll give us asylum."*

He said this as if it were simple.

"As soon as you turn on your father, he'll come for me. Both of his sons, traitors—he'll blame me, he might even kill my mother."

"MI6 is going to stage our deaths first. Sergei and I will be in protective custody before they arrest him."

"And what of me? If this trip lasts for more than two months, our baby will already be born."

He pressed an envelope into my hand—thick with cash, more money than I'd ever seen. "When they pull us out—when they make it look like we're dead—I'll mail you a blank postcard from our safe house. Take a train to whatever city is on the card and we'll be free."

I couldn't believe what I was hearing. He was describing an intricate plot with so many things that could go wrong, and yet he smiled the whole time, his eyes sparkling.

"Dmitri, this is crazy."

He pressed his lips to my forehead. "I thought you'd love it. Exposing injustice, prosecuting criminals, unraveling global terrorism; it's the makings of your greatest novel."

"If anything goes wrong, he'll never stop hunting us."

"He will once he's executed."

Even death didn't feel like it would break the circle of violence. Ivan himself wasn't a cruel man; he was just doing an evil job—one he'd probably been forced into by his father and generations of fathers before him. He was loyal to his family, all members of it, but I suppose that's why betrayal was the only way to escape.

"What if you send this postcard and I'm in the hospital? What if the baby is born sick, and it's weeks or months before we can get away? There are too many open ends for this to be your whole plan."

"I'll call you from the road as things develop. Vladi, I promise you, the agent I'm working with is going to make sure you and the baby get out."

"I hate this."

"And I hate the idea of our little Petr becoming what I am."

"Petr?"

"You don't like it?"

I looked back toward the bronze skeleton of our angel coming together. "I was thinking about Michael for a boy."

"I hate the name Meisha. Everyone with this name is an asshole."

"Ok, Petr. Petr Dmitrivich."

"And whatever surname our new Intelligence friends give us. He'll never go by Zdrastkova. I promise you that." He kissed his fingertips and pressed them against my belly. "I need to go, but the next time I see you, we'll be free. Subjects of Her Majesty the Queen of England."

"Wait." I reached into the collar of my shirt and unclasped the silver necklace Sergei had given me all those years ago on my eighteenth birthday. "Tell him a piece of me is still with him."

"He knows."

Alexei let me know a week later that they had crossed into Poland and their journey had begun.

"My cousin asked me to look in on you while he's away in case you need anything once the baby comes."

"That isn't necessary," I assured him.

"But he ordered it."

Ordered it. Something about that was chilling. Otto's son, charged with my protection, like those medieval stories where the unborn king is placed in the hands of the one person who benefits from his demise. I shook the fear. If Dmitri trusted Alexei, I would try to as well.

The little king didn't remain unborn much after that. I didn't realize at first that he was coming, but I couldn't sit still. The aching, the pressure—Mama recognized it.

They wheeled me into the Rapid Assistance, a ward which hadn't been updated since the Soviet era. Paint peeled, lights flickered. I thought I would be forced to give birth in a hallway in front of an elderly man with a broken arm and a child with pneumonia. A nurse pushed my knees open and decided I wasn't 'urgent' yet.

"You can wait out here," she said. "We'll come back when the head can be seen."

"This is unacceptable!" Mama screamed. "You put her in her own room!"

"We don't have delivery rooms here," the nurse answered.

"Then give me your phone so I can call Ivan Zdrastkova to give us a ride somewhere that does. This is his grandson."

The nurse registered the name with fear.

"Or, I'll have his people empty this hospital however they see fit, and the whole place will be her private room."

I'd never seen Mama threaten anyone before, but I had my room within minutes. Not only did the lights work there, but it even had a small television.

I stared at this screen as I floated in and out of consciousness, riding the current of whatever they were putting into my IV. I watched, hoping deliriously, that I'd see Dmitri or Sergei in one of their important meetings, gathering these names that were going to save us. All the footage was of some American scandal involving senators who'd purchased military secrets from an admiral, and the young witness being made to testify that it hadn't happened. I remember thinking that if even the American government is corrupt, what chance does Ukraine have?

Petr was born at 23:59 on 2 October 1994.

A life created in sorrow but welcomed in joy.

I prayed to God for the first time in that moment. I'd never believed that this—man? spirit? fiction?—was with me, but who else could bring this perfect, beautiful boy to me and pave a road to happiness with the people I love?

A discharge nurse wheeled me from the hospital, holding my sweet boy toward the sidewalk.

Alexei.

He stood waiting, propped against one of Ivan's big black sedans. I clutched Petr closer. "Did you call him?" I asked Mama.

She shook her head.

"Vladi," he called out, darting to my side and steadying my elbow as I stood from the chair. "Everything is ok, yes?"

"Are you taking us to the mansion?" I asked. Where else would he be taking us if he were meant to keep an eye on me?

"No, Dmitri said to take the mansion to you."

"What?"

"I'm taking you home."

The place where I lived wasn't home. I had never found a home in the world—one where I felt I belonged, where I was whole—except when I looked at that child.

When we arrived at the house, I found it filled with brand-new baby supplies. A crib, toys, diapers, clothes for Petr, clothes for me— everything I could ever want or need.

Everything except Dmitri.

CHAPTER TWENTY-FOUR

He wasn't sure when he'd fallen asleep. He wasn't even sure how many times the light had come and gone. Time, for Mike, had moved from Petr's birth in October 1994 to a cold winter where Delilah marked every day by checking the mail for a letter that never came.

The chill seeped into the apartment as it had into Kiev. Delilah was at least continuing on with her life, going through the motions, caring for another living person. All Mike was doing was lying in bed under covers, occasionally reaching to the empty spot next to him, hoping it was a portal to her.

The slam of another car door snapped him back to consciousness, and he was at the window, pointing the gun before he realized it was daytime and he was waving a pistol at M Street like a complete lunatic.

He recognized the car whose door had slammed.

A BMW.

Kristin's BMW.

"Shit," he muttered, tossing the gun down.

He pulled a hoodie on and started toward the door, pulling it open just before Kristin had a chance to knock.

She startled back at his timing. "Ok, do you have cameras out here or something?"

"I should," he muttered, relieving her of a brown paper bag she had balanced in one arm. "What is this?"

"Breakfast," she said, passing him a large coffee and setting hers onto the countertop so she could take off her coat.

The smell of a bacon, egg, and cheese bagel sandwich permeated through the bag and reminded Mike that the last thing he remembered eating was something Sarah Wallace had shoved in his face to make it look like he was having breakfast with the future president. He tore through the paper, distracted suddenly by the hunger that a moment ago he'd been ignoring completely.

"Why did you bring me breakfast? Are we celebrating the Stockton win?" he asked, his mouth full.

"Ha. No. Rothschild told us we could come in late since everyone stayed up watching the polls last night."

"Wait, was that only last night?"

"Yes?" Kristin shrugged, brushing off the comment. "I had some time on this side of town and figured I'd look in on you. "

"That wasn't necessary. How's Rothschild feeling today?"

"He'd be feeling a lot better if he knew how to beat Stockton."

Two to one, he's the one we face in November.

"You think the DNC gives him the nom and not the VP?"

"Everyone in the Jacoby Administration is poison—thanks to Stockton's illegally obtained military records…"

"A Senate Committee ruled that never happened," Mike reminded her.

"Right. The Great Snow Job of October '94."

…All the footage was of some American scandal involving senators who'd purchased military secrets from an admiral, and the young witness being made to testify that it hadn't happened…

Kristin kicked off her heels as she stood at the countertop, picking at the egg-white wrap she'd brought for herself. "You're still reading this? I would have figured you stayed up all night and plowed through it."

Delilah's book was sitting on the countertop next to a stack of research notes. Mike didn't remember leaving it there, but there were a lot of things he couldn't remember lately. He made a mental note to check his computer and see if he'd written anything in between his conversations with the dead girl.

"The Stocktons got in the way."

"They always do. Are these your notes for the next 'Joe' book?"

She held up his notepad, a scribbled mess of words tied together with arrows and little boxes linked by dotted lines. The last word he could make out in the serial killer scrawl looked like "Petr".

"No, that looks like Delilah's writing."

"I'm sorry?"

"Not her handwriting. Notes from her book. Names, places, known associates…"

"Known associates? You sound like you're investigating her death, not enjoying her novel."

"Enjoying wouldn't be the right word…"

"Mike, just because you have a Crim-Justice degree and pretend to be a detective doesn't mean you are. If professionals investigated this girl's murder and let it go, maybe you should too."

"They didn't know her the way I do."

"Know her?"

"You know what I mean."

"No, I don't. You need to throw this thing away before it does any more damage to your head."

She tossed the paperback into the breakfast sack, then wadded her breakfast up and threw it on top.

Mike lunged to yank the book out before the grease transferred from the trash onto Delilah's only words. "Jesus, Kris..."

"Sorry, I'm not trying to pick a fight with you."

"Felt like it was moving in that direction."

"I yield," she said, throwing up her hands in surrender, and then landing them on his chest. "My motives aren't purely innocent, though. I never found the underwear I left here the other night."

"I thought it was a bra."

"As I recall, you ripped through both," she said, grinning.

"I didn't find anything when I cleaned, but have a look around."

"Wait, you cleaned? And you spent Super Tuesday with the Stocktons? Who are you?" she called from the living room, as she peeked under the couch. "You aren't doing coke, are you?"

She moved down the hall into the bathroom next, checking behind the door where she'd changed into the lingerie.

"No, in fact, I was on a clean streak until you dosed me."

"It was worth it, wasn't it?" Kris called as she moved from the bathroom to the bedroom.

He remembered the pistol at the exact moment she located it.

"What the fuck is this?"

Kristin rounded the corner, the grip in her hand and the muzzle angled at a forty-five-degree angle toward the floor. A flick of the wrist, and it could have been level, though her finger avoided the trigger, resting instead along the notch.

"Jeez, don't point it at me."

"Answer me! Why do you have a Sig nine?"

"I thought it would be a good idea to have one in the city."

"You've lived in the city for years."

"Well, now I think someone might be following me."

"Someone is following you?"

"I don't know. Probably a reporter looking for dirt on Rick or something."

"So you're going to shoot a reporter!?" She continued to hold it—her thumb hovering over the safety.

"No, I'm... I'm just..."

"You're just living in a fiction, spending too much time reading about a girl being chased across Europe with her baby."

With her baby?

Mike wondered if she'd been reading the book when he found her awake in the living room the other morning.

"Take a break, Mike." She checked the safety once more and then set the piece on the kitchen counter. "Go to a museum or something. Clear your head. I worry about you. I don't want you to hurt yourself. Or someone else."

"Yeah. You're probably right."

He picked up the gun and tucked it into his boxers before she decided to take it with her.

"I'm always right," she lifted onto her tiptoes to kiss him. "Still can't find my panties, though."

"Maybe you left them somewhere else."

"You're not funny. I've got to get to the office. Call you later." Kristin closed the door behind her, leaving him with the empty to-go cartons and paper coffee cups to clean up after.

Mike returned to the bedroom, pausing to watch through the window as Kristin got back into her BMW. She was already on her PDA—already deep in whatever business Rothschild needed her into.

...Unless you can flip her into being a mole for the campaign...

"I would, Linds, if I didn't think she'd agree and then turn out to be a double agent."

CHAPTER TWENTY-FIVE

I continued to check the mailbox every day, waiting, thinking I'd been forgotten—abandoned. Their business trip was the longest I'd ever heard of. I passed the time imagining the women Ivan bought for their entertainment along the way and if Dmitri would indulge in their services to avoid his father's suspicion.

The snow came with silence. Holiday lights twinkled in City Center before I heard anything. Then a knock on my bedroom window made Petr scream.

"Alexei, use the front door like a normal person!" I scolded. "The baby was asleep and now..."

He held out his mobile phone. "I have Dmitri."

"What?" I grabbed the device from him as he crawled through the window. "Hello?"

Petr wailed in the background as I tried to put him back down. He was already restless, like his father, and it was impossible to hold him and the phone.

"Is that my...?"

"Son."

"My son!" Dmitri cheered, presumably at Sergei.

"I named him Petr, like we agreed."

"And you're both all right? I've received Alexei's updates, but it's been hard to get a private moment to call you myself."

"We're both fine. Anxious to leave, what's happening with your plans?"

I turned away from Alexei, clawing for one semi-private moment with my baby's father.

"Everything is in place. It's going to happen in Germany. My contact needs a photo of Petr to create his documents. Can you give one to Alexei?"

"I don't have a camera… I'll figure something out."

"Perfect. I can't wait to hold my son. And my wife."

"Your wife?" I would hardly make an attractive wife, covered in formula and spittle, and my own body still not reclaimed from being a vessel.

"That's what the documents will say. We can do it for real later. In a church, if you want."

My fingers laced around the bars of the crib. "You promise it will be soon?"

"Any day, but we need that photo. We need to be extracted while we're in Germany; otherwise, we might get too close to Ukraine to go through with it. MI6 would have to send someone to get you in person."

A spy coming to my door… Ivan would hear about something like that for sure, if not see it through the eyes of all his soldiers who constantly watch me.

"I'll do it right away."

"It's over, Vladi. It's finally over."

It was over, provided I could get a squirming infant to hold still long enough to sit for a photo. I asked a friend from Mrs. Butsiah's class, who usually takes pictures of protests and crime scenes, to photograph Petr. Once he'd developed the picture at the newspaper, I had to find Alexei.

I didn't want to wait until he appeared again, not when everything was riding on that single snap. As much as I didn't want to go to the mansion, I bundled myself and my child into the new coats we'd been sent, and I trudged through the frozen city on Christmas Eve.

The gates were locked this time, though I could see all four chimneys at work. I rattled them and then looked for even one window cracked open upstairs to let the smoky fireplace scent escape. Nothing.

I tried circling to the garage—an old carriage house where Ivan kept his many cars. Everything was sealed up tight,

"Alexei?" I called out when I'd moved back around to the front of the house.

"He isn't here, Ms. Stromkovietz."

Otto Zdrastkova threw open the front door himself to scold me. He wore only one of those thin white tank tops the old men put on underneath their shirts. It must have been so warm inside that this was all he needed.

"Are you in the habit of screaming at people's closed doors?" he asked.

"No, sir."

"What do you need with my son?"

"I'll come back."

"Give it to me."

"Pardon?"

Otto stormed away from the safety of the doorway and reached through the iron bars to take the photo out of my hand. I clutched it as tightly as I could; that was as good as my passport.

"Come on. Give it to me."

"I can come back when Alexei is here."

"Why? Is it a flyer?" The bitterness poured from his lips with acrid disgust as he yanked freedom from my hand.

"No, I'm not a revolutionary. I'm a mother. Of a Zdrastkova child."

His lip curled as he stared at the print. His grandnephew's face looked nothing like a Zdrastkova and everything like the girl they had all grown to hate. He stared at my child with hatred.

"What would my son want with this photo? Is the child his?"

"Alexei offered to send the photo to Dmitri while he's traveling—so he can see his son."

"Right. My brother's first grandchild—that we know of. I'll pass it along."

He disappeared inside with the photo. Otto Zdrastkova held my fate in his hands. Yes, I could ask my friend to print another photo, and he could do that once the holidays had passed, but another week could change the outcome of everything. I should have waited for Alexei to find me.

He found me moments later, walking home in the cold.

"Vladi, wait up... I heard you back there. I'll get the photo from my father, don't worry. Dmitri will have it."

"You're sure?"

Why was Alexei helping us? What had Dmitri promised him? I couldn't ask. If he didn't know of our plans, I'd be revealing too much. If he did, he was risking his life for us by betraying his father, too, and why would a person do that?

"It's fine. Let me walk with you."

"You don't need to."

"Let me carry Petr at least. He is the same age as my little girl, Marinyshka."

"I didn't know you had a daughter. Does she live at the mansion?"

"No. Even with all of its rooms, the line of succession takes priority in the house."

"When do you see her?"

"Whenever I can."

He looked at Petr's face. The baby was born with a strawberry curl, which Alexei pushed away from his little eye. "You are little heir to a powerful family, Cousin. Do you know that your grandpa is big important guy?"

Petr giggled.

He didn't know. He could never know.

I suddenly didn't want him holding my boy. I just wanted him to get that photograph away from his father and into the hands of the British government, whether he knew what he was doing or not.

"Thank you for walking with us. I can take him from here."

I pulled Petr into my arms as Alexei's cell phone rang. I waited, hoping it was Dmitri again, but his eyes grew wide. He muttered 'shit' and then ran off with no explanation.

The following morning—Christmas morning—I woke to find Mama crying in Papa's arms. Crying doesn't quite describe the wails that left her soul as if she herself were dying. I tore a telegram from her grip.

FRANKFURT: WE REGRET TO INFORM YOU OF THE DEATH OF YOUR SON SERGEI ALEXANDRYVICH STROMKOVIETZ. {STOP} 24-12-94 {STOP}

It took everything to conceal my excitement. This was it— the first piece of the plan unfolding. MI6 had arranged it to look as if they'd been killed—exactly as Dmitri had promised. This must have been the phone call Alexei got. He'd be back soon with instructions if he were in on the plan. Or I'd receive Dmitri's postcard. I hoped the distraction of this ruse didn't delay his ability to send the photo on to them in Germany, because as long as they were 'dead' and I was still in Kiev, I was unprotected.

As my parents sobbed, processing the loss of their son, I backed away slowly to my room. I told them I needed to be alone, but what I needed to do was pack secretly. They'd lose their other child soon, too, but I wasn't the one they loved anyway.

I waited a week. New Year's came. The date that set this life in motion. The night that everything had changed. I had hoped to celebrate this anniversary on the Thames—anywhere else—but still hadn't heard from them. Part of me—that part that always nagged, that part that told me when not to turn down a dark street or whispered who not to sit next to on the metro—that part knew something wasn't right, but I convinced her she was wrong. I told her to stop trying to step on the throat of my happiness and finally trust that things were changing.

There was a reason I didn't trust.

4 JAN 1995 - I received a package.

Postmark: Frankfurt

This was it. It wasn't a postcard, fine, they improvised. It had to be the instructions. It had to be the next step. I took it to my room where I could read it privately, learn where I was to go, and finally pull out that envelope of cash that Dmitri had given me last summer for this very moment.

When I tore the end from the package, my silver necklace fell out. Proof that it was from Sergei, I thought. I stared at it in my palm, barely breathing. He made it out. They made it out.

Then I read the words.

Three men had been killed on the autobahn when their vehicle left the road at a high rate of speed. Ivan and Dmitri were killed instantly. Sergei, taken to the hospital, only regaining consciousness enough to ask that someone write to me and say 'this isn't part of the plan'…

The package held what was left of their lives: Dmitri's wallet, Sergei's keys… what was I supposed to do with any of it? What was I supposed to do without them, without the hope of escape? My only choice would be to go to Otto. Zdrastkova is written on my son's birth certificate, but would that be enough to buy his safety? Would Otto take my child and then dispose of me?

I sank to the floor, weeping. I'd have kept sinking—all the way to hell—if the ground hadn't stopped me. It was the only thing keeping me anchored—suspended in grief and terror.

Petr cried from his crib, but I couldn't respond, couldn't hold this fatherless child, couldn't look at him. He was the tie that would bind me to the Zdrastkovas, to Kiev, to this life.

I left him crying there and crawled out the window, the way Dmitri had left me the morning after Petr was conceived, the way Alexei had come and gone to deliver news. I was coatless, already numb anyway, wandering through Kiev like a tethered soul, haunting the places where my life had come undone—the campus, the cafe, the mansion. Finally, I sat down under the transitioning stonework. There was supposed to be an angel there already, but even the goddamn angels had abandoned this place.

"You son of a bitch, Meisha. Some protector you turned out to be."

"I'm sorry," Mike said.

When he looked up, he realized he was sitting in the same open green space where he'd had his last panic attack—staring at the Washington Monument, but seeing the Maidan Nezalezhnosti. His spire. Her spire.

Neither had been particularly watchful.

He removed his coat and put it around her shoulders.

"How do I fix things for you?"

"You don't. You can only fix them for yourself now."

"How do I do that?"

"You get to the ending."

CHAPTER TWENTY-SIX

Mike walked home. He had to—he hadn't taken his car to the park, and actually, he had no memory of how he had gotten there. He dragged Delilah's empty shell—or maybe it was his coat—back into his apartment and took the stairs, one foot in front of the other.

"Oh my God!" she shrieked.

"What? It's a take-out menu. The Chinese place downstairs leaves them all the time." Mike plucked the flyer from the doorknob and unfurled it to show her.

WHEN I'M DEAD, IT WILL BE BECAUSE OF ZDRASTKOVA

"Look again!"

A thick red marker obscured the original claim, and someone had scrawled their own over it:

DON'T LET YOUR CHILD SUFFER THE SINS OF THE FATHER. LEAVE KIEV NOW. - A FRIEND

She frantically twisted the doorknob, trying to get inside away from the flyer—away from Mike. He threw open the door and let her inside.

She rushed straight to the bedroom.

Straight to the pistol.

"I need to leave," she said, wringing her hands.

"Where are you going to go?"

"I don't know. Anywhere the Zdrastkovas aren't. Anywhere Dmitri's cash will take me."

"Now, hold on! Would Otto really kill your son because Dmitri is dead?"

"Yes!"

"Why? He got the empire! He wouldn't even know Dmitri was working with the authorities. It never got that far!"

"You've read *Hamlet*?"

"*Hamlet* is your answer? Jesus Christ…"

Mike paced with her, trying to think like a cop: Cause and effect. Motive and opportunity. He never expected that his voice would suddenly be the one of reason. Then again, he was talking to a dead girl, so reason was relative.

"Someone warned you. You had an ally. Someone wanted to help you get out of Kiev."

"Someone wanted me to think that, so I would let my guard down!"

"Couldn't you tell MI6?"

"I didn't have the evidence they wanted. I was useless! Like I said to Dmitri."

"Did you talk to Alexei?"

"Otto's son!? No! He called Petr the 'little heir'! He had as much reason to kill Petr as any of them!"

She threw open the closet door and pulled Mike's suitcase from it.

"Delilah, let's take a beat. Where are you going?"

"Anywhere."

"Don't Ukrainians need a visa to cross the border?"

"I don't care! I'll figure something out. I just need to leave."

She shoved everything she could into a single bag. She didn't think she would need much. She didn't think she had anything left.

The last thing she picked up was her journal.

"Are you coming?" she asked him.

"Am I coming? You haven't even said where you're going? At this point, you're just a girl being chased across Europe with her baby."

The words echoed in the empty room, vanishing like cabin pressure backing up into his skull. He'd heard that line somewhere recently.

Was it Gestapo Joe?

He spun in all directions looking for her, but she was already gone.

"D?"

Mike checked the living room and the kitchen, then the bathroom, where his hand floated near the medicine cabinet, though there wasn't anything in there for a complete psychotic break. The thing was—he didn't feel like he was breaking.

For the first time, he felt like he was processing his emotions clearly.

Filling the void with another substance, one that would leave him aching and emptier in twelve hours, wasn't the answer for him any more than it had been the answer for Delilah to take her child and disappear on a train with no terminus.

You can only fix them for yourself.

He drew his hand back from the medicine cabinet and backed away from the pills inside.

Get to the ending.

I had to get to the border. I wrapped a blanket around Petr and a scarf around my head, and I left with one bag. My life, reduced to what I could fit into a knapsack.

We left Kiev on the first train — first to Lviv and then on to Krakow. I didn't have documents to enter Poland, but I had eight hours on that train to figure out what to do.

The east-bound train was departing the station at the same time my western train arrived. It was difficult with Petr, but I slipped out of one car, dropped onto the tracks, and climbed back onto the opposing train to exit the platform on the Polish side.

I had made it out of Ukraine.

That should have signaled victory. I should have faded into the sunset.

But that isn't how things work.

From there, it was Germany, followed by France. I kept moving toward the northern shores of the continent—toward England. When I reached Calais, I felt like I could see the Cliffs of Dover, but they wouldn't sell me a ticket without a visa.

Visas had to be obtained from the embassy.

The embassy was in Paris.

More trains. More cities. More of Dmitri's money gone from the envelope.

The embassy there was a din of Ukrainian voices, frustrated ex-Soviets with expired visas and lost passports. The noise crawled into my brain and rattled there, sounding like more enemies, more hunters. I kept my eyes down, looking at my child. He stared in wonder at all the stimulation. The boy watches everything, examining things as if he already recognizes patterns.

"Next?"

The consulate worker entered my passport into a computer and then asked me for my host's invitation.

"You must be hosted locally to obtain a visa to England."

"Hosts?"

"An employer or a family member. If you aren't living with a host, you can only apply as a refugee."

"How long does that take?"

"It takes as long as it takes..."

Would it take longer than the cash in the envelope lasted?

"... but you're missing your entry stamp. Where did you enter? Poland?"

Could I claim an error?

Ignorance?

Would it have been better if my passport had been lost?

Would she deport me?

It wasn't worth finding out. I pulled my passport from her hand before she could wave over the military guard, and I left.

It was no use trying to get to England. Maybe if I knew the name of Dmitri's handler—if I knew anything at all...

But I didn't. I was worth more to Otto dead than to anyone alive.

But Paris in the springtime was beautiful and fresh. I saved money by sleeping in parks around the city. Cheese and bread were inexpensive, and fruit grew on trees in the public gardens. I thought I could stay a *while. I thought I had time to come up with a plan, maybe call Mama. If Ivan left her something in inheritance, she could send it to me. Maybe some of my former classmates—government subversives—would make me a new ID or introduce me to their network abroad.*

I thought I had time to think my way out.

But I saw Yuri.

He was leaving the metro, rising from the underground like a demon who'd escaped hell, the smoke from his cigarette wrapping around his bare skull. Everyone else's face blurred, faded, melted into an impressionist painting—but Yuri...

No, of course you didn't see Yuri, I told myself. Why would he be here? I did as I was told. I left. I had been gone almost two weeks, and no one knew where I was going or how I'd gotten there. No one had even...

...entered my passport.

I grabbed Petr and ran. I ran to the nearest train station and snuck onto the first cargo train in the same way I'd dodged immigration—on to the track and up the steps to a concealed car.

Otto must have sent him to collect my son for payback. I wondered what they'd been ordered to do to me?

We rode the train until it stopped, then rode another train in a different direction. No borders. No tickets. No evidence.

I held Petr all night so I would know that he wasn't taken from me. Infants need a routine, and this one had been forced to stay awake, moving around at odd hours, and only sleeping if he's pressed against me. I hope this is the only damage I have done to him. It can't be, though.

Delilah rolled onto her side and tightly spooned a pillow from Mike's bed, like it was a child she was afraid of losing. She slept like she hadn't slept in weeks as he read next to her.

Switzerland.

Italy.

He rustled a page, and Delilah sat up quickly, startled and confused.

"Where am I?"

"Austria," he answered.

Peace crossed over her face, but the expression soon faded into bittersweet remorse as she lay down again. "I loved Austria."

The candy-colored streets of baroque Europe all started to look the same, like the set of a movie that was too perfect to be real and so must be a facade. I hadn't slept in weeks, not for more than a few minutes at a time. And eating. I wasn't even trying to do that. We'd been out of money for so long, and there was only one way I could think of earning it.

But not with Dmitri's child watching.

My life would be little more than if I were taken by the Zdrastkovas then.

I rested for a moment in a doorway out of the early summer sun. When I jolted awake, Petr was gone.

Panic set in. I cried out for him, clamoring as I looked under cars and on the sidewalk. "PETR! Gde ty?"

"He was crawling into the street." A man held him in one arm, cradling his sleeping body as he looked him over. "Are you all right?"

"We're fine. Give me my baby."

"Only if you tell me where you're going. Where will you get a meal today? How about diapers? This one is... not fresh."

This stranger—could he have been sent by Otto? Sent to offer kindness, lure me in, and then kill us both? My hands started to shake.

"What's your name?" he asked.

I couldn't speak. I just reached for my baby and started to cry. "Please."

"Take a deep breath, I'm a friend."

- A FRIEND

I heard echoes of my fear everywhere.

"I'm Jack. Jack Grennan, M.D. Wow, that was lame. You can call me Jack."

"Jack? American?"

"Yeah, I'm from Washington, D.C., Virginia, really, but most Europeans don't know where that is. Wow, that also sounded lame. Do you understand anything I'm saying?" He pressed his dark glasses back against the bridge of his nose and smiled awkwardly, but genuinely.

"Washington is the capital of the U.S."

"That's right. Ready to tell me your name?"

"Delilah."

He raised an eyebrow. "And you picked that?"

"What do you mean?"

"It's not a Russian name."

"I'm from Ukraine."

"It isn't a Ukrainian name either. The only things named Delilah are cats and Philistines."

"Cats?"

"It's a Queen song... doesn't matter. Why are you sleeping on the streets of Austria, handing out a fake name, Delilah?"

"Austria?"

"You didn't know you were in Austria?"

"I move around a lot."

"With an infant? What is he, six months? Are you still able to breastfeed?"

"Excuse me?"

"Sorry. Doctor, remember?"

"From Virginia."

"Right. Let me get you a meal. If you're not eating right, your milk won't sustain his nutritional needs. He definitely looks undernourished. Maybe anemic."

"Why are you helping us?"

"Why don't you want to be helped?"

There were a thousand reasons not to trust him, but Petr was already asleep in his arms, and he was already moving up the stairs of the candy-box building to the loft he kept there.

"Why would you help a stranger?" I asked, following him.

"I've helped a thousand strangers—helped them get back to the golf course and the Senate chamber. I'd rather help someone who needs it."

"What kind of a doctor are you?"

"A cardiologist."

"I don't know this word."

"I heal people's hearts."

There was no chance he'd heal mine. "Then what do you know of babies?"

"I know they need to eat and have their diapers changed."

He opened the door to his loft—a luxurious space with the finest Western fixtures—everything minimal, expensive... Even Jack's shirt was a fine-thread knit that fit so perfectly I wondered if he'd had it made to order. I worried that Petr would spit up and ruin something.

Jack laughed. "Trust me, I've had worse things on me than baby spit. Doctor, remember?" Petr was already eating from his hand.

And I was, too.

CHAPTER TWENTY-SEVEN

"You're kidding?"

I giggled at Jack's story as we walked back from the Marktplatz toward Jack's flat. We'd been together a month, eating well, sleeping well—living well. I'd never known the ease that came with living as Americans do.

"Nope, I took that exam in nothing but my underwear—in the winter—because I lost the bet."

"It is too cold in Ukraine for this bet."

"It was too cold at Hopkins, too, but I did it. I'm a man of my word."

"And what year was this?"

"Wow! Was that an age joke? It's the salt-n-pepper throwing you off, isn't it?"

"What is this? Salt and…?"

"Aww, jeez. You're killing me, 'Lilah. I'm only thirty-seven. Medicine is stress—"

He trailed off, following my eyes. I'd locked onto the front door.

"No, no, no!"

"What, it's just a take-out menu. The Chinese place downstairs leaves them all the time."

He handed me the page as he unlocked the door.

It was the flyer I'd seen so many times in my nightmares—my words sent to remind me of my crimes.

Red felt marker scrawled across the top had changed the headline to read:

PETR'S DEBT WILL BE PAID IN HIS BLOOD OR YOURS

"Well, what's it say?"

"It's a threat— Dmitri's people. I don't know how they found me, but they're here."

"Shit."

"What, shit?"

"I took your passport to the American embassy to see if I could get you a visa to come home with me."

"What? Why would you do that?"

"You're always talking about how much you want to see the U.S. I can't get you to England, but I can get you both to America."

"Is that what they said at the embassy?"

"They said it would be easier if we were married." Jack hoped his humor would lighten the situation, but I was already trying to decide which of the beautiful clothes he had given us I would leave behind. "They're processing the application, but I had to give them a copy of your passport for the forms."

"This must be how they find me. This syndicate network has loyal soldiers everywhere. Otto is probably using them to track me."

"I'm sorry, I didn't know."

"Can we go to America now?"

"I paid for the expedited application, but it could take a couple of weeks."

"In a couple of weeks, we'll be dead."

I found the filthy knapsack I'd dragged through so many countries already, and filled it with food this time, then I reached for Petr.

Jack stepped back, angling his body away as if he'd shield my own child from me—as if I was the danger.

"I'm not letting you take Petr. You aren't going to drag this baby around while you're hunted like prey. You're safe with me."

"I'm not safe anywhere!"

"I won't let you put this child back on the streets!"

"I need to lose them! As long as I don't use my passport..."

"Don't use your passport. That's the answer."

"What is?"

"All we have to do is keep moving until your visa comes through. We move through Europe's capitals, check in with the consular office each time, and as soon as the U.S. approves your entry, we leave from the nearest airport."

"Anywhere my Soviet passport lets me go, they can follow."

"Not America. Look, this is the best option for Petr. It's the best option for you. It's the best option for everyone."

"Not for you."

"Sure it is. Look..." He placed Petr in a playpen he'd purchased and took my shoulders into his hands to steady the panic attack that was running through my body. "I took a sabbatical from medicine because all the adrenaline in the world couldn't raise my pulse anymore. I held people's lives in my actual hands, and I felt nothing. You make me feel something. Let me do this."

"And we'll live in Virginia?"

"Sure. Or New York. Or New Orleans. My family has a lot of properties..."

"I want to stand in front of that tall monument."

"Deal."

Mike wondered if she ever made it there, knowing that even if she did, it didn't matter. She could have stood, staring at the Washington Monument, at the exact moment he was also mining it for inspiration. They could have bumped into each other, shoulders rubbing on accident, the way people do in crowds— her, trying to get lost; him, trying to be found.

So close.

He fanned the pages, looking for an entry that began in Virginia. If she had made it here, if somehow he'd intersected her living life, maybe it would explain their connection. Maybe it would explain Rick's connection.

LINK TO SEN. RICHARD STOCKTON III: **DISMISSED**

The European cat and mouse game went on for twenty pages —Brussels, Zurich, Rome... they'd arrive, check into a beautiful hotel like tourists, and then as soon as the embassy hit her passport: Yuri. The luxury of world travel masked the terror of the hunted.

In Istanbul, Yuri was waiting in the bazaar with three local Turkish hires. A headscarf helped her disappear.

In Athens, he was spotted with a platinum blonde woman. Delilah pinged on her fair complexion and perfect blonde hair. She wasn't Slavic, not with that coloring. Probably sold to him as a prop, hoping a woman would have better luck getting close to the child.

She appeared again in the flower market in Amsterdam and on the Chain Bridge in Budapest.

Either that or Delilah was losing her grip on reality—seeing ghosts the way he was.

She was good at staying one step ahead, hiding in plain sight, and always staying on alert.

The kid's got street eyes.

Because the key to thinking like a detective wasn't to look for what was suspicious or out of place, it was to assume everything was.

London.

The country that should have been my new home. The country that had rejected us.

"I was able to secure you a work visa through the National Health Service," the man told Jack. He was some kind of ... Jack called it 'fixer'. I don't know what he fixes. "As long as you're consulting for the hospital, your dependents' visa status is granted as well."

His dependents. They couldn't refuse us entry with an important American doctor.

"Thank you. And the consulate has our contact information here?"

By 'here', he meant the multi-room suite overlooking Hyde Park that he'd secured along with his lecture series at St. Mary's Hospital.

"Yes, and the furniture for the baby will be delivered within the hour. Will you require anything else for your stay?"

"Nothing comes to mind," Jack said.

"Actually...?" I said. I hadn't discussed it with Jack, but suddenly, there, realizing how easy it had been to get into the country with him...

"Yes, ma'am?"

"What if...what if we wanted to get married while we were here?"

"What?" Jack was as startled as the fixer was.

"It takes seven days to set up an 'address' of residence for the paperwork and then twenty-eight days from the notification to the registrar's office."

"Five weeks?"

Jack knew what I was thinking. We hadn't stayed anywhere for five weeks, but Yuri would have the same problem getting into England on his passport that I'd had.

Unless Otto had someone in MI6.

"Would you like me to fetch the paperwork required to start that process? We could have the ceremony in the garden. Next month, it will be beautiful, too, right before the fall chill arrives."

"Yes, please get us the paperwork," Jack said.

When the fixer had gone, Jack crossed the room and brushed the hair from my face. "Are you sure?"

"I want to change my name. The judge who marries us can make me Delilah Grennan. You can adopt Petr and change it to Peter Grennan, with the American spelling. We'll go to America as a family."

"When I suggested that before…"

"When you suggested that before, I thought you were kidding."

"You thought I was some old guy trying to get into your pants."

"You are still this old guy…"

He stopped me with a kiss—a simple kiss, not one filled with danger or controversy, just affection.

England was where I would get a new name after all.

Petr wanted to be a Grennan, too, I think. Since that first feeding in Austria, he preferred Jack. He'd only settle down in Jack's arms or take the food he offered. He can either sense the goodness in Jack's heart, or the Zdrastkovas' hate for me is genetic. Worth it to know that my son will never have to kill anyone in the street or wear the star tattoo of a made man. And for that, everything has been worth it.

The morning of the wedding, he was fussy, twisting in his crib and whining. I brought him back to the bed and placed him between us, where he could feel us both on either side, protecting him from the world. As soon as Jack's hand steadied him, he drifted off.

Jack caressed Petr's tiny, peach-soft cheeks. "He looks like you here."

"His cheeks?"

"And his eyes."

"Ok, maybe the eyes."

"And his giggle."

"When I look at him, I only see Dmitri."

"Is that hard for you?"

"It shouldn't be. I wasn't even certain I wanted to be with him. I loved him. Petr was a mista—not planned."

"A happy accident, as Bob Ross would say."

"Who is this? Bob Ross?"

"It doesn't matter. Are you certain about me?"

"I've spent more time with you than I ever spent with him. He never even met Petr... You're the only father he's ever had. Of course, I want to be with you."

"Good, because it's too late to back out."

He smirked and rolled over, falling back to sleep, as men find it easy to do. I stared at the ceiling, hoping I was making the right choice.

"How did you know that he was the right choice?" Mike rolled over to face her there, thinking about the ring in his overcoat. "How did you know that you weren't attaching yourself to someone so you could stop worrying about being alone?"

217

"Jack knew exactly who I was, and he still loved me. Without him, my only hope would have been asylum or witness protection—lying to everyone I met for the rest of my life. A made-up identity, a fake past... I couldn't live like that—pretending to be someone else."

"I've always lived like that."

"No, you haven't. Not really. You have Jennifer, Tom, Rick... Besides, you prefer to be alone."

She swept her arm around the room, with its lack of sentimental trinkets or a woman's touch.

"I prefer to know someone is there when I want them to be."

"That isn't how relationships work. You don't get to come and go from them."

"I never go. I've never walked away from someone because I know what it feels like to be left."

"There's a difference between giving a child the chance at a better life and getting out of a bad relationship. I believe your mother loved you. I don't believe your girlfriend does."

"How did this get to be about me?"

"I don't know. It's your head. I was walking around Hyde Park."

Winding through the park's paths helped to unwind my thoughts. The cool air reminded me of home—those beautiful fall mornings in University Park, after the humidity left and before the snow came. Sergei and I played there as children, rolling in grass, jumping in leaves... Maybe I could give Petr a sister to share this kind of joy with—the joy that comes from experiencing childhood with one person who always understands where you come from.

Even if they don't share your blood.

The thought of Sergei brought tears to my eyes.

"Are you all right, dear?" A jogger stopped when she saw me crying. "Are you lost? Do you need help getting to the embassy?"

I don't know why she assumed I was foreign. I guess I don't look British.

"No. Thank you. I'm fine."

"You're sure, love?" She had a kind face—beautiful—the kind of perfect green eyes and high cheekbones that Hollywood movie stars have. *I would love to look like this woman.* "If you're in trouble, I could take you..."

"I'm not in trouble. I'm getting married today."

"Some would call that trouble."

I forced a polite laugh. "No, really. I'm fine."

"You're sure? Second thoughts?"

"About Jack, no. About myself, always."

"You'll be fine. I promise."

Her eyes darted, caught a distraction, and then snapped back to mine. "Congratulations, darling. I recommend Budapest as a honeymoon location. You should go there."

She squeezed my arm and turned toward her distraction to jog away, her ponytail bouncing behind her.

Her platinum blonde ponytail.

CHAPTER TWENTY-EIGHT

My eyes scanned the garden, almost missing the cue I'd been given to say 'I do'. Since I'd left Hyde Park, wondering if that blonde woman had been the same one I'd seen in all the other cities across the continent, all I could think of was leaving London. Immediately after the ceremony, I told Jack.

"She offered to take me to the embassy!"

"That's weird, but not what a kidnapper would say. And that woman with Yuri has never spoken to you before. Why would she do that suddenly? Why would she get close to you and tell you to go to Budapest but not... hurt you?"

"I don't know! Why do they leave notes? Why not wait inside a hotel room and kill us when we come home? It's a game to them!"

We spent our wedding night back in Vienna, at the Palais Coburg—one of the most beautiful buildings I'd ever seen—but I couldn't appreciate it. We were back on the run.

Jack needed to sign paperwork with his Austrian attorney to close the sale of his flat and add me to his estate, and the American embassy there was one of the more efficient. With our marriage documents and Jack's adoption petition, they had everything they needed. They just had to issue our new identities. Three to five business days, they said.

Yuri found us in two.

A flyer. Folded inside the napkin of a room service tray.

"We have to go to the authorities! You're my wife now, with the rights of a U.S. Citizen. We can contact the FBI."

"No! No governments."

"Look, our government has problems, sure, but it's not the corrupt mess that the Soviet Union was!"

"Every time my name is documented, they find me! This means they have people monitoring us from inside the government—your government, every government, maybe! I don't know!"

"But if you keep running, we'll never get home. You have to go to the Americans for help."

"We can go to Munich or Praha without showing a passport. Let's hide there and come back in a week when all of these papers are ready. Then we leave."

"Will you talk to the authorities when we get to D.C.? I'm sure the CIA would love to hear about this crime syndicate."

"Once we are on American soil, I will talk to anyone you want me to."

He pinched the corners of his eyes. Doctors are accustomed to not sleeping, he told me, but I think even Jack was exhausted after almost a year of running.

We reached Prague that night, planning to stay in our suite and order in, leaving no record with the rail or the hotel that I was there. Three days of fine wine, "movies on demand," and my two boys. Heaven.

Jack left once to visit the consular office and learned that our documents were ready—waiting for us in Vienna. We gathered everything in the morning and started for the train station across the street.

Jack carried Petr as he always did. His little eyes darted around, drinking in the world, or perhaps watching for the danger that he'd been programmed to spot.

They stepped free of the revolving door ahead of me.

A tourist, wrestling a stubborn bag into the merry-go-round, stalled the motion. When it finally resumed, it sent me stumbling into the open.

Crack.

I thought it was a car's exhaust, maybe a storefront door snapping closed.

I didn't think it was an assassin's bullet.

Jack slumped to the ground, dropping Petr, and all I did was stand paralyzed—waiting for the second shot. A professional hit. A sniper aiming from a rooftop in the Old Town. I knew I was next.

Someone screamed and snapped my stasis.

I think it might have been Petr, or a woman on the sidewalk who'd been hit with Jack's blood when his head shattered against the pavement. I sank beside him.

The entry wound in his forehead had killed him instantly.

He was the lucky one.

Chaos erupted. Police from the train station, bystanders—everyone screamed, diving for cover into the lobby of the hotel. I felt someone lift me from the ground.

An angel?

Meisha?

"Where's the baby?" he asked.

The crowd swarmed around us.

"Where's the baby, Delilah?"

"Where is Petr?" Mike spun in a circle, trying to visualize the unraveling scene: a sidewalk cafe on a cool fall morning, sipping those tiny European espressos outside a train station, when a bullet rips through the air and kills an American.

Was the murder a distraction to grab Petr? Had one of Dmitri's men been standing there waiting for Jack to exit, given a signal, and then grabbed the boy while everyone was in shock?

He ran from the cafe, shoving dumbfounded tourists and gawking onlookers out of his way. "Move it! Police coming through!"

Then he saw her closing in from the other direction, her platinum blonde mane bouncing in time with her footfalls as she broke into a run, aiming for the child still sitting there in the ever-growing pool of blood around him.

Margarita?

No.

Wrong Blonde.

Wrong story.

He locked eyes with the green-eyed beauty as both ran toward the child writhing on the ground. Before either could reach him, Petr was carried away by a man.

"Hey, get away from him!" Mike yelled.

Someone yelled, 'Get away from him,' and my attention snapped from Jack's corpse to my son's little body disappearing.

HIS BLOOD OR YOURS.

They would need to take both.

"You'll have to take us both!"

"We will, madame," the medic said, placing Petr into the ambulance. Two had pulled around; one to move Jack and the other to take us to emergency.

I don't know why they brought an ambulance for Jack. He was dead. Hope was dead. We were all dead.

"Miss... miss, do you understand English?"

"Yes?"

I think it was a doctor speaking.

"Miss you and your baby are both fine."

"Fine?"

"No outward injuries. The authorities are coming. Is there anyone else you'd like us to call?"

No, don't call anyone! Don't tell them where I am!

I thought it, but the words didn't come out.

A nurse yelled for assistance. A critical patient, one who they still might be able to save, was rushed by on a gurney.

All I saw was her blonde hair.

Two men in suits came next.

"After we get you to the safe house, we'll send someone to get your things."

"What things?"

"Your suitcases. The baby's supplies."

"Why? Who are you?"

"We saw your application with the American embassy. This should grant you immediate asylum."

Shouldn't it, though?

He handed me an envelope and kept talking. Documents, inheritances, legal things. Did I need a lawyer? Did I want help with travel arrangements?

"No." I wanted all of these things for the last year, before it cost a man his life.

They deposited us into a home in the suburbs outside Prague, some place unmarked and quiet. Two agents were to stay back with us and make sure there were no further attempts on our lives.

Unless they were the ones sent to take it.

"You'll be safe here," one said.

"I'm not safe anywhere."

I sat on the floor next to Petr, underneath the window, so there was no line of sight into the room. He bobbed back and forth, making a low humming sound like bad electricity. He wouldn't take food, wouldn't sleep, wouldn't even let me hold him. His small eyes had seen too much before his first birthday; he'd be ruined forever, and he blamed me.

I left in the middle of the night, out through that window while it was safe to move. Trains are easy to sneak onto, even when you can afford to buy tickets. I sat in the rear-most car, my back against the wall, where I could see every passenger that came and went. It didn't matter where the train was going. They'd find me eventually.

But they'd never find Petr.

When the light had come and gone again, the train stopped, and I slipped through the rear door onto the track. I saw the black spires of the church and knew what I had to do.

Perhaps he was always meant to be orphaned. This was simply a stolen year I was never supposed to have with him. At least this way, he has a chance, and when he grows up, he won't ever need to know that *his blood is poison. Any life he has will be better than what I could give him.*

I placed him on the altar under the golden cross with a note begging for someone's mercy, and then I left him to God's will.

CHAPTER TWENTY-NINE

"You'll need to surrender your Soviet passport."

I tossed that evil booklet, responsible for tracking me for months, at the consular officer. "Gladly."

"And we've got one here for Petr Zdrastkova too."

"Keep it. He's dead."

I wanted to start my new life in Washington, D.C., but the first direct flight was going to New York. I would have flown to the dark side of the moon to leave immediately.

Good riddance, Europe. Never again.

I'd dreamt of New York—of America—the lights, the shopping, the music. But none of it matters now. These are things you share with the people you love, and all of them are gone.

I left on a train to D.C. Another train. The endless hum. It won't stop, even if I can. That hum is the same sound Petr made the night we huddled in the safe house.

In Washington, I signed papers with Jack's lawyer that gave me everything he had. It was a complicated language I didn't understand, but it doesn't matter.

Nothing matters.

I had hoped to stay there. I wanted to believe that their democracy—the very thing that we fought to bring to Ukraine, the same principles that got Ludmilla killed—was where I belonged. But Jack's penthouse was empty and silent— a tomb. And I don't know how to stay still anymore.

Something drew me to Jack's second home. He'd described the smells and the damp warmth of this New Orleans—a maze of scrolled iron work and music floating on the air that he said felt like France if France had been wrapped in a wet towel.

The City of the Dead.

That was where I belonged.

His Louisiana flat draped across the second floor of a two-hundred-year-old building, the ground floor supported by some kind of trinket shop that sells trinkets to tourists.

The paperwork Jack's lawyers gave me listed the shopkeeper as the caretaker of this apartment and said she'd have a key, so I entered this strange shop. Tiny vials of animal bones, strange powders, and dolls with pins sticking from them crowded the walls. Something about the objects felt forbidden. I couldn't believe they were being sold there off one of the main streets.

A tiny bell on the door announced my arrival.

"You're Jack's wife?" the shopkeeper called from the back room. She must have had a camera pointed at the door. I tried to spot it among the masks and the beads hanging along the crown molding.

"Yes..." I answered, unable to find a camera. "How did you know that?"

"He told me."

An intoxicating cloud of bourbon, tobacco, and vanilla rounded the corner ahead of her as she appeared from behind the wall.

"When did he do that?"

"Just now."

She smiled at the space beyond my right shoulder as if something hovered behind me. This is a gimmick for tourists, I'm certain, along with the dolls and the colored potions.

"I'm Veronique." *She was draped in a bright, colorful fabric that popped against her cocoa skin, her hair twisted around a scarf of the same material. I'd never seen anyone who looked like her. I had never heard her accent either — a mix of French and African.*

"Delilah. His lawyers told me you keep a spare key to the apartment?"

"I do. I'll find it for you, child." *She moved like she was parting invisible water, a stack of bangles jingling around her wrist, as she rummaged through a drawer of oddities searching for the key.* "Are you moving in or just visiting?" *she asked.*

"I haven't decided. Why?"

"You brought a lot of loa with you."

"I don't know this word."

"Loa? They're the spirits of the dead. Noisy ones, too. They'll be getting louder here, fo'sure." *She motioned to the air around her, maybe to the room itself, or even the city.*

"The dead aren't the ones who bother me."

"That's because you're half in their plane. Your people aren't bound to the physical world. You're part French?"

I laughed. "No."

"Yeah, you are, girl. On your mother's side."

Voodoo Veronique was full of bullshit, trying to trick me into buying something — a protection spell or a doll to make these spirits go away. I think they call this a 'con-artist.'

"Have you found the key yet?"

"Here you go, honey." She stared into my eyes as she placed the key into my hand—lingering there—before a frown crossed her face. "Let me know if you need help."

I climbed the stairs and let myself into Jack's place. The furniture was covered in heavy cloth, as if the room were haunted by the ghosts of children. I got the nagging sense that someone had already been murdered here.

It's been two days. I spend my time sitting on the balcony, escaping the oppressive heat inside the walls, watching the street, the front door to Veronique's shop. From here, I can see who is coming for me. I could sit here writing a masterpiece if I could think of anything but myself.

Something in the air here feels like electricity—like the dead are kissing me with cold air. It would be a relief from the heat if I didn't know what they wanted. They have Dmitri. They have Jack.

They probably have Petr.

Now they want me.

When your time is marked by how long it's been since you've seen the people you love, it's time to join them. I won't run again. I won't leave this City of the Dead. I will join them here. The loa can have me. Yuri can have me. Maybe when I die, I'll find those I'm meant to be with.

PUBLISHER'S NOTE: A worn, leather-bound journal arrived to the publisher on November 2nd, 1995, attached to a scribbled note that simply read, "Someone should know – D"

The New Orleans Police Department found a woman murdered in the home belonging to Dr. Johnathan Grennan, the same day. Details surrounding her death remain sealed.

Rest in peace, Delilah. Finally,

Mike turned the page, aching for something more, though he knew there were no pages left, no more answers to be found. The story was over. She was gone, though her death had not been as simple as the surrender that she'd written. She hadn't simply met it, not according to the morgue photos. Yuri—or whomever—hadn't let her meet it with that grace.

The emptiness he usually felt at the end of a story closed in, bringing with it the walls. Completion felt like loss. Loss felt like mourning—mourning a person he'd never met, the end of their time together, and his own glimmer of hope that somehow he'd found something to fill the Void longer.

Every time he let someone else's voice take over his head, he stayed under a little longer. Resurfacing got harder, and it took more to satiate the need—the same way it was with alcohol and pills. Delilah was merely his latest addiction, and now he needed to brace for the crash.

"I still don't know how to fix it," he whispered to the medicine cabinet, but he didn't draw his hand back to open it. The answers weren't in there anymore.

Mike pulled on his overcoat and turned up the collar. He didn't know where he wanted to go, but he knew he couldn't be alone. The isolation she felt before her death lingered with him and suffocated the apartment. He needed human contact. Living human contact.

He pulled the Lexus from the garage out into the spring rain and pointed toward the Washington Monument, jutting into the skyline.

No, it's too much like Independence Square.

He corrected, steering into a lane that would take him onto 66 and out into the suburbs around Alexandria.

To Jack's house.

No.

Tom's.

Mike reached across the front seat to the glove box and found the bulky cellular device he kept there for emergencies. This felt like an emergency.

"Good, you're up. Got anything left in those bottles I hooked you up with this week, or did you swallow them down like a girl at a frat party?"

"Hello to you, too, buddy." Tom had been rattling around the estate, waiting for his parents to leave again.

"Do you have anything or not?"

"No. Sarah took it all. Like, confiscated, not consumed. Could you imagine Sarah getting high? That would be pretty fun, actually."

"What's the point of a best friend if you can't count on them when the world is threatening to crush you?"

"Holy shit, you sound like me. What's wrong?"

Mike merged onto the bridge, his headlights bouncing off the falling rain as a tailgaiter's headlights reflected off of him.

"The motherfucks on 66 for one thing. I swear, every time I've driven somewhere this week, some prick has been up my ass."

"Score some weed so you can chill the fuck out."

"I don't need weed. I'm already paranoid. I need Xanax or Ambien."

"I think Annabelle has a bottle of Valium somewhere. I'll see if I can get to it when she goes to sleep."

"Your mom has Valium, and you haven't stolen it already?"

"What do I want her Valium for? I'm already depressed. I'm in my opiate era."

"Maybe we could just… hang out."

"Sober?"

"Yeah. Is there a game on or something?"

"A game? At midnight?"

Mike pressed down further on the gas, accelerating toward the end of the bridge and trying to put a space cushion between him and every other car.

"Tom, I need to not be alone right now, ok?"

How many times had Tom asked the same of him in the past eighteen years? Countless. Rarely had Mike been the one asking for support.

It took Tom a second to snap into the reversed role. "Yeah, brother. I got you. How far out are you?… Hello? Mikey? You there?… Your carphone's a piece of shit."

"Tom?" Mike held the phone away from his ear and checked the screen to see if the call had dropped. "Hello?"

The Lexus lurched sideways, hydroplaning across the asphalt. Mike's eyes shot back onto the road, but he was already spinning.

"Ne pereuserdstvuyte!"

What?

"Don't overcorrect," Dmitri instructed, but it was too late. Sergei couldn't regain control of the car once its bumper had been tapped at speed.

233

A second thump ensured their car spun off the road.

Metal tore against the guard rail. The Lexus caught air.

The hood took the full impact, setting off the airbag, as Mike's seatbelt ripped from the floor, tossing him across the cabin. His head smacked the gear shift, cracking his right temple open. The wound filled with heat as he sat blinking, trying to figure out if he'd stopped rolling.

And why Dmitri was lying dead in the passenger seat with a bullet in his forehead.

The horn blared, the rain pounded through the broken sunroof, and Russian voices filled the air as they swarmed on the car. He was in sensory overload, his brain fighting to distinguish time and place, hot and cold—life and death.

Mike put his face against the airbag and closed his eyes.

Sound faded.

Then he heard Ivan's voice from the backseat.

"Predatel."

Traitor.

CHAPTER THIRTY

Everyone in the emergency room moved in synchronous harmony, a sea of blue and green-toned scrubs, their faces covered by masks. Whatever they said to each other was unintelligible noise. They lacked the sense of urgency one would expect from an ER staff, but they'd done this a thousand times, and this time shouldn't be any different.

Within minutes, there was a wail—exactly the kind you expect from a newborn when its mouth is cleared of amniotic fluid and it takes its first breath of air.

"Good job," the doctor said, although who he said it to was unclear. He cut the boy's umbilical cord and then passed him off to a nurse, who wiped him clean.

The young mother started to relax, gasping for breath after the pain of labor.

"The nurses will take care of you from here, honey."

Before he made it out of the room, the girl let out a scream. Blood spilled from her onto the floor, and the nurses couldn't contain it. Something was wrong. Something inside had ruptured.

The doctor gloved up a second time and inserted two fingers, trying to locate the source of the bleed.

Another baby.

"She's got another one coming," he said calmly. The nurses left the infant boy and returned to deliver the second child, the one whose placenta had torn its mother's uterine wall and was drowning in her blood.

The doctor pressed down on her abdomen, squeezing the baby out from above.

A girl.

"Get Mom into the OR!" the doctor instructed.

The labor and delivery nurses split focus, dividing themselves among the two babies, while their mother was rushed into surgery.

She never met her children.

She never even woke up.

"Let's hit him again."

"Charging," the nurse said.

"Clear!" the doctor instructed, laying paddles across Mike's chest.

"That's asystole. Switching to compression."

"When did he first code?"

"Three minutes."

"Charge again," the doctor said.

"For asystole?"

"His brain is alive. He still has pupillary reflex. I'm willing to try it for a twenty-three-year-old."

"Charging for asystole," the nurse agreed.

The paddles grabbed Mike's chest and shot electricity through his body, attempting to restart his heart.

Mike watched from the corner of the GW Emergency Room. Two different hospitals. Two different memories. But Delilah was with him in both.

"I die and I'm stuck watching? What kind of a sick afterlife is this?" he asked her.

"That wasn't the end of your life. It was the beginning. For both of us."

BROTHER (1): [REDACTED]

Delilah took his hand. The cold electricity she'd described feeling in New Orleans passed through his body, crawling from her fingertips into his arm.

"How is that even possible? How does an American baby end up in the Soviet Union in the middle of the Cold War?"

"Papa left Kiev when he found out Sergei wasn't his—got a visa to work in Los Angeles building aircraft parts like he'd done in the war."

"They didn't think he was a spy?"

"Maybe. Perhaps that's why he adopted a child, so they'd believe he was a family man. Or maybe he was trying to rub it in Mama's face or lure her to America, too. When they canceled his visa, he took me home with him."

"You were a souvenir from L.A.? Like a snow globe?"

She elbowed him in fake protest—the way a sister would.

"A reminder. Of the life he wanted."

"Charge to three hundred. Come on, buddy. Five minutes in asystole, and I gotta call it."

"CLEAR!"

The paddles blasted three hundred joules of electrical current through his body a second time.

The lights flickered. Or his sight did.

"You've got to go back," Delilah said, letting go of his hand. "We still need you."

"Who's we?"

"So many people still need you, Meisha."

"To do what?"

"Go back to the beginning."

"Make it to the ending, then go back to the beginning. Could you make up your mind?"

"Another milligram of Epi. Keep compressions going."

"Prepping." The nurse drew back on a syringe and inserted it into the IV line. "On board."

After a moment, Mike sucked in as much ragged breath as he could with a collapsed lung and blinked, fighting the glaring overhead lights.

"Sinus rhythm," the nurse announced.

"Ok, that was step one. Before we push anything else, draw blood for tox. Let's address the pneumothorax now. Needle thoracostomy," he said, inserting the large-bore needle through the intercostal space into Mike's lung. His chest hissed and then expanded again.

"Better?" the doc asked.

"So much," Mike whispered.

"Let's do a complete set of X-rays, a head CT, and a full blood panel. Do you want something to sedate you for the CAT scan?"

"Ketamine?" he answered, a touch too quickly.

The doctor moved straight past it. "Ativan. One milligram."

"What's one milligram supposed to do?"

"Keep you calm, not get you high." He scribbled something onto Mike's chart and handed it back to the ER nurse. "One milligram of Ativan. No narcotics. I'll be back when I have the labs."

The nurse nodded and prepared the syringe, snapping the air bubble out with a flick of her fingernail. As she carefully drew back on the plunger, Mike reached out and touched her arm gently.

"Can you make it three? I have a tolerance."

His trademark smile slid across his face, the charming handsomeness amplified somehow by the two black eyes and the blood smeared across his face.

"Three is a lot," she said.

Mike bit his bottom lip with manufactured innocence.

"I'll give you one and a half," she said, succumbing, drawing her plunger back a touch further than one milligram before pushing the drugs into his system. "And then I'll have an excuse to come back and see if you need anything else."

"You're an angel."

An angel?

Next to a gold cross?

He hadn't been trying to get high, or even dull the stress of what had happened—he was trying to find his way back to Delilah. He wanted to sit quietly in the dark, with the chatter of the outside world dulled enough to hear her again through it. He kept trying to remember her face, the way he'd seen it in his—

dream? Coma? Afterlife? Could any of that have been true?

No. Twins separated at birth is just a bad plot device.

Still.

As the CT scan pulsed deafening magnetic tones into his brain, he tried to remember everything she'd said—or what he'd dreamt she said—but it was all lost, drowned in the vibrations of the machine.

CHAPTER THIRTY-ONE

After scanning, photographing, and charting Mike's injuries, orderlies wheeled him toward a private room—past the elevator, down a hallway, and through a checkpoint guarded by men in suits.

The Secret Service?

"Holy shit," Tom said when he saw how close his best friend had come to death. He reached out for a fist bump until he realized the IV line was taped to the top of Mike's hand. They low-fived instead."Hope they're giving you the good stuff."

"You gave us a real scare, kid," Rick Stockton said, giving the stubble on Mike's cheeks a gentle pat.

"What are you guys doing here?"

"The hospital hit the redial on your phone. Imagine my fucking surprise when I answered and got the emergency room."

"Imagine theirs when they dialed and got the Stockton residence. Are my parents here?"

Parents?

He saw the dying girl again, screaming as her womb tore open.

"They're downstairs, but the floor is sealed on Decker's orders," Rick said.

"Why's Lindsey involved in this?"

"Possession of an illegal firearm," the senator said, threading the needle between disappointed father and irritated public figure.

"Fuck," Mike said, rolling his head back onto the pillow where it could take the weight of the incredible pain in his cracked skull. "I'm sorry, Rick. You don't need this right now."

"Well, like I said. Decker is on it."

"I'm here," Lindsey said, blasting through the door, her coat flaring out behind her like she was riding a broomstick. She reeled around and threw a hand up against the chest of the State Trooper attempting to come through the door with her. "I need five minutes with my client before you question him. Or, this agent can shoot you for attempting to take a run at the candidate."

"How do you have time to run a campaign and be this kid's lawyer?" The crusty old trooper glared at her display of power, as if they had a history of run-ins over illegal activity in the area.

"Agent..."

"I'm going," the trooper said, backing out.

"Tom, you too."

"Linds..."

"Out!"

Lindsey stood at the foot of the bed, flipping through a black folder as she waited for Tom to excuse himself from the hospital room.

"Mike."

"Lindsey. What play are we running now?"

"I don't have a Play Code for Tom's idiot best friend rolling his car off the Key Bridge with a ghost gun in his pocket."

"Guess you will now." He landed his smile in her direction, knowing it didn't usually work. The bloodied face helped in this case, however.

"Christ." She rolled her eyes, softening for just a beat, then she composed herself again. "Ok, your tox screen came back clean—somehow—so we can move past a DUI. The part of the embankment you rolled down has no municipal facilities, so they can't get you for property damage. It comes down to possession. Let's talk about the gun."

"Why did you have a gun, Mike?" Rick asked.

Leather Jackets.

Thugs.

Russians chasing me.

"Sometimes, I think I'm being followed."

"Followed? Then you call me! That's why I bought you the cell phone!" Lindsey yelled. "First of all, they might be mine, and second, if they aren't, I always have someone close enough to deal with things like that! For all intents and purposes, you're a Stockton. You need anything—ANYTHING! —and it goes through LDA!"

"Yeah... I... I'm sorry."

"Where did it come from?" Rick asked. With Mike's condition stabilized, Rick had moved on to thinking about damage control and fallout.

"From Tom."

"Fuck me," Rick said, throwing his hands up, exasperated. "And where did Tom get the gun? One of mine?"

"I think I know," Lindsey said. She closed the file, pleased. "Ballistics will come back clean, so they won't have a crime to tie to you. The weapon won't be registered, which is sketchy, but I'll figure that out—something about national security. Possessing a weapon without a permit is a crime in the District but not in the great State of Virginia…"

"And where was I?"

"Tox screen negative, huh? Let that State Trooper in, please," she instructed the agent in the room.

The cop returned, smacking gum like he was chewing a cow's cud. He hated Decker. He hated all these people with their wealth and privilege, and their belief that they could buy the law.

"Officer, to be clear, you may ask my client about the circumstances surrounding the motor vehicle accident only."

"What else would I want to ask him about? Mr. Michael Green?"

"Yes."

"Can you tell me what happened?"

"A car accident?"

"Well, you're a smart ass, ain'tcha. Some details, perhaps?"

Ne pereuserdstvuyte.

A bumper tap sent the car into a flat spin.

A second thump sent it flying off the road.

Dmitri—dead in the passenger seat with a bullet in his forehead.

"Mr. Green?"

"Someone tapped my bumper. I overcorrected. Then I think they hit me a second time, and I spun out."

"There was no report of a second car."

"Then it was hit and run. Check my bumper."

"You don't have a bumper. You have a pancake that the Jaws of Life barely got through."

"Then, ask Tom. I was on the phone complaining to him about the guy who was tailgating me. He probably heard the whole thing happen."

"Tom? Stockton? Is that where you were going at that hour, carrying a gun? To visit a presidential candidate?"

"That falls outside the scope of your questioning," Lindsey interrupted.

"And I don't suppose you'll let me question the young Mr. Stockton, will you?"

"No. I suggest you pull footage from the cameras monitoring the Key Bridge and direct all further questions to my office. We're done here."

The trooper scowled, probably deciding then and there to vote for Rothschild out of pure spite. "He can't leave until the ballistics come back on that gun."

"He'll leave when he's medically cleared," Lindsey said, pushing the door closed behind him. "Rick," she said, turning back to the senator, "can you give us a minute?"

She passed her boss a look that was equal parts respect and command, one of the few who dared do that. He acknowledged her silently.

"I'm sorry about all this, Rick."

"Nonsense, kiddo. Belle and I are just glad you're ok."

Stockton leaned forward as though he were going to offer Mike an embrace, then stopped. He couldn't figure out how to negotiate the wrap holding Mike's broken ribs together or the lines running in and out of the boy. And Rick Stockton wasn't good with tender words, only filthy jokes said in their place.

"There once was a girl named Brits, with a gorgeous pair of round…"

"Oh, for Christ's sake, get out." Lindsey angled him toward the door as she shook her head in irritation. When she had the room to herself, she sat next to Mike on the edge of the hospital bed. "What the actual fuck?"

"What the fuck, what?"

"First, you get a gun because you think someone is following you, and then you're run off the road? Are you in bad with a dealer?"

"No. Nothing like that."

"Then what am I dealing with here? And don't fucking lie to me."

Mike hesitated. What was he supposed to tell her? He started seeing dead Russians, and maybe now also live ones? That he thought some mafia thug named Yuri was after him because he read a book? That there was a chance he was related to a murdered revolutionary journalist, but the only evidence he had was the fragmented memory of a near-death experience?

Every single sentence he formed was more ridiculous than the one before.

"I stumbled on a file that I maybe shouldn't have seen."

"Where? Rick's office?"

*LINK TO SEN. RICHARD STOCKTON III: **DISMISSED***

"No, in the National Archives."

"What the fuck were you... never mind. What kind of a file?"

***OPERATION CODE:** ["ORANGEBLOSSOM" // D-10-F]*

"Intelligence, maybe. A murdered asset in New Orleans."

"Murdered by who?"

"A European crime syndicate."

Lindsey stood and paced to the far wall, not out of nerves but because it helped her think. "Who knows that you've seen this file?"

"Just Kristin."

She stifled a growl aimed with hatred toward Mike's girlfriend.

"An MI6 memo had a note about dismissing a link to Rick."

"What?" She reeled around. "What link?"

"I don't know. The whole thing was redacted."

"And you've had this for how long?"

"Since last Friday. I didn't mention it to him..."

"You're goddamn right you didn't mention it to him. And you won't! This is my problem now."

"Do you want me to go get the file for you?"

"No! I don't want you to steal a file from the National Archives! Go home to recuperate, and stay inside for a week while I figure this out."

"A week?"

"Yeah. Finish your book or something."

Shit. That.

Mike couldn't even remember where he'd left off, or what he'd been writing about. He'd lost the thread and would need to start over.

Go back to the beginning.

"I'm going to go press that ballistics lab to clear that weapon. Did you want me to let your mom in, or keep this floor locked down so she leaves you alone?" Lindsey winked. Sometimes Mike could appreciate her wicked sense of humor.

"Let her in. Thanks, Linds."

"You don't have to thank me, I bill for it. I built a whole career around you idiots, remember?"

"I remember."

"Anything else pops into your stupid head, you call me. I don't care what it is. We're too close to the finish line to derail over something like a car accident or a dumb file."

"I know."

"You'd better." She booped the tip of his nose with her acrylic nail and left to put the fear of God into some helpless ballistics tech.

CHAPTER THIRTY-TWO

Everything about Mike's head hurt—the weight of it on the pillow, the effort of turning it away from the shard of light cutting in through the nurses' station window—but most of all, the strain of using it to think.

Mike had been thinking since Lindsey left. He thought about the felony he might face, about finishing his book, and about St. Augustine's. He thought, and thought, but no panic attack came —the second shot of Ativan he'd hustled prevented that.

He closed his eyes, thinking about New Orleans, morgue photos, and…

Photos.

Why hadn't he seen it before? Blue eyes, dark hair…

A lot of people have blue eyes and dark hair. It doesn't mean anything.

Mike reached across to the bedside table, pushed the small water pitcher away, and flipped its aluminum tray up to use as a mirrored surface.

He couldn't tell if there was a resemblance behind the swelling. At that moment, the only feature that aligned with Delilah's was the hole in their right temple. Mike traced the open wound with his finger, grateful that it wasn't a matching gunshot wound.

"It shouldn't scar, but I'll get you a plastic surgery consult in the morning if you want."

Veronique?

The light from the hall obscured the recovery nurse into a darkened outline in the doorway until she took a step forward and flipped on the overhead fluorescents. Her hair was pulled back into a tight bun, rather than wrapped in a scarf, but her Creole accent jolted him to another time and place—over a voodoo shop.

He blinked away the lens flare and returned to the present—to the hospital room in D.C. "I'm not that vain."

She gave him a skeptical look. "Boy, you're using an instrument tray as a mirror."

"Ok, you got me."

"I'll try to keep these small. You got that pretty boy face to protect," she said, laying the suture kit onto his chest and examining the side of his head where she needed to close the opening left behind by the gear shift.

Her hospital badge dangled from the pocket of her scrubs, close enough that he could see it despite the migraine.

Lana.

"Lana, have we met before?"

"I don't know. You spend a lot of time in the recovery ward at GWU?"

"No."

"Then I don't see how we would have. I don't cross paths with many rich white boys in my neighborhood."

"I'm not rich."

"The senator I saw in the hallway suggests otherwise."

"Are you from New Orleans?"

"N'Awlins? No. Went one time for a bachelorette party. I won't tell you how that went since you're supposed to be keeping your heart rate down," she said, winking and taking the stool next to the bed.

"Lana, don't make me laugh, it hurts."

"Yeah, I'd give you something for that, but somebody stamped your chart."

She held up the front of his medical chart, which had what looked to be a pediatric sticker on the front—a cartoon puppy.

"What does the puppy mean? Cute eyes, might pee the bed?"

"Dog sticker. D.S..." she said, threading the first thin piece of Vicryl through his forehead.

"Ahh," he said, deciphering the substitution code quickly. "Drug-seeking?"

"Uh-huh."

"I wasn't, you know. I just asked what they were giving me. I can't help that I know the names of things from researching detective novels."

"I ain't judging, baby. It was probably that Statey walking around with the stick up his ass."

"The gun wasn't illegal either."

"Whatever you did or didn't do, I ain't here for. I'm here to stitch you up and run your concussion protocol."

"Concussion protocol?"

"I've got to keep you up all night and make sure your brain is stimulated."

"Ooh, how do you plan to do that?" Mike punctuated with his smile. He wasn't trying to flirt—Lana was old enough to be his mother—he just had a natural propensity for charming women in scrubs and girls behind cash registers.

"Oh, you're going to be a fun one."

Lana finished the final stitch and wiped the area with one more spread of alcohol before putting a bandage over it. "I'm going to send in your mama now, and if she's anything like me, it won't matter that you're 6'4" and grown. She's gonna bend you over her knee and whoop your ass for giving her a scare."

"I don't think my mom is anything like you," Mike said. In the five minutes he'd spent with the caretaker, she'd exhibited warmth, kindness, and a cheeky sense of humor. Jennifer Green possessed none of those things.

When she was finished, Lana collected her supplies and deposited them into the red bio-bag as she opened the door. "Mrs. Green, you can come in now."

"It's Ms." Jennifer blasted past the nurse in her way toward the patient. "I don't even know where to start with you. I guess I should be glad that this is your first DUI."

"I wasn't drinking. Someone hit me and I spun out. Are those my things?"

Mike nodded toward the bag in his mother's hand, a garbage sack filled with whatever the state troopers had managed to recover from the debris on the roadside.

His coat. His notebook. The ring.

"I didn't realize you were going to propose," she said, passing him the bag.

"Because I probably won't."

"That's quite a stone for being undecided."

"Also, you went through my stuff?"

She brushed off the teenage indignation. "Have you called your future wife and told her what happened?"

"I'm not sure I want her to be my future wife. Can you stop?"

"Fine."

Since the cat was already out of the bag, he spread the contents across the bed next to him, taking inventory.

"Would you go ask Lana for a pen? I'm supposed to stay 'stimulated.' Maybe I can finish my draft so I don't lose my book deal, my car, and my dignity in the same day."

Jennifer moved over to the doorway and flicked her wrist toward the nurse, looking more like she was asking for a restaurant check than a pen. "I heard you finalized a film deal."

"Lindsey finalized a film deal. I haven't even finalized an outline."

Mike flipped the notebook to the last written words and locked on his scrawl.

Where did you leave Petr?

His vision blurred on the sentence. The spires, the pews...

A gold cross.

"Are you all right, dear?"

"Did they ever tell you how I ended up in the orphanage?"

"What? No. What difference would that make?"

"I don't know. Medical history. Long lost siblings... I just thought if you knew something..."

"If I knew something, I would have told you long before now."

"So nothing? You get a more complete background check on a used car."

"I hope this is your brain injury and you haven't turned into this much of a jerk."

"Sure, let's go with that."

Jennifer pulled a chair up next to the bed and put a hand on his arm. "Where are these questions coming from?"

"When I was dead for five minutes, I think I saw Sister Catherine."

"Which one was she?"

"The one with red hair."

"I wonder if that's why you are always dating redheads."

"Oh, God, that's the most fucked up thing I've ever heard. I'm going to need therapy now."

"You need therapy anyway. I've been telling you that for a decade."

Lana snickered as she dropped a pen next to the bed, not bothering to conceal her eavesdropping or her amusement. "You're both mean. Leave me to be concussed in peace."

"Irritability is a common symptom of a head injury. Ignore him," Lana interjected.

"Look, sweetheart, it makes no difference what landed you in that orphanage, or even why your fosters didn't work out. You ended up exactly where you were meant to be."

"I hope so."

"Put that place out of your mind. I'll get your spare keys from Marta and make sure you have a change of clothes to go home in."

"Thanks, Mom."

Lana lingered, checking his vitals until Jennifer Green had shown herself out.

"Name, birthdate, and current President of the United States?" Lana asked.

"What?"

"Your cognitive test. Hit me with those answers, and you win yourself a nap."

"Michael Grennan...nope. Sorry. Michael Green. October 10th, 1973. The current president is Jacoby, but not for long.

"Did you say Grennan?"

"Oh, come on, it was an honest slip of the tongue."

"Reminded me, we had a Dr. Grennan in cardiology here a few years ago. Nice man."

"Is that so? What happened to him?"

"Ran off to Europe."

That wasn't all that happened to him.

"Can I still get the nap even though I biffed my name?"

"Go ahead and rest a bit, baby, but I'll be back for you."

Mike closed his eyes, the pain persisting behind the lids as it had in the light. With that stupid sticker on his medical chart, the only relief he was going to get from that pain was sleep. It should have come easily. It should have passed over him like a soft current, washing him away from the mess of the night, but he was only circling the drain. He tried counting backwards...

100… He was walking toward the Washington Monument…

95… *No, it's the Maidan Nezalezhnosti. The statue is finished now…*

90… He stepped into the National Archives building…

85… *The candy-colored streets of baroque Europe all started to look the same…*

80… Highway 66 between Falls Church and D.C.—the only place his thoughts could flow freely…

75… *I wanted to start my new life in Washington, D.C., but the first direct flight was going to New York…*

70…He focused on the ocean; each wave, swelling on an inhale and breaking on an exhale…

65… *Go back to the beginning…*

50… Heat—a dry heat he hadn't felt since he was five years old.

Los Angeles.

Mike's eyes shot open.

Zero. He was still in the hospital.

CHAPTER THIRTY-THREE

"Honey, some angry woman is on the phone for you," Lana said, nudging Mike gently and handing him a cordless receiver from the nurses' station.

"Shit..." There were a number of choices, but he had a feeling he knew which angry woman it was. "Hello?"

"When were you going to tell me you were in the hospital?" Kristin screamed through the phone.

"In the morning."

"It is morning!"

"How did you find me?"

"The news."

"Lindsey let my name hit the news?"

"No, I saw your car being craned up off the embankment!"

"You recognized a generic black Lexus? You can just say my mom called you."

"I heard you died! I freaked out and called every hospital trying to find out what happened!"

"And they told you? That's unsettling."

"Why didn't you call me!?"

"I was in trauma recovery."

"When are you being released? I'll pick you up and stay with you."

"I don't know..."

"You don't know? Mike, you almost died. I need to see you, baby."

"If that were true, you'd have rushed to the hospital instead of wasting ten minutes on a phone call."

"Wow…"

"Sorry. Head injury talking."

"I should say."

"I'll find out when I'm being released and call you back."

"Or don't."

The line went cold, not unlike everything else with her lately. Calling her back wouldn't change the fact that they didn't fit, and seeing her wouldn't get him the other answers he needed. Kristin was a problem for another day.

Lana grabbed the receiver and tucked it into her scrubs, as she verified his vital signs for the dozenth time since he'd come under her care.

"I ain't none of my business, but…"

"Lana, we spent the night together. You know my name, birthdate, *and* the current President of the United States. It's all your business. Lay it on me."

"That rock is too nice for a female like that."

"I've been getting that a lot lately."

"You wanna know something else?"

"Hit me."

"Your discharge paperwork came through."

"Oh yeah?"

"And the police are gone. That scary lawyer lady you got unleashed on them. No ballistics. No charges. Even that silly stamp got crossed off your file. You're free to go."

"With painkillers?"

"Boy, don't make me put that puppy back on your file." She unthreaded the IV from the top of his hand and pressed a gauze swatch against the opening to stop the blood from trickling out.

"Can I at least get a cup of coffee?"

"In six weeks."

"Seriously?"

"They shocked your heart several times; caffeine is not recommended. And no more smoking!"

"Jesus, I was better off dead."

"All right, smoke then. You don't need that lung we re-inflated; you got yourself another one." With her free hand, she flicked his ear like she was reprimanding a child.

"How about flying across country?"

"How about going home and taking it easy for a few days?"

"There's something I need to do, though."

He'd been thinking about it all night. Going back to the beginning didn't mean flipping to page one of Delilah's book; it meant returning to Los Angeles—the place they'd been born.

"Don't make me call your mama."

Lana slid a piece of gauze tape over the cotton to hold the blotter in place, and Mike closed his hand around hers before she could pull it away.

"She's not actually my mom. I was adopted."

"Yeah? Did she ever wipe your ass?"

259

"Sure."

"Has she yelled at somebody who spoke to you the wrong way?"

"Of course."

"Did she bring you a fresh change of clothes in the middle of the night after you rolled your damn car into the river, even though you were a bit of a jerk to her?"

"Yeah, that happened."

"Then she's your mama."

"In fairness, you essentially did all those things for me last night, too."

"Because giving birth don't make you a mother." Lana moved her hand to check the dressing on his forehead stitches, but she just held his cheek in the warm pad of her palm. "Defending your babies makes you a mother. Making the choices you gotta make to give them their best life—even when they're ungrateful —makes you a mother. Sacrifice makes you a mother."

Mike could hear Petr's cries as Delilah placed him in a church pew and turned away. He could hear his sister's sobs as she tore herself away from the child, knowing it was the only chance he had to escape her fate.

"Lana, do you want to move in with me until I get better?"

"Do you wanna give me that ring you're holding, worth more than my house?"

"Sure. I'm not doing anything else with it."

She laughed and unhooked the last of his monitor lines. "Get up slow, now, honey. And you holler if you need help with your pants."

"Really putting out for that rock, aren't you?"

She laughed. "You're the best concussion patient I've had in a long time, honey."

"You're the best mom I've had in a long time, Lana."

The nurse gave him the same look Marta gave him—reassurance mixed with a sprinkle of sympathy—then she left too.

Mike took his time standing, placing weight on the side of his body that wasn't shattered first, before dragging the other side along for the ride. Three broken ribs, a concussion, a re-inflated lung, and a flatline—all said, he made out pretty well, he thought, sliding on the suit his mother had dropped off overnight. The pants weren't the problem. Socks and shoes were a different story.

When he was finished, he stood in front of the full-length mirror on the back of the room's door and surveyed the finished product, and then he slipped on his overcoat.

Camels and coffee.

The stench of the coat was as close as he was going to get to either.

Outside, he hailed a cab.

"Dulles."

"That's like a hundred-dollar fare," the cabbie eyed the suspicious-looking passenger through the rearview mirror.

"I've got cash," Mike said, waving his wallet.

"You get mugged and lose your luggage or something?"

"No, I rolled my car and decided to go see the Pacific Ocean. You want to ask me anything else?"

He pulled the split window closed between them and sank back into the seat for the trip.

The terminal was bright with sunlight and promise. Most people traveling on a weekday were business travelers, and Mike would have fit in stealthily among them in his suit, were it not for the stitches and the busted face that earned him extra scrutiny from security.

The flight would give him six hours to think about what exactly he was doing—if he was making a pilgrimage or a mistake. When the pilot announced their final descent into L.A., all Mike knew for sure was that he would need to rent a car.

He felt the warm, Western air as soon as he passed into the jet bridge. Low humidity, even that close to the water, and the smell of fast food and fuel riding in on the breeze—unmistakably Los Angeles. It was air he hadn't breathed in twenty years, but it resonated in a place deeper than memory. He wanted to suck it in deeply, but his ribs only allowed for small sips.

In the time it took for the rental car shuttle to make the loop around the terminal road in traffic, Mike had already peeled off his blazer and rolled his shirtsleeves up above the elbows. He could feel the sun soaking into his skin and the back of his shirt getting damp with sweat. It felt like freedom.

He got a convertible with extra insurance and pulled onto Century Boulevard before pulling directly back into a gas station that shared its parking lot with a strip club. This wasn't the part of L.A. they put onto postcards—four people asked him for change between the car and the payphone.

The Yellow Pages, hanging limply by a chain in the phone booth, had been used for many things, but so far, no one had tampered with the "Catholic orphanages" section, which surprised him, given the proximity to multiple potential unplanned pregnancy scenarios presenting themselves in the parking lot.

According to that edition of the directory, St. Augustine's still existed. He tore out the page and hopped back in his car, opting to head west a few blocks before disappearing inland.

The urban jungle ran smack up against the Pacific Ocean, a bizarre ecotone where nature and man squared off for a brawl. He found a metered parking spot after a few passes and walked out onto the sand. With the sun as hot as it was, the water looked silver, a vast blanket of mercury sparkling and winking. He focused on the ocean; each wave, swelling on an inhale and breaking on an exhale, like he did whenever he needed to calm his mind.

And it's always been in this spot.

A classic foreshadowing.

He sat down in a pocket of coarse dry sand and searched for the address of the orphanage on the cheap fold-out map that came with the rental. It was about twelve miles inland. He didn't want to leave this ocean, but it held no answers. At least not any he needed then. Maybe some other time, they could unpack each other's mysteries.

Go back to the beginning.

Twelve miles took him over an hour. L.A. mutated from the casual beach vibe along the coast to the frenzied intensity of Mid-

City. People moved from intolerant to outright angry. Los Angeles was inconsistent and undefinable, attracting archetypes who had figured out what they wanted to personify and assimilated into the appropriate zone. It struck him as an easy place to get lost.

And a better place to write.

Before Western Avenue, he hooked north past a Korean spa and an all-night clinic, and found street parking on a side street with no demarcation between the main thoroughfare businesses and the small bungalow homes squeezed in between them.

He couldn't think of one single person in his life who wouldn't be furious with him for checking out of the hospital and flying to L.A., but he wasn't worried about what anyone else thought.

Except Delilah.

He owed this to her.

CHAPTER THIRTY-FOUR

Mike had never seen St. Augustine's from the front.

He'd spent five years on the playground in the back and wandering inside its stone walls, but when he'd left this place, his eyes were closed, and he never looked behind him.

In his child's mind, he'd imagined it as Notre Dame—spires, buttresses, saints staring down from stone. In reality, it was a WPA job from the '30s that gave Mid-City a few paychecks and a squat brick chapel that fought to keep itself clean of graffiti.

The orphanage had always been adjacent to the sanctuary, with a small courtyard joining the two and acting as a playground for the children. Since he left, it had been enclosed behind a chain link fence, padlocked to keep out random strangers with two black eyes and a head laceration.

Mike took himself to the front door—another thing he'd never used—and paused, remembering the rules: dab the Holy Water, cross yourself, light a candle for the dead.

He'd hated everything about the nave when he was a child. The room was dark, the bleeding Christ was unsettling, and the services went on for too long. But as an adult, he wanted to believe it was safe inside the walls. He wanted to believe that they held answers. Like Delilah, he wanted to believe in something that offered a sense of peace, or if nothing else, nostalgia.

He approached the altar—the same place he'd taken communion and spat the wafer out the minute no one was looking—took a gentle knee and stared up at the apse. The clean, white cross hung there, suspended the way it had always been. It was so much larger in his memory than it was to the grown man kneeling below it.

"Do you really think the answers are here?" he whispered, hoping Delilah would answer him.

"If they aren't, I've made poor life choices," the priest said, appearing from a passage that connected to the rectory.

Mike's eyes snapped to the young man in all black, startling him with the state of his face.

"Sorry, Father, I didn't mean to scare you."

"Are you ok, friend?" the priest asked.

"Yeah. Car accident last night."

The priest nodded to the statue of Jesus Christ watching over them. "So the two of you have already spoken today."

Mike couldn't help but chuckle. The young man didn't embody the terrifying and austere discipline that the clergy had in his day. He was there to serve his community through faith and generosity, not slap little boys with a ruler and lock them away at night.

"I may not have given up church if I knew you guys were doing tight-fives these days."

"When was the last time you attended mass?"

"1979. The day I was dragged out that front door by a stranger."

"You were one of our displaced children?"

266

Displaced children. What a PC way to say orphan.

"Yeah. If that's what we're calling them now."

"1979… Sister Mary Catherine would remember you."

"She's still here?"

It was less a question and more a flicker of hope awakening inside of him. Getting his answers would be a whole lot simpler if he could ask someone who'd been there when he was.

"Sure, let me find her."

The priest disappeared into the private offices again, and a moment later, a woman appeared cautiously. Her red curls had begun to gray, but the sweet, round face encircled by her habit was unmistakably the same woman who'd raised him those early years.

"Hello? Father Joseph said you'd like a word?"

The voice ushered a wave of memory through him. She'd always been the one to fold him back into her garments when he'd been returned from a foster home that didn't work out. She'd been the one who corralled him back to bed when they found him wandering with insomnia. She'd been the one who told him he was leaving and introduced him to Jennifer Green.

"Sister Mary Catherine."

"Do I know you?"

"I grew up here. Mike Green. You called me 'Your Little Michael,' though I'm realizing that probably wasn't as unique as I thought it was then."

Her eyes twinkled as the memory of him returned. "My troublemaker. It would appear you haven't changed."

"This?" He pointed to his busted face. "Yeah. The doctors need some family history details when I go back in for follow-up. I was hoping you still had some information on my birth parents."

"I'm sorry. You would need a court order. You should have no trouble getting one if what you're saying is true."

"Would I lie? To a nun? In a church?"

"Yes, I believe you would, Michael."

He needed another approach.

Meisha...I need to show you something.

"Sister, would you mind if I saw the old playroom while I'm here?"

"Why?"

He could have lied again. He could have downplayed the ask into something about old times' sake, but that woman had been his protector for years; she didn't deserve that. He gathered up his courage, pinched the corners of his eyes, and let the truth out despite how foreign it felt to do.

"When I was in the hospital, my heart stopped. I didn't see a light or a tunnel—I saw this place. I saw you."

Her ideology may not have allowed for the belief in near-death experiences, but she could tell that he believed what he was saying. She tucked a stray red strand back into her habit and took his hand. "Let's go for a walk."

She led him back through the courtyard, through the dormitory, meandering the halls past the staircase that led down to the basement.

Meisha.

"Remind me what that was?" he asked, pointing to the empty staircase.

"The basement. There's the playroom," she said, pointing. The nightmare clowns and the gold cross were exactly how he'd seen them in his dream.

"No kids right now?"

"We have a few, but we place them quickly these days."

"May I have a moment alone? I realize as I say that I'm just a creepy guy asking to hang out where the kids do..."

"I understand what you must be going through. I can give you five minutes while they're still playing outside."

"Thank you."

Once she'd gone, he darted back toward the wooden stairs that cut down into the earth. Los Angeles rarely had basements the way the East Coast did, and this one, under a church, felt like a catacomb—where records had gone to be buried.

He moved through the hall the way he'd moved through the archives, skimming the surface of each doorway with his fingers like he could tell what was beyond each one through psychometry. But he was no longer exploring; he was being led.

His hand finally landed on a locked door. The old lock was simply a slit that he defeated with the edge of a coin and pushed inside, closing it behind him.

Three more minutes.

The old green filing cabinets hadn't been touched in thirty years and had no apparent organization, but illegally searching through records was what Mike did best.

He quickly landed on the file, as if it had been pointed out to him.

Green, Jennifer.

Single. Thirty-five. LAUSD School Board. Moving to D.C. to serve on the National Board of Education.

And set her sights on a cabinet seat.

Two minutes.

He was running out of time. He tossed Jennifer's application, financial records, and application essay aside and looked for his birth certificate.

He'd never seen it before. No one had. His legal existence started with those adoption papers, and they had been the only documents he ever needed to get an ID or passport.

This was the beginning.

TYPE OF BIRTH: MULTIPLE

ORDER OF BIRTH: ONE OF TWO

MOTHER: MICHELLE GILMOUR, 18, NO OCCUPATION

FATHER: ALEX BARRETT, 20, U.S. ARMY

It was all true.

He sucked in a short sip of air, as much as his lungs would allow, and his eyes traced the words a second time.

"I wasn't expecting a father," he whispered to himself, checking his watch.

Time's up.

Mike tucked the folded page into his pocket. No one had ever needed it before—including him—so no one should care if it went missing.

Like me.

He didn't have time to process the truth or justify his grief yet; he needed to leave before he was discovered and go somewhere else to do all of that.

Back in the hallway, he pointed himself toward a window at the far end of the hall that—if he were navigating properly—would dump him out in the alley behind the ward. It was four steps to the window, and he made it three.

"Michael."

He froze. "Shit."

"Come here, please."

Instinctively, he offered his knuckles for reprimand as he walked toward her. "Listen, I can only remember the first two lines of the Hail Mary…"

Instead of rapping his hands, Mary Catherine took them into hers. "I should have guessed. You've been obsessed with this basement since you were four years old. Come." She escorted him back to the stairs and up into the playroom again. "Do you remember Sister Grace?"

"The one who liked to hit?"

"She didn't like it…yes. One night, a friend of hers came to the private quarters."

"Nuns have friends?"

"We develop bonds with parishioners. This young woman was a nurse. That night, a teenage girl died giving birth to twins. There was no next of kin, so the county was going to take them."

Mike replayed what he could remember of that vision. The scream. The blood. The nurses rushing to help both babies and move the girl to the OR.

"She brought you here instead."

"She kidnapped us?"

"There are safe harbors now, but nothing like that existed then. She'd have rather seen you with God than lost to the system."

"What about the father?"

"The girl told the hospital he was in Vietnam. She had no way to find him."

"What happened to my sister?"

"We only housed boys then. We sent her to a girls' facility in the Valley that had space. That's all I know, truly." She crossed the chapel, clutching her rosary, and pressed open the large door to the street.

"I appreciate you telling me what you could."

"I hope you found peace in the answers. You're always welcome here, Little Michael."

He smiled at the irony as he easily stood a foot taller than her. "Thank you, sister."

Mike put a hand on the door of his rental car and looked back at St. Augustine's. The dozens of times he'd been escorted out, he'd said goodbye to Mary Catherine and hoped—*prayed*—that he'd never be back. This time, he left hoping he'd have a reason to see this place again.

CHAPTER THIRTY-FIVE

The front desk agents at the Century City Hotel assumed the handsome, yet bludgeoned, stranger with no luggage would have call girls coming and going all night, and while that could have been entertaining, Mike was more interested in staring at his birth certificate and lying very still.

FATHER: ALEX BARRETT, 20, U.S. ARMY

The man who'd donated sperm to the cause of his life. Vietnam, his mother had told the hospital.

A lie?

Maybe. Or maybe that was how she'd ended up alone. Had the young soldier abandoned his responsibilities, or never even known? Had he been killed like so many others—like everyone else in their story?

If any of it were true—the name, the age, the occupation—the man might be alive. Alive and only forty-three years old. Mike paced over to the East-facing window and stared out over the landscape of the LA basin, toward downtown's skyline, twinkling, not because of a gentle atmospheric pulse, but because of the chemical layer in the air quality.

He'd attempted countless times over the years to imagine what his life would have been like had he known his birth parents. He'd written the scenes, sketched the dialogue, and recited the lines to polish them. Never had he cast his father a Vietnam soldier or his mother a teen runaway.

Instead of imagining all of the experiences he didn't have, he tried remembering the things from his life that he would have missed out on.

He wouldn't have grown up in Virginia with its seasons and cherry blossoms. He wouldn't have had the Washington Monument as his compass needle. He wouldn't have gone to Georgetown, and definitely wouldn't have been Tom's best friend.

If someone else had been Tom's roommate, they might not have kept him from overdosing that night. The scandal of their son's overdose would have ruined the Stockton family. America wouldn't have its presidential candidate.

Everything had gone reasonably well in his life, and yet he'd spent it focusing on what he lacked, filling that Void with toxic women and substances instead of leveraging his looks, talent, and social status to get ahead in the world.

Meanwhile, Delilah's adoption had fractured her family and gotten everyone killed.

One life improved, the other impoverished.

The butterfly effect game isn't helping.

He either needed to go home, file that birth certificate away, and be at peace knowing the circumstances around his birth, or he needed to find and confront Alex Barrett.

It would have to be the resting in peace option, he thought, because finding a person with one piece of information and a twenty-three-year gap in data would be impossible. He rolled onto the side of his torso that wasn't shattered and closed his eyes.

If you were a real detective, you'd figure it out.

"Fuuuuuuck," he groaned, standing up again delicately, and finding the phone on the hotel's desk. "Can't believe I'm about to do this…"

"Decker," Lindsey answered from her suite in the Jefferson Hotel. Sarah had taken the next leg of the Stocktons' campaign swing so she could stay closer to home and whip up more sludge on his potential opponents in the Democratic Party. Even though it was the middle of the night in D.C., she was wide awake, energized by scandal and potential outrage. She thrived in the night like a vampire, something she and Mike had always had in common.

"Lindsey, it's Mike. I'm sorry about the hour."

"It's fine, Mike. What do you need?"

"Can you find people?"

"Can I find people? I guess it depends on the people and where they are."

"Well, if I knew where they were, I wouldn't need you to find them."

"Would you stop being weird and just tell me what's happening?" She leaned back in her chair, waiting to hear the boy's needs, which seemed like they might require her dedicated attention, not the split focus she was giving to a black folder full of secrets.

"I'm looking for a Vietnam vet, Alex Barrett."

"Why?"

"I didn't think 'why' was part of the criteria for helping me."

"You want me to find some lunatic Vietnam vet who's probably got a heroin addiction and lives on the street, and I want to know why."

"He's my birth father."

Lindsey sat quietly, absorbing the development.

"Can you find people, or not? He was in the Army when I was born and was twenty at the time. He would have been stateside at least nine months before, so…"

"I know when you were born, Mike. I know everything about you that exists on paper, and I didn't know this one."

"You never fail to creep me out."

"You don't get to sit in Rick Stockton's private office if I don't have your kill file memorized. How did you get this Barrett's name?"

"I found my birth certificate."

"Where? I looked for it, and there was nothing on file with the State of California."

"I stole the original from the basement of the orphanage I grew up in."

"Ok, that's a little impressive, actually. Fax it to me at the Jefferson."

"So you'll do this?"

"Oh, now I fucking have to do it. Where do I get the information back to you? I know you aren't home."

"You know I'm not home?"

"There's a reason I'm the best."

"I'll be back in D.C. tomorrow."

"And where are you now?"

"If you were the best, you'd know."

"Keep fucking with me, Green, see how that goes for you."

"You like it. It turns you on."

"Maybe a little."

He tucked the phone back into the cradle and stared east again. Past St. Augustine's. Past downtown. Toward City Hall, the 110 and everything in between. There was so much more he wanted to do in Los Angeles. He wanted to put the top down and drive Pacific Coast Highway. He wanted to eat tacos, sit on the beach, and feel the sun on his face.

But not at midnight.

At midnight—with pain racking his sober body and a metropolis out the hotel window—all he could do was write through the darkness.

Dead Girls Tell No Tales

Chapter Forty-Seven: That goddamn warehouse smelled like wet cheese. The wet made sense. The whole of the Florida Peninsula was a mold bucket, damp—no, dank—a spore on the groin of America. The cheese...? Yeah, I don't know. It could have been me by that point.

Fat Ivan had us both tied to chrome diner chairs, and if my ass was sticking to the vinyl, I was certain Margarita's was too. I was still thinking about her ass when my jaw took a wake-up call.

"You look at me when I'm talking to ya!"

Fat Ivan looked me straight in the eye with one of his steel ones. I don't fancy looking at .45-caliber eyeballs, so I turned away. Much as I could turn, what with being tied to the chair and whatnot, and so forth.

"Why would I look at your sour mug when I got a pretty dame like her to check out?"

"Yeah, the dame's a fox, all right. Got's a sister looks just like 'er."

"What do you know about my sister?" Margarita asked. "Why don't you spell it all out for me, since I'm just a dumb broad."

"I did a number on her. What kind of a number would be ungentlemanly of me to comment on." He bit down on his stogie and cackled.

"Killing a pretty girl. What's wrong with you, pal? We got plenty of ugly dames you can whack," I said.

"Yeah, but with that one, we had a spare."

"Still, that killin' wasn't your style, Fatty. It was too clean. Who'd you have do it for you? Pinky Pete? Tony Two-Toes? Mugsy Brown?"

He spat the little flecks of wet tobacco from his mouth and cackled again. "Kate O'Leary!"

The moron should have remembered that you never reveal the truth to the hero right before the end of the story, even when you're the only one holding the steel, because I knew that I still had an ace in Margarita's hole.

While he was blustering around, making his posse laugh, she was wiggling a pearl-handled Dillinger free of her garter. I knew it was there because I'd taken it off of her the other night—the garter, not the Dillinger.

"That's it, you rat! You had my sister killed, and now you're under arrest!"

She jumped up, drawing on that clown with her thigh piece. She'd never even been tied to the chair. The jabroni in Ivan's gang who'd done the honors was working for her all along.

"Didn't see that one coming."

Fatty and I looked at each other with the same dumb man-look. Both of us: Duped by a dame.

Not just a dame—a fed.

She slid her pistol and her badge back into her garter while her team of G-men rushed into the joint and arrested the whole lot of them.

"Of course, Joe, you understand I needed you to do the dirty work and keep it off the books in case it came back that my sister had been involved in something illegal. I couldn't have Hoover stripping me over something she did."

"Nope, sure wouldn't want anyone stripping you."

"You aren't mad, are you, baby?" she asked, pressing the tip of my nose like a button.

"Mad? Nah. Why would I be mad? It's not like I got punched in the face and tied to a chair while you sat there."

"Good. See ya around, sweetheart."

She swung her hips through the door and out of my life.

"Hate to see you go, love to watch you leave."

One of the feds finally bothered to untie me.

"You all right, fella? You look like you seen a ghost?"

"A ghost? Nah. Those I believe in. This was a broad with a badge. What'll they think of next?"

I stepped free of that cheesy warehouse and lit up a cigarette. It was time to be getting home. Like it or not, my job here was done. Schmitty's *was calling, but it was on the wrong coast. I was on the wrong coast. I belonged somewhere else.*

After all, L.A. was my town.

I'm just a devil from the City of Angels.

CHAPTER THIRTY-SIX

Mike balanced a venti Americano on his lap and aimed his right leg down the aisle. He was already breaking his discharge instructions—coffee wouldn't kill him. He might, though, kill someone else if he attempted to do the first morning flight out, in economy, with no caffeine. Business was sold out; otherwise, he wouldn't have been attempting to wad his broken body up and shove it into a seat designed for someone with ten fewer inches on him.

He re-read the scribbles he'd written the night before after talking to Lindsey. They were good—in need of a polish—but they were good. He could email them to his editor when he got home and call this first draft done. Something was bothering him about his antagonist...

"Excuse me, I've got the window."

Mike looked up slowly—mostly because moving hurt too much. The woman was almost six feet of languid perfection in a navy suit. Skin, the perfect alabaster. Eyes, a rich jade. The dame looked like she walked out of a black and white film.

Or a Gestapo Joe novel.

No. Wrong blonde. Wrong story.

"Yeah," Mike said, attempting to lever himself from the seat and into the aisle so she could slide by without the indignity of the seat-shuffle.

They stood nearly eye-to-eye for a moment, blocking the rest of the passengers from passing.

"Are you all right? I mean, other than your face," she asked. Her low, breathy whisper forced him to lean in and watch her lips to make out what her British accent had said.

"Yeah. It's been a rough couple of days."

"Hopefully not a plane crash?"

Mike stifled a laugh that would have torn a hole in his compromised lung. "No. Car accident."

"You'll be on the mend once you're home." She took her seat at the window and quickly lowered the shade. Mike repositioned himself in the aisle seat, angling toward her across the empty space between them.

"How did you know I was going home?"

"That's your coat in the bin?"

"Yeah."

"No one in LA owns a coat like that."

"You some kind of profiler?"

"Hardly. Art collection curator."

"Well, *madam*, I was born here, but you're right, I'm going home."

He closed his eyes, hoping that was the end of it. He wasn't the guy who talked to people on planes.

"Where should I eat in Washington with only one night in town?" she asked after a few minutes had gone by.

"One night? I guess the Old Ebbitt," he answered without opening his eyes.

"The Old Ebbitt?"

"Right next to the White House. Lots of famous politicians eat there. Just don't sit at the bar alone. They'll think you're working."

"I beg your pardon."

Mike sat up fast. Too fast for his injuries. "Shit, I didn't mean you look like... I'll shut up."

Her mouth widened into a laugh as the cabin crew announced takeoff. When they'd finished the instructions, she turned back to her seatmate. "Violet Martel."

She extended her long fingers to shake Mike's hand. He expected delicate and slightly cold skin offering a light greeting, but got a firm, confident grip.

"Now, what exactly made you think I was a call girl? Mr...?"

"Mike Green, and I never said that. I just know old married guys would spend the night soliciting you if you sat at the bar by yourself."

"And why do you know so much about it?"

Mike didn't have a great answer. He personally knew a woman who made stories like that disappear, so of course, he knew they were happening, but couldn't volunteer that.

"Is there any version of the next four hours where you let me off the hook for this rough take-off?"

"No. None at all."

She bumped over from the window to the middle seat, so she could lean closer and continue their conversation at a lower volume. Mike wasn't usually the guy who talked to people on planes. He wasn't usually the guy on a plane. Hell, he wasn't usually the guy fresh off a near-fatal accident and holding his birth record. A lot had changed in the last thirty hours. Maybe this was who he really was.

When the cabin crew instructed everyone to prepare the cabin for landing, hours had gone by, and they'd barely paused their conversation to decline drink service.

Mike wasn't usually the guy declining drinks either.

It was the most words he'd used off the page in as long as he could remember, and he didn't want it to end. Violet had infected him against his very will or intention while there were already too many women occupying his mind: Delilah, Kristin, Jennifer Green, and, now, Michelle Gilmour.

The last thing I need is to get involved with another dame.

"It's my luck," she said. "I get the handsome fellow on the quick flight. Tomorrow, I'll probably be stuck next to a dodgy bloke with wandering hands."

"You're only in town for one night?"

"One night. Don't suppose you'd like to take me to that restaurant? I'd let everyone believe you've already paid for my time."

"I deserved that, but I can't tonight."

The real answer wasn't that he couldn't; it was that he *shouldn't*. There was about an eighty percent chance he'd run into someone he knew at the Ebbitt, and of that eighty, at least half a chance it would be Kristin. The stupid ring in his pocket wasn't going anywhere, and neither was she.

"I could give you a ride into the city, though."

"In your car that's flattened?"

"Shit. You're right. You want to split a cab?"

"I couldn't be a bother."

"No bother at all," he said, attempting an English accent. He quickly backpedaled when it came out sounding insulting. "Not sure why I did that. Thought I was done making an ass of myself. Guess I have an unlimited well to draw from there."

The plane hit the tarmac with a thud that jolted Violet even closer to him as the tires squealed and the fuselage fought against gravity. The cold air that rushed in when the forward door opened was familiar, a combination of jet fuel and woodland decay that lasted all the way to the taxi stand. Violet drank it all in, her eyes surveying her surroundings for every detail she could record. While she took in her environment, Mike ran at the mouth like he was a Virginia tour guide coming off of opiates.

"I grew up twenty minutes that way," he said, nodding with his nose as he put her bag into the trunk for her. She tried to insist she carry it herself, given that he was struggling with the chest brace holding his ribs together.

"You live in the city now?"

"Logan Circle," he said, sliding into the backseat.

The cab smelled like tobacco, and not the 'it's Virginia and we use tobacco as an air freshener' smell. No, this was the real thing —an ashtray holding a straw stack of spent butts. Two-days-ago-Mike would have bummed one and lit up immediately. His pleurisy begged him not to, even as his nerves craved it.

"Is that where you're headed?" the cabbie asked. "Logan Circle?"

"Sorry, no. What hotel are you at?"

Violet checked her purse for a small slip of paper with the reservation's info written on it. "The Jefferson."

"Of fucking course you are."

There was a one hundred percent chance he'd run into someone he knew at The Jefferson, and of that one hundred, he already knew it was going to be Lindsey.

"Something wrong with it?"

"Not at all. Just don't sit at the bar alone."

Lindsey stared into a glass of deep red wine, pretending not to eavesdrop on the couple seated at the bar next to her. When a black folder slid under her nose, she followed the direction of the file to find her young Navy minion leaning one elbow on the bar, waiting for a reaction.

AJ wasn't in uniform. When at all possible, he didn't wear it, but especially when moving through the streets of D.C. on an LDA errand. He didn't want to associate those lives with one another—the Navy officer with a pedigree and the clandestine operative moonlighting as a fixer.

"Tony, have a drink, you look uptight," Lindsey said, snapping for the bartender.

"That's just what eight years of boarding school, Annapolis, and a Navy Career does to your face," he said dryly.

"Then please get laid, before you snap and go on a five-state killing spree. I don't have time to deal with something like that right now. Why are you here? I didn't call for you."

"Alex Barrett." He wagged his chin toward the black file, urging her to open it.

Lindsey lifted the cover. All her black files held the subject's headshot inside the front flap, and this one was an Army ID photo. He was Mike Green in twenty years, with a buzz-cut. She flipped it closed again, pretending it hadn't piqued her interest. "And it's good enough to drive over here and hand deliver?"

"You tell me."

"I haven't read it yet, Commander. Want to give me the Cliff Notes?"

"Alex Barrett: Grew up in Long Beach, California, fought in every major campaign since '73. Current rank colonel."

"Colonel? Sounds like a patriot. Where is he stationed now?"

"Lindsey, I know this was a test. I keep my sources anonymous, so you up the ante and ask me to go after some random JSOC colonel to see if I can get into the Pentagon."

"JSOC? He's black ops?"

"I don't know if they're black, but they're definitely special. He's classified under something called Operation Iron Veil, but you know that already because this was a phish to see if I could get in. Either that or you're punishing me for giving Tom Stockton a gun."

"You think I have time for games, Anthony?"

"I think you hate lacking information, like who I have that can penetrate a firewall like the DOD's."

"I don't care who you're penetrating. Where is he stationed?"

"Unclear. His file was locked SCI Level-3 last year."

"Ok, well, find out. I need to vet him. For Stockton. *Our boss.*"

"I can't do that without stealing special compartmentalized military files."

"Oh, please. That move runs in your family. This is a very tiny espionage. You've done far worse."

"To be clear, you want me to illegally access Joint Special Operations Command records to locate Colonel Alex Barrett. I want to make sure I have the order correct."

"What, are you wearing a wire?" Lindsey scoffed. "Get me his location, Commander."

"Ma'am." He spun and started for the door.

"You know I hate being called, ma'am!" she called after him.

AJ returned to his car, still idling in the valet circle, and pulled away, passing an inbound taxi.

"I hope this wasn't too far out of your way," Violet said, as the cab pulled into the valet drop-off in front of The Jefferson.

"Not at all. Happy to. It's not every day I meet a gorgeous older woman on an airplane and fall in love."

"Wow, I'm not sure what to do with that comment, because I heard 'gorgeous', but then I heard 'older woman'."

"Right! Just before I dropped an L-bomb. I should go home now before I get real stupid."

"I'm sure that's not possible."

"You'd be surprised." Mike crossed around to the trunk and helped her with her bag again despite the racking pain.

You picked a shit-dumb time to give up painkillers.

"Ms. Martel, it was lovely sharing six hours with you."

"Likewise, Mr. Green. I hope you feel better soon."

The dame swung her hips towards the door and out of my life. Calling after her would be a mistake. The things I'd do if she actually turned around would be a mistake. Or, maybe the mistake was letting her leave.

"Violet," he called after her. "I can't go to the Ebbitt, but would you like to have a drink here in the lobby?"

"I would like that. Would you give me fifteen minutes to check in and freshen up?"

"If you think you need to be fresh around me. I'm practically a corpse at this point."

She laughed endearingly and continued inside.

Let the mistake-making begin.

CHAPTER THIRTY-SEVEN

Mike crossed the black and white checkered tiles of the Jefferson lobby to the bar—the same one he warned her not to sit at. The Jefferson, in particular, had a reputation. Its proximity to the White House made it an exceptionally convenient location for the power elite to meet in the rooms upstairs without being seen, or right there in the lobby, specifically to be seen.

He rested one hip on a barstool, careful not to put pressure on the rest of his skeleton, while the other half draped over the side like a rumpled overcoat.

"Get you something?" the bartender asked.

"Johnnie Walker Blue," Lindsey answered. "Right? That's your drink?"

"It is when you're buying," he answered. Mike didn't even want a drink. He *did*, he always did, but in that exact moment, he was trying very hard to remain clear-headed. The second he declined a whiskey, Lindsey would dig in, and he'd already let her get too close when he asked for her help. She was a useful weapon, but not one you wanted to carry around loaded.

"Los Angeles?" she asked with a smile.

"You are the best."

"You had any doubt?" She picked up her stack of ominous reading material and slid to the barstool next to him. After the bartender on her payroll slid a plump little glass into his hand, she proceeded to open the front cover of the top folder. "I'd say there's a strong family resemblance."

Mike focused on Alex Barrett's eyes, zeroing in on the familiar feature that held constant through not only him, but the photos he'd seen of Delilah. Crow's feet around the corners suggested that Alex Barrett had spent a lot of time in his life smiling.

"I'm still working on his current location, but there's a lot of good reading material in there. I'm having a copy sent to your apartment as we speak."

"A copy?"

"I'm not giving you an original intelligence file, Mike. First, because it's illegal..."

"The copy isn't?"

"And second, because I still need this one to vet for Stockton's proximity."

"You think the dad who doesn't know I'm alive is a threat to Rick?"

"We don't know that. We don't know that he didn't skip out on his pregnant hippie girlfriend because kids are a fucking pain in the ass, and once he sees your picture in the paper next to F-POTUS, he doesn't show up looking for a promotion to General."

"You're a peach, Linds, really. Always a ray of positivity. Speaking of pictures, how did the news have my car getting craned out of the river?"

"It absolutely didn't. I buried that accident before you were even discharged. No records exist."

"Huh."

It wasn't the kind of reaction that Lindsey Decker let slide. "Huh, what?" she asked, sitting up straighter. "Why do you ask? Who said you were on the news?"

"Kristin..."

"You know I don't fucking like her."

"No one does."

"Want me to bury her, too?" She flashed her wicked smile.

"I can break up with my own girlfriend."

"Let me know if you change your mind. There are some parts of my job I love more than others."

"So, what's the going rate on a stolen intelligence file?"

"We could just go upstairs."

Mike smirked, sliding the still-full glass to the side. "I think you require full lung capacity."

Lindsey snickered and set her empty wine glass back onto the bar as she stood to leave. "Consider it a favor to the campaign."

"You don't do favors. Everything is on trade. I know that much about you."

"I'll put it on Tom's tab. A little thing like this gets lost in his ledger."

"That I believe."

"Now, stay out of trouble, would you? I don't have time for more of your bullshit." She leaned forward and kissed his cheekbone, below the sutures. "Plus, you know, I kind of like you."

"Yes, ma'am."

Lindsey rolled her eyes at the moniker she despised and disappeared toward the elevator that would take her to her suite upstairs. As she passed a stunner of a blonde in the doorway, the two women sized each other up.

"I said stay out of trouble," she whispered to herself as the woman slid onto the barstool Lindsey had vacated.

Violet eased into the spot next to Mike, glancing over his shoulder, watching the elevator doors close. "I thought you said you didn't know a lot of gorgeous older women."

"Actually, I said I don't fall in love with them on planes. And Lindsey isn't a woman, she's a lizard queen who drinks human blood to sustain her earthly corpus."

"You should write that book."

"I should! That would be a great sci-fi novel: Lawyer by day —alien vessel of evil by night."

"Your lawyer? Well, she's busy this week."

"You have no idea."

She helped herself to his untouched whiskey glass and took a sip. "Is she the Stocktons' lawyer, too?"

He knew it had been too good to be true. Women who registered a ten on the Richter scale didn't give him their undivided attention for six straight hours unless they were after something. A chill ran down his spine as he determined how to extract her agenda.

"Did I mention the Stocktons?"

"No, but I saw the newspaper when I was checking in. 'Prominent D.C. Author and friend of the Stocktons'."

"Ahh. Well, I'm just buddies with their son—nothing to get excited over."

"What should I get excited over?"

Nighttime Violet was so much more distracting than Daytime Violet. The suit had been complimentary to say the least, but the form-fitting number she'd slid into upstairs had one purpose and one purpose only—total manipulation.

If he had really been Gestapo Joe, he'd have already kissed her and suggested they go upstairs. If he were rolling on E like college, he'd have skipped suggesting they go upstairs and slid his hand up her skirt right there under the bar. If he were anyone other than 'Baby Boy Gilmour, birth 1 of 2' on a piece of paper, he'd have done anything other than what he chose to do next.

Mike slammed the shot of whiskey to find the courage to leave.

"Miss Martel, I should go."

"Already?" She deployed the low whisper again, drawing him closer. "Old girl can't hold your attention, eh?"

"It isn't that. God, it isn't that." Mike looked down at his shaking hand and then back up at her dark green eyes, only inches from his face. "I'm not having the best week, and with that, I can't be sure that the guy sitting here tonight isn't the codependent Mike with poor self-control."

"I believe we already met in the car when you said you loved me a few hours into our relationship."

"See, codependent Mike only heard 'our relationship'. I want to buy you a drink, take you to the Old Ebbitt, and keep talking all night until we fall into a passionate embrace, but I'm going to go home."

"I see." She cast her eyes down and then looked back at him through her long, coated eyelashes. "Well, you know where I'm staying if you get home and start kicking yourself."

"That's going to happen long before I get home, but, nevertheless, goodnight."

He kissed the top of her hand and walked outside, flipping up his collar to the rain.

On the subway, Mike hunched over, pressing his face into his hands and pinching his tear ducts. He was doing the right thing; he knew that. He absolutely knew that for the first time ever, he'd made the thoughtful and deliberate choice to face his problems instead of compounding them with distraction.

It was right not to fill the Void of his dead mother, missing father, and murdered sister with self-medication in the form of a one-night stand. He knew he was making the right choice. Knew it, but he exited the subway, kicking himself, as promised.

CHAPTER THIRTY-EIGHT

A manila envelope rested against his door jamb, holding a slightly redacted copy of the file Lindsey had shown him. He plucked it from the floor, catching a whiff of Sarah's perfume lingering on the page, and went inside. Coat up. Coffee on. File open.

Alex Barrett's last known duty station was outside of Frankfurt, but that was years ago. Since 1994, the man was a ghost.

That's ok. I'll write a letter, and the Army will know how to forward it.

"But if he never writes back, you won't know if it's because the letter got lost or our father hates us," Delilah said. She hadn't appeared since the afterlife. It had to be the whiskey.

"What do you want me to do? Go to Germany and start asking around?"

"You just flew to L.A. and stole your birth certificate."

"This is a tomorrow problem."

Mike pushed past the vision of his dead twin and sank into the couch. He wanted couch-sleep—the kind that was somehow more comforting and rewarding than bed-sleep, but none of the women haunting him were going to let that happen.

He watched as Delilah paced, reading the biography on their father and making notes as if she were now the detective.

And he still needed to deal with Kristin. It was too late to do it then—that would be a dick-move. He'd wait until he was leaving for Germany. Or when he got back from Germany.

Did I just decide to go to Germany?

Then there was Violet, a few blocks away. He could have gone back for her. He could have walked into the lobby of the Jefferson and asked them to ring her room. He could have enjoyed her company for a few more hours, but he didn't want it to feel worse when she left. Right now, he could still get over her, but if he spent more time disappearing into her, it might not be that easy.

She felt kind of like booze.

Which means you've already had too much.

A knock at the front door broke his untethered thought spiral, forcing him back to his present reality.

It had to be Kristin, hellbent on tracking him down. Someone had probably seen him at the bar with the stunning blonde and called her. Although if that was the case, she wouldn't have been knocking so gently.

He stood and checked the peephole, wishing the state troopers had given him back his gun.

"Mike?" the voice called out. It was British.

He threw open the door and saw Violet standing there with her hair tousled and her jogging clothes askew.

"Jesus, are you ok? What happened?" He led her inside, helping her to the couch.

"I'm so embarrassed. I couldn't sleep, so I went out for a run, and some creep grabbed me."

"My God, were you…"

297

"No, no, he knocked me down and took my wallet."

"Did you call the police?"

"No."

"Why not? What all did he take?"

A few dollars and my hotel room key. But that's why I didn't want to go back to the room. I'm sorry to show up like this. You're the only one I know in town."

"We should call the cops and report it. They probably took the cash and dumped the bag on H. I could probably find it, actually."

"No, we don't need to trouble the police. Could I just rest a minute, and maybe not ride the subway back to the hotel alone?"

"Of course."

He left her recuperating on the couch as he poured a glass of water. "How did you find my apartment?" he asked, extending his arm to pass her the drink.

"Phone book. I found the Mike Green listed in Logan Circle."

He drew his arm back.

"Really?"

There were at least eleven Mike Greens listed in the D.C.-area directory, and he was almost certain he wasn't one of them. Lindsey had scrubbed him from the phone book years ago, before the press could start digging up dirt on the Stocktons and every one of their known associates.

"You must have gotten lucky and found an old edition. I'm not listed anymore."

"Then I truly did get lucky. I'm sorry to have bothered you in the middle of the night," she said, plucking the glass away.

"No, it's all right."

It is all right, it just doesn't make sense. Car on the news. Name in the phone book. Lindsey's either slipping or these dames are wisin' up.

"I'm not sure if it's a good idea to go back to the hotel, with my key floating around out there."

"You don't have to worry about that at the Jefferson. That place has its own Secret Service detail. You just need a new key. Let me get you a change of clothes, though."

He rounded the corner to the bedroom and opened the closet door in search of a pair of sweats to offer his guest, but Delilah was there blocking his access.

"That's her. The blonde."

"A lot of women are blonde," he said.

The same way Jack had.

"Meisha, listen to me…"

"She's English, not Russian, and you're crazy. Actually, you're dead—I'm crazy. Plus, very tired and a little buzzed. I'm seeing book characters everywhere I look. I do that."

"She's one of them."

"Yeah? She's also the femme fatale in my novel, and Lindsey is an alien vampire. Violet is a real person. A live person whose appearance is an imaginary central casting coincidence."

"Violet isn't even a real name."

"Ok, *Delilah.* How? How would she have found me? Hmm? My *kill file,* as Lindsey would call it, is as fabricated as one of my stupid novels. Mike Green and Vladienka Stromkovietz are as far removed on paper as two people could be."

"Somewhere that file isn't redacted. Someone at MI6 had to do that, which means they read it! Otto and the syndicate he's part of have people in every level of government. They can access all sorts of files!"

"Just because she's British, doesn't mean she's British Intelligence! Now... go haunt someone else!"

Mike slammed the closet door in her face and took Violet his sweats as intended.

"Here you go. I'll get my coat and walk you back."

"I really am sorry." Her eyes looked up at him through her lashes, a vacant distance clawing its way back from somewhere scared as she slowly took the garments from him.

...Like booze...

"You know what, this is dumb. Don't go back there tonight. You can take the bedroom. It locks from the inside if you're worried."

"I couldn't put you out of your bed. My strict English nanny would never have it."

"The nannies are usually better than the mothers in my experience."

"I wouldn't know. I lost my mother when I was young. First, it was the nanny, then boarding school. My father didn't know what to do with a girl."

"My father didn't know I existed. I certainly didn't know that he did until yesterday."

"Yesterday?"

"I was in L.A. picking up my birth certificate. I told you it's been an intense week." Mike moved back to the kitchen and located the file folder, then handed it to her.

"Well, the resemblance is undeniable," she said, flipping past his headshot. "Where has he been for the last two years?"

"The last two? I want to know where he's been for the last twenty-three! I want to know if he knew she was pregnant and still left! I want to know if he looked my mother in the eye and said, 'Nah, not for me, thanks. You're on your own!' I want to know what he was doing while I was sitting in an orphanage, wondering why I wasn't good enough!"

"Ask him."

"You sound like my sister."

"Your sister?" Violet buried her face in the folder, searching for a clue about the girl.

"Yeah. Turns out he bailed on two of us."

"Maybe he's still in Frankfurt."

"I'm not going to Germany. He might not be there. Or refuse to see me. Or he *might* see me, resulting in the most painful interaction I've ever had, and that's coming from a guy who was rejected by multiple foster homes. I don't know if I can take that after just coming back from the dead."

"Now you're making excuses."

"Guess you've met that Mike now, too."

"Well, you shouldn't stay in D.C."

The comment filled the room, sounding more ominous than it should have.

Or that's Delilah's paranoia seeping in.

"Why not?"

"I meant, stay here, wondering. If I had even one chance to speak to my mum again, I would."

Frankfurt though.

Dmitri, assassinated on the side of the road covered in broken glass, flashed in Mike's mind.

"I know someone who was killed in Frankfurt. Three people."

"One of them probably deserved it."

Mike blinked. "What?"

"Statistically speaking. I wouldn't blame Frankfurt for that."

"Come with me."

Everything he'd been saying to himself about impulse control was out the window. Women, alcohol, fiction—they were usually the catalyst for poor decision-making. Now he could add death and detox to the list of excuses.

"*Aus Deutschland? Ja, natürlich.*"

"You speak German?"

"*Ein bisschen.*"

"You'd do that for me?"

"I would."

There was something resolved in her voice, like she owed him, but for what he couldn't figure out. He'd paid for a cab and answered the door when she was scared. It didn't balance out to the offer of a world tour.

"I'm going to Europe anyway. It's not even out of my way."

Not sure who's crazier here.

"All right then. Germany."

"All right then." She stood, all five feet ten inches of her rising proudly as if renewed by the decision. "Mind if I take the bed after all?" she asked.

"All yours."

Violet collected the change of clothes and disappeared into the bedroom. He thought of a thousand reasons to follow her, to pick up where they'd left off at the bar, edging closer to an inevitable climactic ending. He stood, working on his courage, wondering if he still had a bottle nearby to help himself along.

The bedroom lock flipped.

A small sound, but it landed like a gunshot.

She must have been worried after all.

CHAPTER THIRTY-NINE

"Time to go, traitor."

Delilah's eyes snapped open as the gloved hand pressed against her mouth.

"Uh-uh, sweetheart. You don't get to scream. Tell me where the boy is."

Yuri's breath smelled like cigarettes and rotten molars. He grinned, millimeters away from her face, examining the prey he'd spent the last nine months hunting. He was close enough to smell her French perfume and a voodoo potion on her lips.

"Get up," he said, dragging her limp body from the bed by the neck.

"Fuck you, Yuri."

"If that's how you want it."

He slammed his forehead into hers, knocking her down with a thud. She hoped Veronique hadn't heard her body hit the floor. It would be a shame if the poor woman died at Yuri's hands trying to help her when she was already dead.

Her eyes fluttered, blacking out from the force as he used the phone cord to tie her wrists together with such force that he split the skin apart. He tore away at her shorts and spread her knees apart.

"No, no. You don't get to sleep through this," he said, slapping her face to keep her conscious. "It's better when you fight me."

He unbuckled and thrust himself inside, as she clenched her jaw. She wouldn't give him the satisfaction of screaming out.

"I was the last thing Dmitri saw. I'll be the last thing your boy sees, too."

She writhed, struggling to move her bound wrists toward his waist, but she wasn't fighting the rape. She didn't care about that anymore. There was only one fight she wanted to end. Her own.

She wanted his gun.

When she had it in her grip, she pointed it to her temple.

"You never let them win," she said as she pulled the trigger.

Mike sat up with a jolt, the sound of a gunshot resonating in his skull as he got his bearings. He was on a plane. He was on a plane next to a woman he'd just met, going to look for a father who might not be there.

He'd been shocked when, in the morning with the clear light of day and a nap, neither had decided this was a bad idea. He'd called them another cab to Dulles, certain that she'd end up on her original flight back to London, while he chickened out and went back to D.C. to deal with Kristin.

"Look, Violet, if you don't want to go through with this, I get it. It is not lost on me how absolutely insane it is to escort some lunatic on a wild goose chase to Germany because he thinks his birth father might be there. Particularly one that looks like he's taken a hockey stick to the face."

She blanched, perhaps at the graphic reference or at his constantly resurfacing self-esteem issues.

"You deserve answers. A resolution no one else can give you. I'm still in if you are."

Resolution.

He'd never been good at Act Three. He was wired for slow-burn complications and never tying up plot threads.

Not this time.

After buying a ticket, he made a call from a payphone to an office on Capitol Hill.

"I don't know how else to say this, so I just will," he said while he still had the nerve. "I think I'm done."

"What do you mean you're done?" Kristin asked.

"With this. With us."

"You're breaking up with me over the phone?"

"You'd rather I'd done it at the Ebbitt?"

"Ok. Break up with me fresh off of a near-death experience and a morphine drip. You'll be back in a week."

"No, I don't think so. Not this time." He had no intention of telling her he was leaving the country, but the PA system overhead betrayed his location.

"Are you at the airport? What the hell are you doing, Mike?"

What the hell *was* he doing? In that moment, he was breaking up with his girlfriend and boarding a flight to Germany. Seven hours later, he was reliving Delilah's death in his dreams. An hour after that, he and Violet were checking into separate rooms at a Frankfurt hotel.

"Tenth floor," he said, holding the card key envelope.

"Same."

"Do you want to get dinner or something?" he asked as they squeezed into the small lift.

"I didn't sleep much on the plane. Even if it is my own time zone."

"Right."

The elevator car was hardly wide enough for the two of them and the duffels each carried. It forced them to hover—circling the obvious as Mike clenched his grinding teeth. The tenth floor came a single moment too soon.

"What I could really use is a cigarette," he said, stepping out.

"Don't. Your lungs can't take it. Plus, it's disgusting. Have you ever smelled someone's breath in your face after they've been smoking?"

"I know. I'm just used to having something occupy my hand."

"How's this?" She slid her fingers between his a second before they reached his room. "You have to learn how to fill the empty spaces without hurting yourself."

"Where have you been for the last ten years?"

"You don't want to know."

"I do want to know." He lifted her finger to his mouth and took a drag, exhaling across the moistened tip. Further resistance was futile.

He pressed his mouth against hers as he fumbled behind him, swiping the key in the direction of the card reader until he finally heard it click and give way to his body weight. They stumbled, tangled, through the door, grasping—less at each other but at something they were hoping was there.

The door slammed forcefully behind them, the positive airflow pressing against it. The thud landed with force, making Violet flinch. She held still, staring at the clean bed, perfectly tucked. Unsullied. Neither could say the same for themselves.

"I shouldn't," she whispered.

"Right, sure," Mike said, wiping her from his mouth. "Me neither. Head injury, broken ribs. I'd be terrible. You aren't missing anything."

"Stop doing that."

"Doing what?"

"Thinking you aren't good enough." She slowly let go of the grip she still had on his shirt. "I'm the terrible one. I'll see you in the morning?"

"Sure."

Violet backed out of the room.

Alone again.

Alone should have been a good thing. Alone was a chance to sleep for more than fifteen minutes at a time. Alone was a chance to shower, to let the hot water cleanse his body and his soul, but more to the point, release the pain in every screaming cell of his body. He knew it was an opiate detox, although he'd never gone enough days between them to experience it. Blaming the accident was an easy cover for the teeth grinding, nausea, and dull ache racking his body.

Great way to meet my dad.

At first light, he slipped away from the hotel to the U-Bahn. It was drizzling—a misty, coagulated fog hanging around the city. Mike hoped it wasn't an omen of impending darkness, but if he had been writing the third act of this novel, that is exactly what it would have signified was coming.

The American Army base at Wiesbaden still wore its Cold War DNA on its sleeve. On the surface, it had served its purpose and was now a halfway house for young soldiers waiting to see action in Bosnia and old dogs who'd seen enough for a lifetime already.

Underneath, the espionage machine was still winding down. No one trusted that Russia was done threatening the world, and America didn't like to give up strategy, no matter what Jacoby was telling them. The base was on a short list for downsizing. Stockton would never let that happen.

Two young soldiers, shouldering M16s, closed on the battered stranger approaching their perimeter line.

"*Halt. Wer da?*"

"Sorry, I'm American," Mike said, handing over his passport.

"Sir, this side of the base is restricted. If you're looking for the Visitor's Center…" the other said.

"I'm looking for Colonel Alex Barrett."

"You'd need to contact BaseOps." The two boys whose combined age looked to barely be thirty ping-ponged answers like a rehearsed Tweedle-Dee and Dum duet.

"Can you at least tell me if he's here? Senator Richard Stockton sent me." He rarely name-dropped, but this seemed like a good time to think outside the proverbial box.

"Let me call my CO and see what info I can give you." The first private returned to the guard shack to place a phone call while the other stood on point, guarding the visitor.

Mike remembered his own rule: Make friends with the armed guy at the gate. He talked the boy up about creature comforts, Hollywood It Girls, and found out his favorite baseball team until his partner returned with news.

"Colonel Barrett's been relo'd, sir. He's with IFOR now."

"Sorry, IFOR?"

"Implementation Force, NATO. They've got him training EOD for Bosnia."

"Explosive Ordinance Disposal," the other clarified, noting Mike's lost look with the military jargon.

He'd come to Germany for nothing. Well, not nothing. This was more than he knew a day ago.

"Can you tell me where that IFOR is?"

The boys looked at one another, certain that they were not allowed to hand out that kind of information and definitely not to a tall, dark, shady character like this guy.

"I get it," he said, releasing his trusty smile, slow enough to feel like a resignation and not a deployment. "Wanna give me your mailing address and I'll send you that Jennifer Aniston poster?"

"Thanks, that's really nice of you," the kid said, slinging his rifle around to his back and grabbing a pen from his sleeve pocket. As he scribbled, his partner finally broke down.

"Kyiv."

"I'm sorry?" Mike said, startled.

"IFOR Joint NATO base is outside Kyiv. On the edge of the Chernobyl hot zone. They can blow that shit up for days and nobody's the wiser."

"Ukraine?"

"Ukraine, sir."

"Ukraine." Mike was going to keep saying it until it sank in. "Well...fuck."

CHAPTER FORTY

Once he had returned to the hotel, Mike knocked on Violet's door to give her the news: this had been a twelve-hour detour. She could be getting home to London, and he could crawl back to D.C. and see if Kristin would take him back.

She yanked the door open fast—too fast—like she'd been standing by it and watching through the peephole.

"You should have waited for me," she scolded.

"I think going to meet your birth father is a solo task."

"How did it go?" she said, stepping aside to allow him in.

"He isn't here anymore. Reassigned to a NATO base."

She poured him a cup of coffee and pressed deeper. "Did they tell you where?"

"Near Kiev."

Her eyes closed, just for a beat, just long enough to regain her composure, but not long enough that Mike would have seen the way it rocked her core. "Kyiv?"

"Yep. Russia."

"Technically not for five years now."

"You know what I mean."

"A lot of people died for you to know the difference."

"Yeah, well, they don't teach us that shit in school. If they did, I was high that day."

He paced to the window. This was both a failed attempt at finding himself and a goodbye packaged in the same hotel room. He wanted to get it over with, finish the scene so he could file this chapter and start writing something else. Something with an ending he liked better.

"Well, at least you know where to find him now. You can direct a letter to the base and be reasonably certain he'll receive it."

"Reasonably certain? I stood there thinking I might be a few hundred yards from the man responsible for my existence. I thought once I met him, or saw him—once I had some resolution one way or the other—I could move on. Worst case scenario, he tells me to fuck off, I could at least begin the fucking off process."

"You're closer than you were. One day soon—"

He cut her off with a rare display of outrage. "One day soon? That's what Sister Catherine used to say. I'd watch all the other kids get adopted, and she'd say *one day soon Michael* and that one day would come, and I'd go home with somebody for a week or two... You know, when they send you back, they always give some reason like 'won't go to bed on time' or 'talks back.' They never just say, 'I needed a kid to pass inspection so I can keep collecting my checks!'"

His anger wasn't rare because he wasn't angry. It was rare that he wasn't numbing himself from feeling it. These last few days of sobriety had cracked open a new well, one he didn't care for.

"Mike, I'm sorry... no child should grow up without a parent. I know that as well as anyone."

"No, you don't! You had a parent! You had a nanny and boarding school and money. You're just like Tom complaining about all the things you *did* have. Some of us know what it's like to really have nothing and no one. And today, standing there thinking I was moments away from some version of fucking closure to find out I was basically being sent back again… Where's your minibar?"

"You don't need a drink."

"What are you? My fucking sponsor?"

"Maybe I should be."

She moved to comfort him, but he side-stepped her, reaching into the collection of miniature bottles in the cabinet. She stopped his hand before it reached his mouth.

"Think of something that never disappoints you."

"I don't have anything like that."

"Sure you do. Where's the one place you can always go in your mind that makes you happy?"

He closed his eyes and tried to answer the question. He had a few favorite writing spots, maybe. The National Archives building, the park next to the Washington Monument, and a section of highway between the Key Bridge and Falls Church.

He let the bottle drop onto the desktop. "Until a few days ago, it was the road between the Stocktons' and the city. Until someone tried to kill me the same way they killed my sister's fiancé."

"How do you know how Dmitri died?"

Mike inched toward the door. "I never said his name was Dmitri."

"I peeked at the book on your nightstand."

"No, you didn't. Who are you?"

"No one."

"Like hell…"

"No, really. Right now, I don't exist."

He put his shaking hand on the doorknob, the urge to flee as intense in him as it had been in Delilah the day she left home.

"Mike, I promise, I'm a friend…"

- A FRIEND

"…and I can get you onto the base in Kyiv."

"Why would you do that?"

"Because I owe it to you."

"You don't owe me anything. I don't even know who you are."

"Then I owe it to her." Violet turned away, looking out the window toward the street. "I owe it to Petr for not getting to him in time."

He saw her closing in from the other direction, her platinum blonde mane bouncing in time with her footfalls as she broke into a run, aiming for the child still sitting there in the ever-growing pool of blood around him.

"But you tried to get to him."

"I tried to get to them both."

"You're MI6?"

"No. I told you. I'm no one right now. Do you want to go or not?"

"Why should I trust you?"

"You shouldn't. You shouldn't trust anyone. That's the one lesson your childhood got right." She lifted her bag from the bed and slung it over her shoulder as she left the room.

Normally, he excelled at ignoring reality, but there was a palpable difference between going to Germany to find an Army colonel and going back to the city where the criminally insane had turned on his sister with a woman he was now convinced had been with them while they'd done it. For reasons beyond his own explanation, Mike stepped on the throat of his own reason and followed her from the hotel.

Before the flight landed at Boryspil, Violet gave him strict instructions: don't speak, angle your face away from cameras, avoid eye contact. Then, in a move that didn't do anything to set his nerves at ease, she wrapped a scarf around her hair and tucked it so tightly around her chin that it obscured any suggestion of who she'd been before, sealing the rest of her face off with large, round glasses. She melted into the environment like she'd been trained to do it.

Violet marched quickly through the sparse Soviet-style terminal, intimately familiar with her surroundings, though Mike struggled to keep up past the Cyrillic signs. A pair of uniformed guards leaned against a scuffed metal doorway, not saying a word but watching—definitely watching. The line to pass border control snaked on, only getting longer and not shorter.

"Come with me," she whispered, tapping his arm and pulling him from the line that would confirm their right to enter, and moving instead toward those two drab olive uniforms in the doorway. "Wait here," she said before pulling away her glasses and approaching them.

Her body language was seductive. The two guards weren't prepared for a woman like her—suggestive and teeing up to pass a bribe. They took an envelope from her, and then one cracked the door while the other stood sentry to block the view. She beckoned Mike with a head nod, and they slipped out into the frozen Kyiv air.

"What just happened?"

"I know how things work here."

"You bribed a guy to skip the visa process? So we're here illegally?"

"Yes."

With a wave of her hand, she flagged down a rusty Lada before it could make its way to the front of the airport to pick up arriving passengers, and gave him instructions in flawless Russian.

"I told him to take you to your father and wait there to bring you back."

"Bring me back where? What if he dumps me in a radiated neighborhood?"

She scrawled a frustrated note in Cyrillic and tucked it into his pocket like a child afraid of being separated from its mother.

"Here. Addresses for your father's base and my hotel, in case you need to give them to another driver. Hurry."

She pressed him into the cab and shouted one more thing at the driver with such clarity of purpose that it transcended the language barrier into meaning. "Don't even try to scam him."

He replied in the universal cabbie tongue. "Yeah, yeah, lady."

CHAPTER FORTY-ONE

The cab drew to a stop beside a chain link fence, its rusted steel signs half-buried in Cyrillic graffiti. Mike couldn't read the words, but the bright red skull and crossbones got the point across: *Danger – Explosives.* Above that, a serrated razor wire curled a final warning to anyone stupid enough to ignore the warning about what this was.

Explosive Ordnance.

"Here," the cab driver said in clipped English.

"And you wait for me, yes?"

Being deserted at the edge of a firing range outside a nuclear ghost city went beyond his usual fear of abandonment; it was how people went missing forever.

"Yes. I wait. Your wife yell. Take car number."

My wife.

"Sorry about that. *Prostite'tye. Spasibo.*"

The driver waved him off. He didn't care for the American's attempt at politeness; he just wanted the other half of his money when he got back to the hotel on the slip of paper.

Mike exited the cab and crossed the dirt road to an opening in the fence where a soldier stood smoking. His woodland camo may have been a good choice for the summer months, but the dark green stood in stark contrast to the endless blanket of white that still clung to the ground in March.

"Privet," Mike called out. He wasn't sure where all the Russian vocabulary was coming from.

Yes, I am…

"Are you Mr. Green? From Washington?"

Mike slowed, surprised that the base had advance notice of his arrival when he himself hadn't had advance notice of his arrival. Violet was pulling strings everywhere.

"Yes."

"Walk on through, but wait here," he said, opening the chain link fence for Mike to pass. The soldier scanned the undercarriage of the cab with a mirror to check for explosives, then escorted Mike down a long pathway to the only concrete building tucked into a forest of pine and poplar that had reclaimed the area with unchecked authority since the meltdown a few miles away. Even the building was being strangled by the tendrils of the fauna, though, that could have been intentional camouflage.

He didn't know what IFOR was or what they were doing out there, but he could see how easy it would have been to buy up all the land and blow things up all day without disturbing the neighbors, when all the neighbors were three-eyed stray dogs.

The door opened inward.

"Mr. Green, welcome."

Mike stepped inside to shake hands with the officer in the doorway.

Alex Barrett.

"Colonel Barrett," he said, extending his hand. The Colonel's drawl carried southern grit, although Mike knew he was from California. Barrett missed the uncanny resemblance behind

319

Mike's bruises and stitches the same way Mike had missed Delilah's behind hers. "Looks like you've had a go of it lately?"

"That's an understatement."

"Ops said you were here from Stockton's committee. This about Operation Iron Veil?"

Mike's courage surged—the kind he usually needed whiskey or narcotics to access—summoned now by the women he needed to make this right for.

"No, this is about Michelle Gilmour."

The man cleared his throat, stiffening his stance and focusing on Mike's eyes. "I don't know a Michelle Gilmour."

Unintentionally, Mike cleared his own throat the same way. "All due respect, you did know her. You got her pregnant and then you left for Vietnam."

Barrett's pupils flared, though his face didn't move. He'd been interviewed, polygraphed, and drilled by harder men than this kid from Washington, but never about the girl he'd loved once.

"Gilmour? That wasn't the name she gave me. Has she come up in regards to my latest JSOC clearance? I can assure you that I haven't seen her since 1973, so if she's claimed something…"

Mike dug deep and found Gestapo Joe hiding somewhere inside—the cadence, the swagger… the *cop*. "She's dead. You left her to die alone in childbirth, which means you might as well have killed her yourself."

"Hey! No one speaks to me like that!" Barrett lunged, ready to bring his training, authority, and his raw physical fitness to bear on the cocky asshole, even if the young man did have two inches on him. "You don't know a damn thing about it!"

"You're right. I don't. So clue me in, *Dad*!"

Silence echoed in the damp, crumbling room—a cold silence that rang in their ears until Alex spoke again.

His once booming voice, used to shouting over explosions and barking orders, came out in barely a whisper. "I didn't know. Her father told me she had an abortion at the same time he tried to have me arrested."

"Arrested for what?"

"Statutory."

"She was eighteen."

"She was sixteen," he said, hanging his head into his hands. "No one thought twice in those days about a high school girl and a college freshman, but her father was going to use the letter of the law to get me out of her life."

"Grandpa sounds like a real fucking charmer."

"Look, I was a punk kid. Long hair, protesting the war. That's how we met. She was an activist, a bra-burner. She'd have pulled the whole patriarchy down if she could have. I really loved her. Whatever that meant at that age."

Somewhere, Delilah smiled, her lineage, her passion, finally justified, the argument landing firmly with nature over nurture.

"I was handcuffed in the back of that squad car on my way to jail when the cop pulled over and said he'd let me out if I signed up to serve my country. I was in South Carolina next thing I knew. I made the only choice I had."

"You're right. I don't know anything about it. I know I grew up without either of you, though."

"You can't know how sorry I am to hear that." His thoughts drifted to a place they hadn't gone in a long time. That one moment, that one act, had changed the course of so many lives. He'd given up on college, gone to war, stayed in the Army, and had a career. And this boy had grown up without his parents. "If I'd have known she was still pregnant... or if I'd known you were out there, even before now... Why are you here now?"

Barrett straightened his spine a little tighter.

"I don't want anything if that's what you're asking."

"No, I mean, how have I never learned about you before? I have SCI clearance on multiple programs. They've turned over every inch of my life countless times."

Mike didn't want to lie to his father, not already, but he couldn't very well say *I followed a murdered woman's journal and a spook dragged me across Europe.* It was too early to let his father know he was crazy.

"With Stockton's campaign, the vetting has gotten more invasive."

"You work for him?"

"No. He sort of adopted me."

Barrett's eyes widened. "I wish we had time for that story, but someone's going to figure out that you don't belong here."

"Yeah."

The conversation decelerated naturally, a gentle sinking in of how significant the day had become, when neither had woken that morning knowing it would unfold in quite this way.

"Mike, was it?"

"Yeah."

"Let's get acquainted someplace with a cozy fire and a bourbon someday soon."

One day soon. There it was again.

"I'd like that. Unless it would be disruptive to your family."

"No family. Divorced. No kids. Pretty hard to stay married to a man who keeps detonating the barbecue." His hardened military exterior cracked, and through it shone a man who realized what had been missing in his life.

Mike jotted his contact info on a scrap of Army stationery and handed it to Alex Barrett—his father, Alex Barrett.

"Thanks for this."

They shook hands hard, a facsimile of a hug between two men who didn't naturally do emotion before Barrett showed him back out into the snow.

As Mike reached the rusted chain link gate, he turned back. Leaving someone—leaving the only person on Earth he knew he shared DNA with—should have been hard. It should have been impossible. But as he watched Barrett toss him an honorary two-fingered salute, Mike knew he'd finally met someone who would stay in his life.

CHAPTER FORTY-TWO

Mike pressed his cracked temple to the cold rear window of the rattling cab. It chugged through the capital, sounding like it might die at any moment. He didn't see the powder blue mansion behind the iron gate, or the internet cafe near the campus. He only opened his eyes when the driver spoke.

"Independence." He tapped on his window, pointing proudly at the statue standing tall above their main square. The Archangel Michael, Patron Saint of Kyiv.

"Meisha," Mike replied.

"Ya, ya, Meisha!" The cabbie beamed that the tourist would know about his city's symbol.

"Can you drop here? Maidan Nezalezhnosti?"

The Lada's brakes engaged quickly. "You go see?"

"Yeah. I need to go see."

"I wait?"

"No, no, don't wait."

Mike passed him all the U.S. dollars he had in his wallet and darted across the traffic, just as he had crossed 15th to get to Washington's spire.

The icon had been a hope Delilah held on to; its scaffolding stood vigil over his sister for every significant event in her life. It was fitting that he brought her there to see the finished product on the day they met their father.

Closure.

"That statue isn't closure, but you're in the right neighborhood," her voice whispered.

He moved through the square toward the transit system, seeing Dmitri in every man's face, knowing when to exit, which streets to turn down—how to walk *home.*

As his mind was invaded by memories that didn't belong to him, Mike tried to figure out what to say to the Stromkovietz family that wouldn't sound strange.

Hello, I'm Mike Green. Your daughter, Vladi, is actually my twin sister, who happens to be haunting me. Can I come in, please?

Well, that certainly isn't it.

He approached the dilapidated cottage. If the windows had started to fall out when she lived there, she had never described it in her journal. Maybe the boards came later. Maybe they were warmer than glass in the winter. The porch crumbled under his feet, the concrete degrading under the conditions. He half expected the door to fall from its hinges if they managed to shove its warped bottom across the step.

It struck him that although the house was in poor condition, it wasn't a flat concrete apartment building with a hundred other families all sharing the same water pressure. The fact that they had a small piece of something and had managed to hang on to it had to mean something.

A petite woman answered the door when he knocked, her black hair pulled loosely into a bun, with strands of gray falling carelessly from it. Her dull brown eyes were wary of the stranger at her step.

"Hello. Uhh, *privet*…"

Nadia.

"…Nadia."

"*Da?*"

He spoke slowly, each syllable stilted as he accessed it. "*Ya Michael Green, iz Ameriki. Ya byl drogom Vladienka.*"

Great, you told her you were her friend from America, now what, smart guy?

Nadia yelled toward the back of the house and summoned a frail man with a long black beard. At one time, perhaps he had been a strong man, but age and sickness had taken their toll. Mike extended his hand to the man.

Delilah's father had a firm handshake despite his appearance.

"Mr. Stromkovietz?"

"Alexander."

Our fathers have the same name.

"You know English, yes?"

"Yes?"

"Sir, I'm a friend of your daughter's—from America."

"America?"

"Where you adopted her from?"

The couple's eyes grew wide, and they looked at each other, concerned. "Come inside from the street," he said.

Mike stepped into the house and scanned the rooms. All of it was familiar: the couch where Nadia had read the telegram, the kitchen where Dmitri and Sergei had smuggled in the stolen food. Down that hall, the room where she'd grown up, where

Petr had slept for a few months of his life, when he still had a future.

"How do you know our daughter?" The old man was skeptical, and rightly so. They only knew their daughter had disappeared. One morning, they woke to find her and the baby gone. They'd thought about putting up flyers, but *flyers*, it had been explained to them by a Zdrastkova, would not be helpful in locating her.

Mike pulled the birth certificate from the pocket of his overcoat, where he'd been holding it since Los Angeles.

"*Bpat*," he said, remembering the word and the name of her novella.

Nadia and Alexander passed the page between them. They weren't document experts, but it looked authentic, the paper pulp true to the seventies, and the typewriter's font plausible.

Nadia placed her weathered hands toward Mike's cheeks to steady his face as she examined it. Her lips started to quiver, and she turned to her husband, shocked.

"Look at his eyes! It is like she is looking at us herself." The woman had spoken in her native tongue, but Mike had understood in his soul what she had said.

Delilah's father moved toward him, staring into the bright blue orbs—an obvious genetic match to their girl.

"How have you come here? Why have you come here?"

"I came to give her peace. To feel closer to the sister I never met."

"I don't understand." Alexander repeated himself in Russian for his wife's benefit.

Mike realized then that they didn't know about her journal. They didn't know she'd been stalked like prey, and exterminated like vermin. They'd been holding onto hope that she'd escaped the life they thrust her into and was somewhere raising her child beyond the reach of generational pain.

A puff of air left his lips, releasing the pressure in his damaged lung as he realized he was going to be the one to tell them the truth.

"She was killed. I think his name was Yuri."

Alexander translated, but the name *Yuri* had cut through clearly already. Nadia gasped and muttered something.

"My wife wants to know what happened to Petr."

"She gave him to a church. Ironic, right?"

As he said it, he realized the idiom around irony probably wouldn't translate, nor had it been the appropriate tone for the message he was delivering. Deflection, however, was his only defense against emotion.

"It's for the best," her father said. "If Otto Zdrastkova ever found him, he would kill him."

"Is there anything of your daughter's that I could... hold?" Mike needed a tangible anchor to this reality he suddenly found himself in. Otherwise, he'd convince himself he'd written the scene and deleted it without hitting save.

Alexander snapped his fingers, an idea forming. He left the room, returning a moment later with a man's wallet. He opened the fold and pulled out a three-inch photo square and a silver necklace.

"This is everything."

Mike held the photo of Petr for a long time.

The boy had Barrett Blue eyes and the cheekbones he'd never known how he'd inherited. He could assume now they'd come from Michelle. In fact, if there was any of Dmitri in the baby at all, he couldn't see it. If there had ever been a baby picture of him, it probably would have looked just like the one he was holding.

"Thank you for letting me see this."

"Take it. It's dangerous for us to have these things still."

"I couldn't take them from you."

"Please."

Mike tucked Dmitri's wallet away in his pocket. Even without the gun in there, they were running out of real estate.

"Would you like a tea?" Nadia asked, managing to find words he understood.

He wanted to sip sweet Russian tea and let the Stromkovietzes share their memories. In unburdening their history, explaining it to him in a way they'd never found to explain it to their daughter, maybe it would give everyone closure. But he'd been gone for the whole day. Violet was certainly freaking out, and he still needed to figure out how to get back to the location she'd written on the slip of paper.

Another thing in my pocket.

"I should go, but can you tell me where this is?"

He showed them the address and listened as Alexander described how to locate the former factory-turned-hotel, a block off Independence Square.

"Thank you so much. You have no idea what this means to me. To us."

Again, he was the one deciding to leave when it was still healthy and appropriate. This was some kind of new record, he thought, carefully pulling at the front door so as not to damage it further.

A menacing figure in a leather jacket hovered over the threshold, sucking on a cigarette. Mike would have wanted one if he hadn't wanted to vomit. He didn't just see the rotten smile grinning at him from the porch; he saw it grinning at him in Austria, Prague, and New Orleans.

And even last week in D.C. at the mouth of an alley.

"Hello!" Yuri said, flicking his cigarette. "You leave? Ok, we go."

"Go? I'm not going anywhere with you."

"Yuri, leave our guest alone. He was leaving," Alexander pleaded, he and his wife joining them in the doorway. "We've already paid for the week."

"Yeah, but big boss wants word with Mike Green."

"That's not happening," Mike said.

"I don't ask!" Yuri pulled a shiny pistol from his coat and pressed it into Nadia's forehead. When her husband moved to protect her, Yuri slapped him with the butt end of his pistol grip, knocking him into the melted snow puddle on the porch. "Don't make conversation messier than it needs to be, *kozel!*"

Mike weighed his options:

- *Go with Yuri and his semi-automatic*
Or...
- *Get myself and the rest of Delilah's family executed by her killer.*

"Ok, ok! I'll go with you. Just don't hurt them."

"Good choice, big D.C. man," Yuri said, turning the pistol on Mike and pressing it into his broken ribs. "Good choice."

CHAPTER FORTY-THREE

Yuri dragged Mike by the elbow and shoved him into a dented Mercedes sedan. The car was the newest thing Mike had seen since landing in Kyiv, but it had been used as an instrument to get Yuri's point across when necessary.

The Zdrastkova mansion was only a few minutes away at the pace the driver whipped the sedan around. At the end of the broad art deco street, they pulled through the iron gates and into the carriage house that Delilah had mentioned once. Having just seen how the average person lived, Mike understood the visceral hate people had for the Zdrastkovas' wealth. It was *gratuitous*.

The garage's sliding door rolled back slowly, and Yuri shoved Mike through the opening into the center of the dim garage, illuminated only by a few lightbulbs dangling bare at the ends of the electrical conduit, hazed over by the cigarette smoke cloud that hung in the air around them.

This isn't going to be a conversation.

Mike clocked three men already inside, two wearing the same leather jacket and gold chains that identified them as enforcers, while the third sat waiting behind a folding table. A fourth loitered against a support beam, disappearing into his surroundings as he fumbled with the buttons of a flip-phone.

"Have a seat," the older man commanded, spinning a metal folding chair into the center of the room.

Yuri shoved Mike toward it, and though he didn't protest, he was still met with a kidney punch for his trouble. The strike vibrated through his shattered ribcage, sending more pain than he'd ever felt in his life directly to his internal organs. By default, he collapsed into the chair, windless.

The elder who'd insisted he sit took a step closer and leaned into his face— staring at it, memorizing it...

Perhaps recognizing it.

"Mr. Green, was it?" he asked, though he knew the answer. "Mr. Green, do you know who I am?"

"No. I don't know anything about anything."

"My name is Otto Zdrastkova. This empire was my father's," he said, waving his arm around the room. "My brother was firstborn. Dmitri, his firstborn. Dmitri's son... Do you follow?

"Not really."

Of course, Mike followed, but he didn't want them to know that. He figured his only hope at this point was to play dumb and hope they got bored with him.

"Fathers and sons. This is an important relationship."

"I wouldn't know. I'm not anyone's son—I'm literally an orphan. I'm of no use to anyone."

"I think you could be. You are like someone's son. Someone important."

Otto strolled over to the boy with the cell phone—his son Alexei—and slapped his arm, indicating the boy had missed his cue. Alexei produced a folded newspaper from his waistband, where the others all kept pistols, and presented it to his father. Then he went back to fiddling with his phone.

Last Wednesday's New York Times.

The headline read: **STOCKTON IS A LOCK** over a photo of the Stockton family beaming proudly from their staircase in Falls Church—a photo Lindsey had insisted he appear in.

"Prominent D.C. Author and Friend of the Stocktons..." he read aloud.

"Yeah, I grew up on the same street, so what?"

Otto beamed. "So this is fascinating twist! Yuri kills stupid girl —he does this all the time, who cares? But when American FBI runs fingerprints, they find birth record in Los Angeles. Stupid girl has twin brother. So we look. We find him. And if he has Petr? We kill them. Simple."

"Me? You think I'm the brother? You've got the wrong guy. I don't have a sister."

"I am still telling story!" Otto yelled, sending a shockwave through the carriage house. He paced, picking the tale up where he left off. "Brother knows next U.S. president. Ok, we don't kill him, we use him to get close to Stockton. But brother starts to go poking—raising the dead. So what should we do, brother? Either you are wrong guy and we kill you, or you know Stockton and have use."

Mike thought quickly. If they were willing to keep him alive to flip him and send him to spy on the Stocktons, he might have a chance. All he needed to do was get out of this goddamn place long enough to contact the FBI or the CIA—or LDA. He might live.

"Yeah, I know the Stocktons. You want me to plant a bug in his office? Easy."

Otto Zdrastkova laughed to himself. "No, no, we have already bugged this home. We want you to get job in White House."

"The White House? I have no skills for that. Rick would never hire me for something important."

"Then maybe we do have wrong guy."

Yuri stamped out his cigarette and stepped closer, understanding he was about to be called on for his specialty.

"Wait! Look, just because I can't work in the White House doesn't mean I'm useless. I'll have access to the residence, the family secrets—stuff that employees can't get close to. What kind of things do you want?"

"I want to own this man! Twist him to disrupt his agenda in Eastern Europe. Claim the President of the United States for the Syndicate."

"Ok. Tell me what to do."

"Whatever she was having you do."

"She? Who?"

Yuri gnashed his teeth and then growled the answer. "Anya." To punctuate the taste this Anya left in his mouth, he spat—like he was spitting on her future grave.

"I don't know anyone named Anya," Mike said. "I really don't."

"Anya!" Yuri yelled into Mike's face again before landing a fist across his jaw—penance, Mike thought, for every bad guy he'd ever had Joe beat on for sport.

"MorningGlory. Josephine. Whatever name the agent has given you this time," Otto said.

"I don't know who you're talking about. Look, tell me what you want out of Rick and I'll get it. I have zero principles, ask anyone who knows me."

"Yes. We've heard. Self-loathing, addicted, easily manipulated by women, lacking self-esteem, but somehow arrogant... You make easy mark, Meisha," Otto said with a laugh. "Easy mark make good *suka*."

Mike didn't know the actual meaning of the Russian insult, but he could feel the disdain seeping off Otto's tongue. He was used to owning people, degrading them until they were empty soldiers marching on his orders. He was the embodiment of the oppression that his sister had fought. And he somehow had Mike's whole emotional profile already committed to memory.

He was all of those things Otto had said. He walked around in an expensive coat with the collar flipped up, pretending to have swagger, flirting pill bottles away from nurses, and sparring verbally with the power elite because the alternative scared him. He'd only felt healthy for a couple of days, but he'd been toxic his whole life. He didn't have the activist dog in him the way his sister and his mother had, and he didn't have the broad chest and authority he'd seen his father display. He was absolutely a 'suka'—whatever that meant.

He rubbed his jaw with a free hand. They hadn't even tied him to the chair; they thought so little of his threat level.

"How do you know so much about me?"

Otto wagged two fingers in the direction of the leather thugs. "Malkin, Federov, bring her," he commanded, though he'd done so in Russian that Mike couldn't follow.

From the shadows, they dragged a semi-conscious body, hooded and bound. He could see bare legs and feet, the woman's toenails dragging behind her across the concrete, smearing the dirt and oil of the garage with her blood. Malkin tossed the broken pile at Mike's feet and stepped back in line.

She writhed, an involuntary muscle flinch as adrenaline tried keeping her alive, though she probably wanted it to be over.

Like Delilah had.

Otto reached down and tugged at the hood. Mike expected blonde hair. That would have been full circle revenge, closing the loop—bookending the story with a satisfactory plot wrap-up.

The hair was red.

"Kris?"

He bent to the floor and rolled her onto her side so he could get a better look at her face. He touched the arms that had wrapped around him in lust, while entangling him in betrayal, and the bleeding mouth that had been his kiss of death.

Mike's mind couldn't even reconcile the reveal; how the girl he'd been dating since last fall and who he'd broken up with before getting on a plane would have ended up tortured on the floor of a Kyiv carriage house. He broke his memory of her down into bite-sized pieces to attempt to digest it.

She approached him.

She flirted her way into his bed.

She'd spent most of their relationship picking apart his routine, his personal effects, and his morale.

And it had started last November, right after Delilah was killed.

"When we need them, we wake them up. Kristya was a soldier, trained to keep you entertained while we decided if you were useful—or a threat."

"Awesome. I wasn't just dating a Democrat; I was dating a Russian spy. Really, this week can't get any better."

"You keep poking her instead of poking around Vladienka; everyone has better day," Yuri said, laughing. "But now we are all friends, we don't need her."

Yuri drew his pistol with a casual grace that said he'd done this before, a hundred times. The crack of the gun filled the garage—louder at close range than the movies prepare you for. Louder because it echoed through Mike's memories, knocking Jack to the ground and bursting Delilah's head open.

Blood and brain splattered across Mike's coat and pooled around his feet. He recoiled to the chair, his ears ringing.

He hadn't just watched Kristin get executed—he'd *felt* every murder the Zdrastkovas were responsible for.

"Holy shit," Mike whispered, wiping the blood spatter from his face with the back of his arm, which only smeared the tissue from his sleeve across his forehead.

"Don't feel so bad, Meisha!" Yuri laughed. "She tried to kill you."

Laughter erupted from the goons.

The headlights.

The car following aggressively close, knowing my schedule and where I would be going.

Roofie'ing me to see if I could tell if I was being poisoned…

"I told her," Yuri said to the laughing trio, "you never just run someone from road. You stop and make sure they get the *point*."

On the word '*point*,' Yuri tapped his muzzle in the center of Mike's forehead, exactly where Dmitri had been shot, exactly where Jack had been shot.

Otto stopped laughing. "If she did, we wouldn't have that blonde back here with her little American toy!" All the laughter ceased. Malkin and Federov knew when their boss wanted levity and when he meant business.

Alexei had disappeared.

"What does Anya want?" Otto asked, returning to the interrogation.

"Really, I don't know who that is."

"You've been with her since Los Angeles! What is she planning?"

Los Angeles?

Blonde.

"Margarita?... I mean, Violet?"

"Yuri's favorite until she called the authorities in Prague," Otto said, as though the wistful recollection of human trafficking and assassinations were a family tradition.

"Fucking traitor whore," Yuri spat, though the words were obscured in his native Russian.

"I don't know why she's here," Mike answered honestly. "Using me, it would appear."

As he stared at Kris, still oozing in a pool of her own lies, he resigned himself to the same fate. If he was going to end up on the floor next to her with a matching head wound, then it didn't

339

matter what he did next. He was Delilah, putting the gun to her own forehead.

You never let them win.

He took his feet, rising inches above the rest of them.

"Kill me or send me back to Washington. This intimidation game—this making me your *suka*—stops now. I won't let you disintegrate my mind the way you did to my sister."

Otto examined his face, capturing it like a photograph to remember. A souvenir. The spoils of his war were people.

His soldiers waited for the verdict.

"Kill him."

A gunshot reverberated through the garage.

Then two more.

The first blasted through Yuri's head from a muzzle no one had noticed peeking through the sliding door.

The second caught Otto in the clavicle.

Had it not shattered the elder's arm at the shoulder, his shot would have hit Mike in the heart instead of the lung.

Both men sank to the floor on top of Kristin's already lifeless body and watched as the other bled out among chaos.

Mike couldn't focus, couldn't turn his head to watch the swarm of uniforms through the door. He didn't see Malkin draw on the assault team, only to be shot from behind by Alexei. He didn't see Federov taken out by the lead agent as she barreled through the room toward Mike.

His vision blurred.

The edges darkened, leaving only the pinpoint of Yuri's face in the illuminated center as he slipped away.

I'll be the last thing you see, too.

CHAPTER FORTY-FOUR

The beeping had gone on for weeks—the only sign his hollowed-out shell was still alive. That body had been through so much: a car accident, cardiac arrest, collapsed lung, broken ribs, a beating, and then, finally, a bullet.

When he died the second time, no one expected Mike Green to come back. Too much trauma, stacked on a decade of smoking, drinking, and drug use, had left his organs ill-equipped to fight.

If there was one bright spot in all of it—one glimmer that suggested he might survive—it was that the bullet had ripped through his punctured lung. Had it nicked the good lung, the one doing the heavy lifting, it would have been lights out.

The shot was a through-and-through. Otto hit him with a nine millimeter—which, as any trauma nurse will tell you, is the best thing to be shot with. Smaller caliber rounds spin, carving more than they need to before lodging inside. Larger calibers are pure destruction, blowing through, leaving nothing behind.

Nines are the Goldilocks of gunshots. They leave something the surgeon can work with. And in Mike's case, the round even tore out some necrotic lung tissue on its way through.

A happy accident, as Bob Ross would say.

The Soviet-era hospital where Petr had been born stabilized him the best they could as the lights flickered and the doctors called upon their military experience to stop the hemorrhaging.

Then he was moved. Mike knew none of that. He hadn't come out of the coma since that horrible March afternoon.

Anyone from his life back in D.C. wouldn't have recognized him. Pounds had melted away, both muscle and fat, as his body cannibalized itself. Dental records and above-average height were the only markers that indicated who he'd once been.

And forget the smell. The wounds, even with treatment, irrigation, and antibiotics, were still healing from the inside out—rotting, debriding, repairing. It all had a smell to it that was not for the faint.

The breathing tube had been out for a few days. His lungs were opening and contracting on their own again, and hair had started to grow on his face—all signs that things were progressing.

When the beeping ticked faster, indicating a rise in heart rate, she called for a doctor. No one knew if his mind would work, or how well, if he even regained consciousness. Everyone on the medical staff at Ramstein was interested in finding out if their patient was a vegetable.

His eyes slowly rolled around, trying to moisten enough to open, fighting against the light that had been sealed out. When they latched onto consciousness, there was only one thing he recognized.

Violet.

She looked at him with anticipation, her hair pulled back tightly into a ponytail that gave its platinum color a darker tinge where the roots were oily.

"I've called for the doctor already," she said, placing a calming hand on his arm.

He pulled it back quickly. Too quickly. He'd used the sum of his energy to recoil from her. His first waking moment in weeks, and it had been in disgust.

"You've been in a coma, so take things very slowly right now. If you're disoriented, that's ok."

"I'm not disoriented. I'm just not sure why you're here."

"Otto Zdrastkova shot you in a raid on the mansion."

"And you're waiting around to finish what he started?"

Mike's last memory was of her working with Yuri. She'd chased Delilah through Europe with the thug, then baited him in L.A. to lure him back to Kyiv, where they had been waiting to grab him up.

She ignored the comment, assuming he was delirious.

"I know why you're here, *Anya*."

It wasn't delirium; he was genuinely blaming her. She stood abruptly, bringing her waist level to his eye line. Along the shirt tucked neatly into her trousers was an ID badge.

"Have you completely missed this?" she asked, ripping the metal clip from her belt loop and throwing it in his face.

Through the tangle of IV lines and the heart monitor clipped to his finger, he brought the plastic card close enough to focus on it. Violet's face in an unflattering mug shot in front of a Union Jack. Along the series of numbers and codes lining the bottom, he could only make out "Vauxhall" and the name Josephine Bradley.

"Yeah, how do I know this is real?"

"Jesus Christ, how do you know anything is real?" she muttered. Violet—or, rather, Agent Bradley—paced over to the door to check if that doctor she'd called for was on his way. "Since your brain is obviously working, I'll give you a brief. You're at Ramstein Air Base. Those are American soldiers in the hall. Do you really think a Russian double agent is roaming around with a fake MI6 badge?"

Duped by a dame. Not just a dame—a fed.

"But you did work for Otto. You were with Yuri while he hunted my sister."

"Yeah, that was a great year of my life."

A young military doctor, wearing fatigues in place of scrubs, breezed through the door, interrupting their conversation. A nurse followed, and the last to enter was a wet towel of a man wearing a suit who immediately scowled at Agent Bradley.

"Mr. Green. Welcome back. How do you feel?" the young doctor asked, as he got to work reviewing the statuses on every monitor.

"Doctor," the suit interrupted with a BBC-style snobbery. "You mustn't use that name any longer."

The doctor rolled his eyes. "Right. Sorry. Patient X, how are you feeling?"

"Empty."

"That's the ketamine. We'll adjust it."

"Ahh. I thought I recognized the k-hole."

"Did Agent Bradley tell you what happened?" the doctor asked.

"We didn't get that far."

"Excuse me," Astor interrupted. "What we share or do not share with our asset will be at my sole discretion, not Ms. Bradley's."

"Ok…" The doctor flipped Mike's chart closed and silenced the beeping monitor, now confident that it wasn't going to flatline. "I'll leave you all to discuss—or not discuss—what happened. I'll check back in a bit and adjust those meds."

He nodded to the nurse to follow him, leaving Mike with the two MI6 agents and a whole lot of questions.

No one spoke at first. Bradley waited, deferent to Astor, and Mike was too exhausted to carry the conversation.

"Well, let's start this debrief," Astor said.

"Bloody hell, Astor, he's been awake for two minutes!"

"Wouldn't want him slipping his medical detail and running off to complete an unsanctioned mission, would we?"

Agent Bradley scowled at the pointed remark. "He's not going anywhere. Let him breathe for a moment."

"You may never need to return to London, Agent Bradley, but I do."

"Hey, coma patient, here. Could I get like an ice chip or a Jell-O or something if we're going to do this?" Mike tried to execute a smile, but only part of it appeared through the pain.

"Fine," Agent Astor reluctantly obliged, grumbling off into the hallway to locate the nurse again.

"Clever," Agent Bradley noted, "but he won't stay gone for long."

"Then talk fast because there are a lot of dots here, and none of them connect for me! I came to Europe to meet my dad, and I ended up with a bullet hole because I'm in the middle of some… British Intelligence operation?"

"We don't have time to get into fifty years of Eastern European crime family trees, but I can tell you that I was Dmitri's handler. I made the deal to get them out after he delivered the identities of the Three Syndicate Families."

"So what happened?"

"Otto had them executed first so that he could take over, and Astor wouldn't let me pull your sister without something on the Zdrastkovas."

"That motherfucker is the reason my sister is dead?" He tried to rise, as if he planned to rush the agent the moment he returned, but collapsed almost instantly back onto the bed.

"Trust me, I'd do it myself if I could."

"Why wasn't Otto arrested for murder?"

"Murder is nothing. The Soviet collapse left them a playground to deal weapons across the entire Bloc. A concentration of wealth that controls the flow of contraband throughout the globe and a network of thousands helping them do it! Preventing global destabilization was more important than one girl. Myself included."

"They hunted her for sport!"

"I know! I was there! Otto only wanted Petr. The rest was a sick game to a psychopath."

"Well, you got to shoot him," Mike said, as if it should have been some consolation.

She smiled despite herself. "Yeah. Lucky me."

"So you decided not to save my sister because she didn't know anything?"

"No! I decided I could save her and the mission if I were inside, and women only have one way into the Syndicate."

"Yeah, you're good at that ruse."

"Hey, spare me your judgment! I spent a year with those monsters, trying to save her and the case. You have no idea what I went through!"

"And you still lost her, the baby, and all your intel. Good job, Violet."

"It's Josie, and you know fuck all about it!"

"Because you didn't tell me! You lied your way into my life, and then you let me walk into Kiev knowing I was already a target!"

"It's Kyiv, and I couldn't tell you. I'm not supposed to be telling you now!"

"You were already breaking the rules! When I stood there in Frankfurt, opening myself up to you about my dad, you could have whispered, *Pssst, British spy here. We ought not to go to Kyiv. Big price on our heads, let's bugger off.*"

Josie couldn't help but laugh at the poor impersonation of her accent. "I did kind of want revenge," she admitted.

Mike could understand that. If nothing else, he could understand the desire for some shred of justice for herself, for the baby, and Delilah. He wanted those things too.

Astor pushed through the metal door carrying a tray of water and a jiggling orange gelatin. "Right, here you are. Let's crack on." He dropped the tray next to Mike's bed and picked up an envelope. "I recognize that this isn't anyone's favorite part, but the sooner we do it, the sooner we can all get on with it."

"On with what?" Mike asked, still unable to look away from Josephine Bradley.

"The rest of our lives. Agent Bradley, I need to ask you to step out. You are not cleared for this debrief."

"Of course."

"I'd like her to stay," Mike said softly.

"It doesn't matter what you'd like. I run you now."

"He's right," Josie said, collecting her blazer from the back of a chair and slipping it on. As she pulled her ponytail free of the collar, the gentleness left her face, and she turned to Astor. "William, thank you for letting me stay this long. Mister... well, right, you'll have a new name soon. You have my sincere and utmost apologies for the situation. I wish you the best."

"Josie," Mike said, halting her escape. He couldn't think of what to say. His chest felt paralyzed. She was standing in the doorway, waiting for something to come out of his mouth, and he didn't have anything for her. She had done her job, and now it was over. If he said nothing, she would leave, the way everyone else had before her. Orphaned again.

Except he wasn't an orphan. Because of her, he knew that.

"Thank you for helping me meet my father."

Josie lingered, waiting to hear if anything else was coming—if he would give her anything to hold on to—a lifeline, a rope to tie around herself so she didn't float away.

Nothing came.

She pursed her lips into a smile, perhaps because that NATO base stunt was another thing she'd done illegally that William Astor would have to deal with in her wake.

"Every child needs a parent."

When she left, Mike let her go.

CHAPTER FORTY-FIVE

"What in the bleeding Christ am I looking at?" Stockton bellowed, slamming his fist into the desk instead of the low-level CIA agent in front of him.

"Sir, it's an intelligence briefing..."

"I've had a seat on the Senate Intel Committee for eight years. I know what a goddamn briefing looks like!"

He threw the folder down, scattering the pages across his desk. The file detailed something out of a Cold War movie. Operation OrangeBlossom: twins separated at birth and a blood trail that led back to a crime family. The part he'd keyed into, however, was the fact that one of them had an SVR Department S girlfriend who had been coming to his family get-togethers for the better part of the last year. Likely, she'd been the one who'd planted listening devices around the estate.

"Sir, this memo states that..."

"Shut up. And I mean, literally, stop talking. Immediately!" Stockton roared. "Clear the goddamn room!"

The senator looked around at who he'd ordered away: two Secret Service agents who had been only recently assigned to him. Recently, as in a week ago, when he became the presumptive party nominee. He didn't want these two unknown agents to hear the rest of the CIA's summary. As few people as possible should hear it because it could destroy him, and he was so close.

In fact, he wasn't even sure why such a crucial piece of information had landed in the hands of some kid from the Eastern Europe desk, and not the director himself.

He hated that he didn't know this Langley rep either, didn't know where his loyalty was, didn't know who else he'd already told about this. Stockton hated anything he couldn't control.

"Kid, do you mean to tell me this man, my son's life-long best friend, was a foreign agent?"

"No, sir. Michael Green was cleared of any suspicion. He appears to have been targeted because of his biological connection to the female."

"Mike has had full access to this family since he was five years old! He was in my office the night they found the devices!"

"Senator, I can assure you we found nothing out of the ordinary around Mr. Green, neither this time nor last fall when MI6 flagged his tie to Ukraine."

"Last fall? You flagged this bullshit last fall, and no one fucking briefed me. Marta!" His voice boomed through the walls of the lower floor, summoning his head of household. "What were they looking for that time?"

"He came up as next of kin to the DOA in New Orleans, but he had no other associates besides your son. It seems the girlfriend came later."

"Came later... You mean, WHEN THE RUSSIANS FOUND OUT HE HAD ACCESS TO ME AND PLANTED HER!? Government fucking ineptitude. My first act as president is going to be firing the Director of the CIA!"

"Sir?" Marta said, peeking her head inside the office door as unobtrusively as possible.

"Lindsey Decker, now! Send a goddamn chopper if she's more than ten minutes away."

Marta nodded and backed out of the room.

"And we're certain Kristin is dead now?" Stockton asked.

"Quite, sir. There's a photo…"

He selected a dossier glossy snapped in the aftermath of the carriage house shootout, and handed it to the senator as carefully as if he were handling an asp. Kristin, the sour puss foil to the last few months of dinner parties, lying in a pool of blood, her head blown apart.

"Mother of fuck," Stockton said, tossing the photo aside. "And Mike was there? Is he ok?"

"Sir, he's in the custody of the British Secret Service as part of their case against the Syndicate."

"Fucking 'syndicate'? You make it sound like some movie plot."

"Sir? Do you prefer 'network'?" The agent was trying very hard not to upset the nominee, but he'd handed him bad news and was almost certain that he, as the messenger, would be shot. "The Secret Service sweeps the estate twice per day now. They've never found anything past those initial devices."

"Goddamnit," Stockton whispered under his breath. Perhaps this was still under wraps at only the most need-to-know levels, and the next news cycle ticker wouldn't read: **RUSSIAN MAFIA OPERATIVE INSIDE STOCKTON CAMPAIGN.**

"Ok, let me read this whole fucking thing one more time."

When he'd reached the back of the brief for the second time, his mood had softened slightly as he thought of his friends Jennifer Green and James Langham. They were about to get word that their son, days after surviving a horrendous car crash, had been killed in a bar fight in Frankfurt. It was the kind of bullshit people expected of Tom, not the markedly more responsible and somewhat less drug-addled friend of his.

And it was horseshit.

It was one thing, Stockton thought, to spin a story in your favor. Taking something that might spark fear and making it so there wasn't a public panic, or coloring a topic to convince someone that yours was the best way forward. It was another thing entirely to tell a mother her son was dead when he was sitting in Ramstein being erased by the British Intelligence Service.

At least someone else got to deliver that news to her. He'd only have to perpetrate it for the rest of his life.

Lindsey Decker dashed across the lawn, ducking under the blades of the helicopter, and stormed straight into his office.

"You need me?" she asked, slowing only to clock the CIA agent she didn't recognize.

Stockton threw the file in her direction. "Read this front to back and tell me what the fuck we're dealing with here."

"Sir," the agent interrupted. "That is a classified document that Ms. Decker doesn't have the clearance—"

Lindsey glared at him, summoning the darkest part of her evil core. "You're going to back out of this room now, or you'll be disappeared to a black site in Islamabad by sunrise."

He didn't know her, but he knew her reputation for destroying her enemies and elected not to find out if the rumors were true. The agent did as suggested and backed out of the room.

She sat, carefully poring through the pages one by one, layer by layer. When she closed the file, her eyes squinted in disbelief. "Goddamn it, Mike," she whispered. In a way, her job had been to protect him as an extension of Tom. She'd failed. And Lindsey Decker didn't fucking fail. "I just saw him at the Jefferson. I didn't think he was the one we needed to worry about."

"Right. The 'good kid.' Poor taste in women."

"Not that night." She remembered the blonde, va-va-vooming herself across the lobby to have a drink with him. Her wheels turned. The Jefferson had cameras—microphones in some places —she could start with that knockout and get to the bottom of this.

The quiet moment of reflection passed, and Rick pounded his fist into the desk again. "How did you miss a Russian operative in my fucking house, Lindsey?"

"Hey!" she said, standing her ground. "I vetted her. She was born here. Her parents were born here. They're from Boston, not Brighton Beach. They weren't fucking Soviets, at least not on paper. I've heard of these sleeper cells left over from the Cold War, but there were no signs, Rick. None!"

"Well, you're going to go back through everyone I've ever met and dig so deep they feel you in their fucking colon!"

"Of course. I'll start with her associates and colleagues in Rothschild's office."

"Fuck! Rothschild is tied to this fuck-stack, too! They're going to brief him on this!"

"I'll deal with it. Who else knows?"

"Fuck if I know. The MI6 agents on the case, the CIA agents on the Europe desk, the shitstick in the hallway, the Director of the CIA…"

"That's a lot of collateral. Can you think of anything you said around the house that could be compromising?"

Stockton had been rolling that around in his mind since he'd learned of the device. He'd been on the campaign trail for the most part, but there had been a meeting with the CNO in there the night he got home.

"That miserable prick admiral was in here one night going on about our deal in '91."

"And MI6 has that now?"

"MI6, SVR, who fucking knows. Goddamn it! I haven't come this far to be un-fucking-done by the British or some Soviet… syndicate. I need those tapes!"

Lindsey licked her teeth, thinking, then bit down on her tongue. "You need to plant someone on the Eastern European desk working this… Zdrastkova…case personally," she said, taking a moment to get the name right from the file. "Someone we own, so we know what they know, when they know it, and know it before it has a chance to go up to the director and be filed in a report. You need a fixer inside the CIA."

The only thing that could ensure Stockton's success was an agent as cunning and calculated as she was, but whose expertise was in the Intelligence Community, not the public sector.

"You got somebody like that?" he said dismissively as if she'd described a unicorn.

"Maybe."

His ears perked up. "Well, let's have it, Decker. Don't keep an old man waiting. There's a lot at fucking stake here."

"Tony McCollister."

Stockton needed a second to compute the name. He was far more used to the nickname he had gone by as a young man than the more adult moniker he'd been using professionally. "Who? AJ?"

"Think about it, Rick. He's proven his loyalty to you on several occasions, he's a trained intelligence operative, and he moonlights for me already."

Stockton digested the suggestion. He did like the young man, despite his festering wound of a father. There was something unflappable about him, and he had always been that way.

"Marta!" he screamed again once he'd made his decision. "Find me AJ McCollister. Now!"

Thirty minutes later, Tony "AJ" McCollister pulled through the guard gate on the Stockton Compound and was escorted to the senator's private office by the Secret Service.

Finding Lindsey Decker there was unexpected, though it shouldn't have been.

"Ms. Decker," he acknowledged. "Senator. How can I be of service?" He stood erect, his eyes fixed forward.

"No need for attention, son. How are you?"

"Fine, sir." Tony relaxed his locked knees but kept his back straight.

"How are things at ONI?"

Tony could have sworn they'd had this conversation just last week. "Sir, would you like to let me know what required such urgency?"

He had noted the presence of a plainclothes federal agent pacing the hallway like he'd lost his kitten, and it wasn't adding up. Stockton seemed to be having trouble figuring out what to say next, a symptom he'd never seen the senator infected with.

"Tony," Lindsey interjected, "I'm holding an intelligence briefing. The senator has started receiving them as the nominee."

"Yes." Tony still didn't understand why he was there. "Am I in it?"

"No. And let's skip past the part where seeing this is a crime and agree that the three of us have all done worse, shall we?"

"Ok."

AJ took the folder cautiously and gave it a read-through. He had no familiarity with Operation OrangeBlossom, or any of the players mentioned by name. He could, of course, see how the infiltration of the Russian sleeper and the listening devices were of concern, but there was no obvious explanation for why he'd been read in on it.

"Sir, I'm still unclear about my involvement."

"Did you meet our Mike at the house last week?" the senator asked.

If this were the same friend for whom Tom had procured a gun, he'd never met him on purpose and was glad for it now.

"I don't believe so, sir."

"Too bad. Loyal guy. Wrote these cheeseball detective novels that were actually pretty good." Stockton moved toward a bookshelf and pointed at his collection. He was obviously proud of the young man. "Sarcastic little shit. I think you would have liked him."

"Sir," AJ acknowledged. "I know he was very dedicated to the family. Tom spoke of him often while he was … away."

"He kept Tom in line the best he could. He probably saved his life more than once. I don't even know where we'd be without him," the senator said.

"Sir, may I ask again what you need from me here?"

"Tony, we're reading this, and we're thinking about how to protect the senator—the Nominee—"

"The president?" Tony completed Lindsey's thought for her.

"Exactly. This isn't just about foreign operatives or political optics… If someone else is holding cards we don't know exist…"

"Then you don't win," he finished. "You don't have to explain the concern, Ms. Decker. I write intelligence briefs. I understand the ramifications. You don't know what was on the tapes, who has them, or what they'll use them for."

"It's not about the information!" Stockton screamed, hitting the table for a third time. If he wasn't careful, his grip and grin hand was going to be sore at his next appearance. "Yes, we need to know if some limey shitbird is holding my presidency hostage from a cave under the Thames, but more importantly, I want to know my son is ok!"

359

His declaration reverberated through the room, landing with enough fatherly emotion that it surprised both members of his audience. His grief wasn't going to be solved with a limerick this time. This time, he was going to bring the full weight of his office.

Lindsey waited until Rick's shoulders had relaxed and he had settled into the chair behind his desk, his emotions subsiding. "I'll do both, Rick. *We'll* do both—find out who knows about the tapes, and track Mike Green's new identity."

"Right," Stockton said, pivoting back into the political animal Tony was used to seeing. "I want to know we're fucking clean in this, but I also need to know that he's doing all right."

"Anything you need, sir." Tony's eyes jogged over to Lindsey, hoping for more of an explanation on how she envisioned the mission unfolding, because he didn't see it yet.

"Tony, let me work out the details to get you undercover. Once you're inside the CIA, you'll have full operational oversight, but obviously, don't bring anyone in that you don't need to. Sarah will be the only one I bring in."

"Ma'am." Tony nodded. Even if he didn't know the operational details yet, he knew Sarah had always been an ally. There was only one other person he could truly say that about.

Stockton took one more glance across the bookcase, where the short-lived Gestapo Joe series held prime real estate next to photos of the boys together since they were five. "Goddamn it, I really liked the son of a bitch," he said with an exhale. "Now, run the Play, Decker. I have to go tell Tom his best friend is dead."

CHAPTER FORTY-SIX

"And with those delegates, Richard W. Stockton III, has become the forty-second President of the United States."

California's delegates wouldn't even matter. Stockton had crushed Rothschild in a landslide—the kind no one had seen in a generation. Yes, Lindsey was that good at spin, but Rick deserved it. The man would open a vein to protect the people he loved, and he loved America.

Mike tipped his glass in the direction of the TV hanging over the bar despite the boos and hisses from the deeply Blue Los Angeles County voters surrounding him. For Mike, it wasn't about the politics, the policy, or even the election. He was just happy someone got the ending they wanted.

And I didn't screw it up for him.

He watched the Stockton machine take the stage to the cheering devotion of thousands: Sarah Wallace, corralling her favorite reporters so they could get the best angle of the First Couple's entrance, Annabelle on Rick's arm, beaming, and Tom on the other side, looking broken.

Of course Tom looked sad; he would have to spend the next eight years asking the Secret Service's permission to take a piss. Well, that and his best friend was dead. Killed in a bar fight in Frankfurt.

At least that's what everyone had been told.

Anyone who really knew Mike Green, and admittedly, the list was short, should have known that it was a lie. Mike had never been in a fight in his life, but the last place that had swiped his passport was Frankfurt, and SIS needed a cover. Put the tourist in the wrong place at the wrong time and bury the story with him.

He looked at President-Elect Stockton and wondered if he knew the truth. Would it have made his intelligence briefing? Surely something as significant as a global crime syndicate having an agent in his house and being the source of the listening devices would have pinged on the radar.

It didn't matter if Rick knew or not. He couldn't tell Tom. All it would take was one drunken coke-fueled rant to let something slip, or a juvenile grudge against his father to let a reporter know he was part of a cover-up.

Stockton couldn't have told his friend, Jennifer, the next Secretary of Education, that her son was alive and she wasn't allowed to know where. He would have to keep that lie along with the rest of the intelligence agencies that orchestrated it. At least, Mike figured, Rick was a professional yarn-spinner.

MI6 let him in on their plan for him once he was up and moving around the hospital under his own weight. Prior to that, he'd been told he was in protective custody because of the investigation around Otto. No visitors. No phone calls. National Security. He'd made friends with the medical staff so that he wouldn't go crazy.

"Looking good, Doug," the nurse said, as he dragged his IV hanger along by his side. They were making him do laps around the hospital, rebuilding his strength, his lung capacity, and, honestly, his will to live.

"Don't say that. They'll make me leave."

"Aren't you excited to get home to your pretty wife?"

"I see what you did there, Lisa," Mike said, winking. "And no, I don't have anywhere to go. At least not anywhere where I get sponge baths and painkillers."

The painkillers he hadn't had a say in. Too many nerve endings, muscle fibers, and bone structures had been destroyed to 'raw-dog' it through recovery. The Army doctors freely administered everything from morphine to oxy with no idea that they were re-awakening the dragon that lived inside of him.

When they started to titrate him off, the nurse who'd been caring for him since his admission was an easy target for his smile. Even if ethically she wouldn't hand over more meds, she was game to rebuild his stamina in other ways, and when she was distracted by his hands on her body, she didn't notice his hands lifting her keys. His lap around the hospital started to include a dip into the med locker.

After all, he was still Mike Green, even if the name on his records now said something else.

"Glad to see you can get in and out of bed without detaching a rib. You're ready to get out of here," the doctor said, examining him one last time.

"And go where?"

"That's between you and that Brit. He's on his way down from London."

"Oh, good."

"Yeah, right? Guys like him are the reason we threw tea in the ocean. Anyway, I'll have you out in the next forty-eight."

"I don't even own pants."

"I'm sure I could scare up a set of fatigues if that smarmy guy doesn't come through for you."

"I have no reason to believe that he will."

Astor didn't. Not really. On paper, he'd tied up the loose ends that Josephine Bradley had exposed on her whirlwind escapade across Germany and Ukraine, disappearing Mike and Alexei after he'd turned on the family.

On paper, though, rarely jived with reality. On discharge day, Astor showed up in person to hand him a padded envelope and send him on his way.

"You haven't given me any instructions."

"I just did," Astor nodded to the envelope. "It's simple. You've been erased. Stay that way."

He remembered it sounding so final. Erased. Not just given a new identity, but made to have never existed. Mike supposed in a way he had never existed. Mike Green wasn't a real name. Barrett, Gilmour, Green—he was never any of those people. He could as easily not be this guy, too.

The photo in the American passport, taken while he was still recovering, looked nothing like him, which he supposed was the point. And he didn't love the name the British picked for him.

"I'm Doug Ross now? You want me to live my life as George Clooney's character from 'ER'?"

"I don't follow."

"Number one show on TV… It doesn't matter."

"I've moved your sister's inherited funds into Mr. Ross's name, and the sale of her assets will transfer to the account as well. When it's gone... well, that's how money works."

"And so what does Doug Ross do for a living? Did he go to school? Where does he live?"

"You get to figure that out. The gift of a clean slate."

"More like Scorched Earth."

"*Po-tay-to, po-tah-to.* I could have handed you over to the U.S. Marshals and kept the Grennan assets for myself. Oh, and technically, I'm supposed to incinerate your belongings, but since you're forbidden from going to D.C. to collect anything, I'll let you keep your coat. It's a touch chilly out."

"What did I ever do to you, Wills?"

"I don't like to clean up other people's messes. Agent Bradley left a trail of collateral for me to deal with—an unsanctioned mission and two witnesses to erase."

"Remind me again why all the cloak and dagger? Why can't I just go home and put this behind me?"

"Because she couldn't even shoot Otto Zdrastkova correctly. He is as powerful recovering from his gunshot in a prison hospital as he is free. We know he paid off a guard to release a kill contract on Agent Bradley. We have to assume you're named as well."

"You assume, but you don't know? You could be erasing me for no reason."

"You were on a contract kill list in D.C. before you knew of your DNA. They will hunt you and kill you if they ever find out you didn't die in that carriage house. You should thank me."

"Your bedside manner is shit, Astor."

"Well, after today, you'll never hear from me again. Will there be anything else?"

"Clothes? Or am I supposed to wear my coat like a flasher?"

"Take it up with the Americans."

Astor evaporated like a mist on the moors. Mike hadn't been told what to do when he got back to the States, or how to apply for a new driver's license without a birth certificate. Hell, he hadn't even been given any kind of cover story to help him find a job.

The doctors released him from the hospital with a set of U.S. Army fatigues, handed him a banker's box stuffed with his coat and the contents of its pockets, and put him in a cab to Frankfurt.

As he crossed the terminal carrying his box, he caught his reflection in the shiny surfaces of the German *Flughafen*. In the fatigues, he looked like Alex Barrett in his enlistment photo. The last thing he'd said to the man was a promise to keep in touch. Now, the contact information the colonel had for his one living child would ring to a dead man. He'd only known his father for half a day and lost him again.

Mike took his box and his new passport and did precisely what he'd been told not to do. He went back to D.C. because *fuck William Astor*. He needed something he recognized to tether him to reality.

When he stepped inside his apartment, Mike stopped—lost. He had nothing to hang on a hook, no coffeepot to start, nothing of his routine—of his life—was left. He grabbed a trash bag and hit play on the blinking answering machine, the only thing that resembled the normalcy of coming home.

"Mike, it's Lindsey. Colonel Barrett is currently stationed at a NATO base near Kyiv, working on a Spec Op program called Iron Veil. You're going to need help getting to him there. I have people, if you decide you want to do it. Just don't try anything on your own. I don't want to see you get hurt...during the campaign."

Mike snickered. "Well, I fucked that up, Linds."

In a sick irony, she probably could have fixed everything from the beginning. If he had walked out of the archives that night and phoned her to ask about the redacted black file, she'd have found out everything he needed to know and done it without a bullet.

Too late now.

He erased the message. The last person's voice he'd ever hear from Mike Green's life. No one else had called to check on him in the days after his accident—not his best friend, not his editor, not even Jennifer Green, the woman who'd chosen to raise him. Of course, had she shown up to do more than pay an adoption fee, he probably wouldn't have been arrested at fifteen and met Lindsey Decker in the first place.

In the end, it was Lindsey, a woman who was paid to care about him, whose voice would end Mike Green's life.

The inventory he took with him was minimal. He grabbed Delilah's journal, one contraband picture of him and Tom from college, and his bean bag chair. Surely no one could identify him by a fucking sack of foam beads. He changed out of the fatigues, into jeans, and his trusty Georgetown hoodie.

He was carrying enough cash to make him nervous, but used a stack of it to buy a used car, loaded up the trunk with the three things that still held any meaning to him, and began heading west.

In fairness, there was no other direction.

Before merging onto the endless highway, he stopped at the Lincoln Memorial, walked up the steps, and breathed in the city one last time. From there, he had the best view of the Washington Monument—his building-friend—the one thing he really thought he'd miss about D.C. and didn't want to miss anything or anyone anymore. He patted one of Lincoln's giant white columns, and then disappeared—a ghost.

In Oklahoma, he mailed his final manuscript to his publisher and put his metaphoric pen down. Though he could have continued to write crime thrillers under a pen name, he knew that every time he described a murdered woman, he'd see his sister, and every time a gun went off, he'd feel his chest collapse. The posthumously published novel and the movie deal would be a million-dollar success—royalties probably going to the Royal Family.

God save the fucking Queen.

He meandered across the country, staying off the grid, using cash and fake names, and taking the time to think about the first quarter-century he'd spent on the planet. When the road got lonely, he could always find another damaged soul to share a drink and fill the Void in the backseat of a car. After everything, it wasn't gone; it had just changed shape.

When he hit water, there was nowhere else to go. He was in Los Angeles. Where his life had started. As good a place as any for it to start over.

Election Night came and went. The air started to cool, and the holiday lights began to appear.

Christmas. The day Delilah lost everything.

He shook the thought and used Doug Ross's credit card to buy some furniture. If he was going to stay in L.A., he needed something to sit on that wasn't a bean bag—a couch that his seventy-four inches would fit on easily and a bookshelf to hold a cheesy detective novel collection he bought as an excuse to talk to a bookstore girl.

After stabbing himself with an allen wrench a few hundred times during the assembly, he collected all the boxes lying around and hauled them down the alley to the dumpster. He hurled box after box into the bin until the last one landed with a thud. It was still full—shrink-wrapped by an airline and tagged by the U.S. Army.

He grabbed it back from the blue bin and salvaged Gestapo Joe's coat from the rubble. It was still caked with blood—his, Kristin's, Otto's—he couldn't tell. The pockets were still loaded with the things that nine months earlier he had thought defined him: a notebook, Dmitri's wallet, and a diamond ring. He pocketed the wallet and the ring and tossed the rest back into the garbage.

"You can't put your coat in the rubbish bin." He reeled around to find Josie standing at the alley's mouth. "A homeless person will pull it out of the dumpster and get picked up for wearing a coat with a bullet hole and blood all over it. Then the cops will run it, find your DNA, and three different governments will light up, wondering how evidence from this case ended up in Los Angeles. You'll have to burn it."

"Well, when you put it like that."

A quiet laugh escaped as she was charmed by his sardonic humor.

"What are you doing here?" he asked, edging back toward his apartment.

"I unwittingly became the world authority on smuggling operations in Eastern Europe. I was offered a position tracking the Syndicate for the U.S. Customs Service."

"You can't just arrest them all?"

"There's a difference between knowing how they operate and being able to identify them."

"You won't have to go undercover again, will you?"

"I don't imagine I ever could. Not with Otto Zdrastkova still alive and an active contract open on me."

"Yet, you didn't have to change your name and disappear from your own life?" He said it with enough accidental bitterness to make her flinch.

"Getting to a federal agent is a lot of work. They'll try, but not for a while."

She followed him inside the apartment, where Mike deposited his salvaged pocket contents on a new $15 coffee table whose legs he'd just screwed on.

"Have you thought of getting a job?" she asked, surveying what had become of him—how he was living. It was Spartan, but she got the feeling it was by choice, not necessity.

"Not yet. I will. I'm kind of taking it day by day."

"Sure." She picked up Dmitri's wallet and started laughing.

"What's funny?"

Josie held up the slip of paper that had been folded in the flap since 1994.

"All this time, you could have just called me."

"And said what?"

She shrugged. He had a point. She couldn't trace the edges of his life and hope to heal it any more than he could come into hers and fix things that had been broken overseas.

She tucked the slip back inside and pulled out the tiny square photo it had been living with.

"God, he looks like you," she whispered.

Mike peered over her shoulder at the photo he'd forgotten about. "How old would he be now?"

"He would have turned two in October."

She passed the infant's photo to him to hold. Mike placed it on the new bookshelf, there next to a copy of *Dead Girls Tell No Tales.*

"Well, he can live here with us. Where he belongs."

Josie set the wallet down and rang her hands for a second, resetting her purpose.

"When they asked me what office I wanted to work in, I chose L.A. because... well, I know how hard it can be to make connections when you give people a fake past. I'm the only one who knows what you've been through and who you could talk to if you needed someone. And, frankly, you're the only person who can appreciate what I went through and why I would never want to speak about it."

She lowered her eyes and looked back up at him through her lashes, but her attempt to reach him fell flat. She was rusty at softening up a mark, and he was rusty at human connection. She fanned the pages of Delilah's worn book until she saw a reference to herself and let it fall from her hand.

"Well, it was nice to see you. Would you like me to take the coat and put it into the incinerator?"

"Sure. Thanks."

When he passed her the coat, he thought he caught her fingers trembling at the sight of the blood—there because of her, though maybe that was his tendency to apply meanings to things where pragmatic people didn't.

He pushed the door closed behind her, flipping the deadbolt out of habit, and returned to the spot where she'd dropped the book. Before moving it to the shelf to be with Petr's photo, he glanced down at the open page—Delilah reaching out again from beyond the grave:

"Jack knows exactly who I am, and he still loves me. Without him, my only hope would be asylum or witness protection. I would need to lie to everyone I meet for the rest of my life. A made-up identity, a fake past... I couldn't live like that—lying to those I love, pretending to be someone else..."

"Violet!" he called from the porch, halting her departure.

"It's Josie," she reminded him.

"Right. Josie. Would you like to grab a coffee or something? If you don't mind waiting five minutes so I can shower the particle board off of me."

"I sat next to you while you festered in a coma. You don't need to shower for me."

"Gross. I'll grab my wallet."

"Or you could just make coffee," she said. "Why risk being seen together in public?"

"Even better."

He held the door open, standing aside so she could step back inside. It had taken nine months, three thousand miles, and too much self-reflection to measure, but he was ready to stop being alone.

He was ready to stop being a ghost.

EPILOGUE

Josephine Bradley dashed through the rain and into the unmarked two-story office building. She stopped to remove her coat and shake the water off just inside the doorway while she was still standing over the thick rubber mat—that's when she caught him staring.

President Richard W. Stockton, III—his portrait hung inside the door next to the Customs Commissioner and the Secretary of the Treasury in a pyramid of U.S. power dynamics she had little interest in. She started back at them: her boss, her boss's boss, and her fiancé's surrogate father.

Fiancé. That had happened quickly. It made sense; neither could form another relationship unless it were based on lies. All they had was each other, and Mike, she knew, had a habit of latching onto people. Still, it had happened fast.

Stockton's eyes seemed to follow her like a haunted painting. She'd never met him, but she'd heard stories. Warm, foul-mouthed, funny, and fiercely protective. The wars he'd declare on his global enemies were nothing compared to the ones he'd launch against someone who'd wronged one of his own.

"So you're the Russian whore who wants to marry my son?"

Stockton probably wouldn't have made a Russian joke. Still, she imagined that if she had met him that fall in the run-up to the election or in the winter months before the inauguration, he'd have grilled her over her past and her intentions—not to mention the whereabouts of certain recordings from his office. Luckily, he didn't know she existed, and as far as she knew, he had no idea where Mike even was these days.

"Stop looking at me," she snapped at the portrait.

"Agent Bradley?"

Josie reeled around toward the receptionist who had called her name, startled and ready to excuse away the fact that she'd been talking to the president's portrait. "I was just…"

"A call for you."

"A call?"

"An Agent Dwyer with the CIA."

"Matt Dwyer?"

Matt Dwyer. That wasn't his name. That wasn't anyone's name. It was a code name—a cover story from a mission he'd been running while she'd been running one on him.

"Yes, Agent Matt Dwyer, Langley. Would you like it in your office, Agent Bradley?"

"I would, thank you."

Josie walked quickly, nearing a jog, to the closet of a space where she now worked a nine-to-five.

"Josephine Bradley," she answered. Her voice was professional and firm, not the whisper she had once used to control his mind. She didn't care about doing that anymore.

"Agent Bradley," he said. There was no mistaking Tony McCollister's calm, deep voice on the other end. It was smooth and unflappable, but it reminded her of betrayal.

"Agent *Dwyer*. How did you find me?"

"Come on, Jo, you're smarter than that."

"Ok, then, *why* have you found me?"

"You're smarter than that, too."

"Tony… I swear if you try to…"

"I'm not going to try anything. I need to ask a favor."

"Of me?"

"Yes. One you're uniquely qualified for."

"I'm afraid to ask."

"I have an asset, I believe you know. POTUS has authorized a Special Compartmentalized Intelligence project around him and wants regular updates on his status."

"POTUS doesn't have anything better to do? He's got a country to run."

"I told you, Mike's family. Stockton wants to ensure his continued safety. Would you be willing to moonlight for me on his behalf?"

"On POTUS's behalf?"

"No, on Mike's. You run him and give me a sit rep every month. You should like that. It's more in line with your training than this Customs ruse you're playing at."

"Every month?"

"Sooner if something feels off, which it already should. He's using the name Grennan? It's like he's not even trying."

"I know. We've discussed it."

"Discuss it harder, Jo."

"We just want to be free of the past. You can appreciate that, can't you?"

He could appreciate that, but coming from her, it felt like salt pouring into his still fresh-gaping-reminder-that-she-had-outplayed-him wound. Tony considered stabbing her back, but this game wouldn't get them anywhere.

"Jo, if others had their way, I'd burn him again and bury him where you can't find him, but alternatively, I'm willing to do it this way."

"Why?"

The honest answer was so that he'd have a reason to hear from her—a leash to yank the way she'd yanked his, but the answer he gave her was, "Because the way you played him to get to Otto wasn't fair, and the way you played me to get to him wasn't fair. This is how you make it up to both of us."

"Fair? Tony, you sound like a child," she scoffed.

"You're not a good person, Josephine. You paint a target, and you neutralize it regardless of casualty."

"You think you're any different?"

"I know I'm not. Which is why you should believe me when I tell you that if you do anything to jeopardize this asset, I will kill you myself on the order of the President of the United States."

Josie knew if she didn't cooperate, Tony would erase Mike for a second time, and she wouldn't have the resources to find him again. This treaty—the one where she was forced to spy on one lover and deliver the intel to another—was her only play.

"Someday, I hope you meet someone who makes you want to be a good person. Someone who erases 'target' and 'neutralize' from your vocabulary. Then you'll understand why I had to use you to find him and why I am willing to do anything to keep him now."

"And if you want to keep him, you'll give me my updates, or Marshalls will WITSEC him overnight when you're not looking."

"That's all I have to do? Update you on how he's doing?"

"And watch for red flags."

"And you'll leave us alone and let us have our life?"

"Such as it is."

She hated it, but sucked in a quick breath so she could spit out an answer. "Fine. How would you like the intel transmitted?"

"You can call my private number. No information regarding Project Helix can go through official channels anyway. It's a Black Op."

"Project Helix? Clever."

"It's an SCI file, Jo, no one named it to impress you."

"Very well," she said. "I'll run him, and you can run me."

"Aww, Jo," Tony said with a patronizing lilt, "Don't sound so defeated. It's only for eight years. Or until one of you is dead."

HELIX PROJECT // FILE: REDHELIX // STATUS: ACTIVE

ASSET NAME: GREEN, MICHAEL (ALIAS: DOUG ROSS, MICHAEL GRENNAN, MICHAEL BARRETT)

CODENAME: **REDHELIX** / **PASSCODE:** 101073

CLASSIFICATION: SCI LEVEL-3 // EYES ONLY

HANDLER: BRADLEY, JOSEPHINE (DUAL AGENCY CLEARANCE: MI6/CIA) **MORNINGGLORY**

MONITORING AGENT: MCCOLLISTER, ANTHONY J. (DIRECT EXECUTIVE OVERSIGHT)

AUTHORIZATION: EXECUTIVE ORDER 12792 (POTUS, R.W. STOCKTON III)

OPERATION STATUS:

EMBEDDED CIVILIAN IDENTITY ESTABLISHED.

ASSET LOCATION: GREATER LOS ANGELES, CA, UNITED STATES.

PSYCHOLOGICAL STABILITY: MARGINAL.

BEHAVIORAL VOLATILITY: ELEVATED.

THREAT LEVEL: LATENT.

NOTES:

ASSET REMAINS UNAWARE OF FULL SCOPE OF HELIX PROJECT AND MORNINGGLORY INVOLVEMENT.

CONTINUED SURVEILLANCE AND PSYCHOLOGICAL FIELD REPORTS REQUIRED.

MONTHLY SITREP

RECOMMENDATION:

MONITOR ALL EXTERNAL CONTACT AND ACTIVITY. VET ALL KNOWN AND NEW ASSOCIATES.

PROJECT HELIX TO REMAIN COMPARTMENTALIZED UNDER EXECUTIVE ORDER 12792. CODEWORD CLEARANCE.

FILED: CWO H. BARBER

ABOUT THE HELIX PROJECT

Beneath the surface of power, loyalties fracture and lives are erased.

DoubleHelix was the first strike in a series that spans backroom deals, global syndicates, and black-ops warfare—where every truth only sharpens the next betrayal.

Come for the politics, the espionage, and the shadow play. Stay because the cost of survival scars those who can't walk away. Once in, never out.

Be the first to get read in on Book Two.

Sign up at www.dwyerstreetpress.com

ABOUT THE AUTHOR

JL Calder, Author and Founder of Dwyer Street Press

JL can remember picking up a pen for the first time as the Berlin Wall fell, aware even then that the event would define a generation. A degree in English Literature from UCLA followed, with a concentration in military and espionage fiction shaped by the tendency to pick courses with guest professors like David Mamet, and a graduation thesis titled *"James Bond's Role in Shaping the Lexicon of Espionage"*.

With three decades in film production, Calder brings a cinematic eye to the page — along with a healthy disregard for taking creative notes.

You can find J.L. and Dwyer Street Press together online and on social.